Rocket/Lemon Duet
A Bones MC Romance
Marteeka Karland

Rocket/Lemon Duet
A Bones MC Romance
Marteeka Karland

All rights reserved.
Copyright ©2024 Marteeka Karland

ISBN: 978-1-60521-898-4

Publisher:
Changeling Press LLC
315 N. Centre St.
Martinsburg, WV 25404
ChangelingPress.com

Printed in the U.S.A.

Editor: Jean Cooper
Cover Artist: Marteeka Karland

The individual stories in this anthology have been previously released in E-Book format.

No part of this publication may be reproduced or shared by any electronic or mechanical means, including but not limited to reprinting, photocopying, or digital reproduction, without prior written permission from Changeling Press LLC.

This book contains sexually explicit scenes and adult language which some may find offensive and which is not appropriate for a young audience. Changeling Press books are for sale to adults, only, as defined by the laws of the country in which you made your purchase.

Table of Contents

Rocket (Grim Road MC 1)	4
Prologue	5
Chapter One	12
Chapter Two	23
Chapter Three	31
Chapter Four	41
Chapter Five	50
Chapter Six	59
Chapter Seven	68
Chapter Eight	77
Chapter Nine	84
Chapter Ten	91
Chapter Eleven	104
Chapter Twelve	114
Chapter Thirteen	122
Chapter Fourteen	132
Lemon (Grim Road MC 2)	146
Chapter One	147
Chapter Two	158
Chapter Three	165
Chapter Four	173
Chapter Five	186
Chapter Six	195
Chapter Seven	203
Chapter Eight	212
Chapter Nine	220
Chapter Ten	229
Chapter Eleven	244
US Agricultural Act of 2018	252
Marteeka Karland	253
Bones MC Multiverse	254
Changeling Press LLC	255

Rocket (Grim Road MC 1)
A Bones MC Romance
Marteeka Karland

Rocket: My life pretty much took a hard left a year ago when I first met Lemon. She's wise beyond her years and as abrasive and sarcastic as they come. The second she busts my VP's balls -- literally -- I know I'd never be able to forget her. A year later I'm still infatuated with the vicious woman. When she runs off to charge hell with a water pistol, I'm right behind her wondering how we're gonna get out of this one alive. But I have a smile on my face and a determination to give this woman anything she wants. Even if it means some things in my club are going to have to change.

Lemon: Look. This is supposed to be all about how Rocket caught my eye and I decided I wanted him but there were obstacles and… phfffffff… Forget all that. What you need to know is when people are stupid, they need a kick in the… Crap. I'm not supposed to swear here. Grrrrr! Anyway, this is where I come in. Grim Road needs fixing. I'm not exactly qualified to do club… garbage, but Rocket? Yeah. I might have decided I'll keep him, so… I'm great at whipping people into shape. Grim Road, meet Lemon. See me, love me, MF'ers.

Rocket: Just pass me the beer and popcorn…

Prologue
Rocket

"I'm so sorry, Scarlet. But you should know, I'm so very, very proud of you. I love you."

Had I known what Claw would do next, I'd have taken him down. I can't say he didn't save me the trouble myself, but he was still my vice president. Without hesitating, even for a moment, Claw put the .45 to his temple and pulled the trigger. He'd shot it only a few minutes before, taking one of Hammer's legs off below the knee. The other man was now gagged, bound securely, and still writhing in pain. And rightly so. He'd terrorized Claw's daughter, Scarlet. But Claw had been as much at fault as Hammer in that. In a way, I suppose Claw had done what he knew had to be done and saved his brothers the trouble.

"Are you fucking kidding me right now?" Scarlet's eyes were wide with both shock and grief. Claw might have sold her out, but Scarlet hadn't known and the man was her father. Mars, her man, pulled her into his arms but she didn't turn her face away from the sight that had been her father. The powerful handgun he'd used had obliterated his head, spraying blood and brains all over the area.

While it was Scarlet I was concerned about, the small woman at her side snagged my attention. Lemon. She was younger than Scarlet in terms of years, but the woman was a force to be reckoned with. She held Scarlet's hand in solidarity and steadfastly refused to leave.

"Holy. Fuck." Lemon grimaced, obviously getting a little more than she bargained for, but she held on to Scarlet's hand like both their lives depended on it.

"Christ." I quickly stepped in front of the women to block their view of Claw. "Can't someone get the women the fuck out of here?" It went against everything I believed to have women witness violence of this nature. It was why I'd kept Talia, the daughter of my deceased best friend, away from everyone and everything to do with life in Grim Road. It was why I'd allowed Scarlet to leave when Claw had requested she do so. It went against everything I'd ever believed in to allow violence to touch any woman under my protection.

"Why? You think just because we're women we can't handle the hard shit? We're here to support Scarlet. She needs us here, so we're here. Seems like supporting each other is something Grim Road has a fucking problem with." The woman who spoke was the woman of Iron Tzars' sergeant at arms, Atlas. I'd heard she'd lost an unborn child fairly recently during a violent attack on their compound. I'd have thought this would be the last place she'd want to be. Given how pale she was, I was probably right. But she stood proudly beside Scarlet without flinching.

"Rose, honey." Atlas spoke gently to his wife. "Let's go. We can take Scarlet with us."

"Only if that's what Scarlet wants," Bellarose said. "If not, we stand by her."

As one, all the women surrounded Scarlet in a protective circle, Lemon at the front.

Lemon seemed to be directly challenging me with fire in her eyes, though she said nothing. I couldn't help but admire her courage in the face of what we had all witnessed. All of the women. But Lemon in particular. She technically wasn't even an adult, yet she stood her ground when I was certain there were men who would have backed down.

I glanced at Sting. "Are all your women like this?"

Sting just shrugged. "They've been through a lot this past year. And they are part of Iron Tzars. No wimps here."

"I'm sorry, Scarlet," I spoke softly to the young woman, never looking away from her. "You didn't deserve any of this."

"I got it anyway. Are you saying this was all about Hammer getting revenge for Claw killing my mother?"

"Looks that way, kid."

"I'm many things, Rocket, but I'm not a kid. Not anymore."

"Point taken. I never thought Claw was capable of betraying you. Or killing himself. Not like this. Every member of Grim Road has secrets they don't want anyone to know, and that was Claw's. I guess it's better this way. For what he did to keep his secret from you, I'd have had to kill him anyway." I sighed, scrubbing a hand over my face. "No one inside Grim knew Claw had killed Madina but me. I honestly hadn't realized Hammer knew until now. Had I known, I'd have overridden his approval of you leaving with that bastard."

Hammer thrashed and yelled behind his gag but no one seemed to pay him any attention. I was eager to get started on that motherfucker, but I would not do it with women in the area.

"It's done now. At least, Claw is done." Scarlet glanced over toward Hammer. "What's gonna happen to him?"

Sting laid out everything he had planned for the bastard. I tried to listen, knowing I fully intended to actively participate, but my attention was focused squarely on Lemon. She had her chin up, her hand firmly clasping Scarlet's. Her gaze flitted back and forth between Claw's body and Hammer, where he lay on a table that resembled an execution table. In a way I suppose it was. Hammer was going to die. Hard. Just not by lethal injection. Oh, no. He wasn't going to get off that easily.

The longer Sting spoke, the more satisfied Lemon's expression grew and she focused her entire being on the man tied to that table. The torture Sting described was brutal. Scarlet looked positively gleeful, almost maniacally so. Nothing I didn't deem appropriate, but I didn't want the women knowing how inhumane we were planning on being. Maybe it made me too old-fashioned for this day and age, but it's who I was. It was who my father had raised me to be.

Scarlet moved to stand over Hammer. "Sounds like you're getting ready to have a fun time. Bet you wished you'd never fucked with me now, huh?" She spat in his face before grabbing a scalpel and slicing a bit of skin off of his chest. Not a big piece, but enough she made the man scream behind his gag. Everything inside me rebelled. Not because I didn't think the bastard deserved everything she'd done, everything Sting described -- and more -- but because Scarlet should never have been led to feeling the way she obviously did. And because Lemon was a witness.

"We should go, Scarlet." Mars, Scarlet's man, looked desperate to get her out of there and back to the clubhouse.

"I can see this through, Mars. He was my nightmare. I can watch his demise."

"I know you can, honey. But maybe I can't."

Mars looked like he was trying not to flinch, but the fact was, the man was lying his ass off. He could totally watch the spectacle about to happen. He was trying to remove Scarlet from the situation in any way he could. I was sure he thought it would make him look weak in front of the men, but I knew better. It made him all the stronger because he thought he'd lose face and was still willing to do it if it was the only way to get his woman out without losing her trust in him.

"I'll stay in your place, Scarlet," Lemon volunteered. "I'll be your witness." I wanted to groan out loud. Did the woman have no sense of self-preservation? This could scar her for life! Probably already had. And that was the whole problem. She wasn't a woman. She was a girl. Seventeen, if I remembered correctly. She shouldn't even be here in the first Goddamned place.

"Not on your life." Danica, Lemon's sister, interjected. "You're coming back to the compound with me and Wylde. Right now."

Lemon, the brat, rolled her eyes. "You forgot to add 'young lady' at the end."

Danica looked ready to spank Lemon. Wylde looked like he was seconds away from a full-on belly laugh. Until Danica tilted her head up at him. Then he looked just as horrified as Danica had.

"I swear to God, Lemon," Danica bit out through gritted teeth. Then she pleaded with her sister. "Can you, for once in your life, please just do what I tell you?"

"If it were your best friend, Dani. If you were in the same position I'm in right now. Would you not see this through when your friend couldn't?" I'd bet my left testicle Lemon knew the answer to that question. She was too smart. She'd never have asked it otherwise.

"Sting can do that for her. He'll see this through." Danica stuck up her chin in a remarkable resemblance to Lemon. She didn't answer the question.

"But he's not her best friend. I am." Lemon looked like she was proud to call herself Scarlet's best friend. Loyalty, to this girl, meant everything. When she put herself solidly in someone's corner, she didn't leave.

Then I did the strangest thing. "Let her stay. I'll see to it she gets back to the clubhouse safely."

"Like hell," Wylde growled. "You couldn't keep one of your own women safe. You expect me to trust you with one of ours?" The fucking guy grated on my nerves something fierce. He seemed like a fun-loving geek, but Wylde was as deadly an enemy as ever I'd faced. And not just with his computer skills either. While I respected Wylde, I didn't appreciate his attitude. I couldn't allow him to disrespect me, but how could I reprimand him when I'd been thinking the exact same fucking thing?

"I'd never have permitted Scarlet to leave the safety of our territory if I'd known she'd be in danger. I know I have a lot to make up for because of Claw, but despite what it looks like, I take the safety of everyone in my club seriously. Especially our women and children." I should have followed up with her. It hung in the air unspoken between us like a specter.

"I'll keep an eye on them both, Wylde." Sting spoke softly, gripping Wylde's shoulder. "I'll bring her back. If she wants to stay, let her. Trust her to know where her limit is." I raised an eyebrow. Sting was a young man but apparently wiser than I was. I was with Danica on this, even if I'd said otherwise. I glanced once at Lemon. Her expression took my breath. It didn't matter what anyone said. Lemon wasn't leaving until she was Goddamned good and ready.

"Sting, I don't want her to do this. This is going to be brutal."

"I got this, Dani. Go on." Lemon actually reached out to her sister and squeezed her hand. She squared her shoulders and gave her sister a small grin. It was the first show of nerves she'd shown since immediately after Claw had shot himself.

Wylde whispered softly to Danica. I didn't hear what he said, but Danica didn't try to insist Lemon leave with her. Wylde guided her gently out of the barn. Lemon moved next to Hammer where he lay on the table. The men from Iron Tzars had started IVs on the guy and he now had one in the bend of his elbow and in the side of his neck. Both had fluids dripping slowly, but steadily through them.

"Looks like we're gonna be here a while, Hammer." Lemon grinned down at him. "I'm new to this whole death by torture bit, but I'm confident I can outlast you."

Just like that, I fell in love. I knew beyond any shadow of a doubt Lemon would be mine. Not today. Not until she was legal and I could be sure she was ready. But this woman would be my old lady. And I would rule her. The fun would be in the taming. It would possibly take a lifetime. But by fucking God, we'd have a blissful time of it.

Chapter One
Rocket

The heavy air in the compound's meeting room hung like a shroud, thick with exhaust and the sharp tang of spilled beer. I stood at the head of the long table, my gaze sweeping over the assembled brothers of Grim Road.

"All right, listen up," I called out, my voice rough as gravel. The room fell silent, every pair of eyes locked on me, waiting. "For those of you who don't know, Claw and Hammer are gone." More than one of the brothers raised an eyebrow, glancing at the man next to him. I'd taken eight of my most trusted men but hadn't called on the entirety of Grim Road. Mainly because I knew in my heart Scarlet wasn't being held against her will by Iron Tzars. As a rule, the men in Grim were a pretty Goddamned secretive lot, so when I'd called on my officers to ride with me, they'd simply done as I'd asked and hadn't said a fucking word to anyone else in the club.

"The fuck?" Spike had been leaning casually against a table, his arms crossed over his chest. He stood up straight, looking around at the others. Spike was also a close friend of Hammer. They'd served together both in and out of the Marines. "What do you mean gone?"

"Dead." I didn't mince words. They all needed to know because that left the VP position open and I needed to really think about who I put there.

There had always been cliques in the club. Men who trusted some more than others. We were all so used to operating by ourselves or in groups of two or three that thinking and operating as a group had never been something we'd adapted to. Grim Road had been around for a long time and hadn't always worked like this, but as the political environment changed over the decades and the old guard ushered in the new, we'd... changed. It wasn't that we didn't trust each other, but we... didn't really trust each other. Exactly.

"What happened?" Bear finally broke the silence weighing down the room. I knew he would be the one to speak for the group. His voice was a soft growl. The man could be demanding without being overly aggressive. His demeanor had always been a direct contrast to my own. Sometimes, he could balance me with the rest of the club without even trying. I was pretty sure he'd be the best choice for a VP. But not just yet. I needed to straighten out this fucking mess before I made any permanent changes in the club.

"There's a lot several of you guys don't know and I ain't tellin'. Not my story. But Claw put Scarlet in the hands of a sadistic bastard, and she was hurt because of it."

"Wait." Mace held up a hand. He was a man I should have taken with us. Of all the men in Grim Road, Mace was the steadiest. But he hadn't been in the compound when we'd left, having stayed behind to clean up from our last mission. "Didn't Scarlet leave with Hammer?" He glanced at Crush. "From what I heard she was supposed to be Hammer's old lady when she came of age. What happened?"

"Again, it's a long story, but Hammer and Claw had... history. I thought the same as you did. That Scarlet wanted to leave with Hammer. But that wasn't the case. Once he got her out of the compound, he abused her physically and mentally. Getting even with Claw for a past incident. One I should have dealt with years ago. So part of this whole fuckin' mess is on me."

"So, they're dead." Bear gave me a hard look.

"How'd they die?"

I shrugged. "Claw blew his own brains out. Hammer… well. There were quite a few pieces of the man when we finished with him."

"We?" Dom raised an eyebrow and glared at me. Hard.

"Yeah. Me, the men I took to Evansville, Indiana, and a few members of Iron Tzars."

"You were there?" Bear looked disapproving. I frowned at him.

"Yeah. I was fuckin' there. A member of this club has to die, I'm the one doin' it. Problem?"

Bear stared at me. Hard. "Yeah. I got a fuckin' problem. You went into another club's territory with only a handful of men. You went lookin' for a war but didn't take enough to back you up." He lifted his chin. "Tell me I'm wrong."

I shook my head. "Not sayin' you are, Bear. But I won't lie. I was pretty sure Hammer was lyin' when he said Scarlet was being held by Iron Tzars against her will. I know some of those men as well as I know you."

Bear grunted. "Mars, in particular."

"Yeah. Scarlet is with Mars. He made her his old lady."

"You gonna respect his claim?" Bear always did know how to ask the hard questions. It solidified my belief he was the right man to be vice president.

"It's what Scarlet wants. Woman's been through enough without us fightin' over her like dogs over a bone."

Ringo snorted. "Well, that and the old ladies of Iron Tzars are more than a little rabid. Especially that one called Lemon. Eh, Prez?" Yeah. Ringo had my number.

"The women of Iron Tzars ain't our problem. But

Scarlet wants her sisters to come to Evansville. I think it's a good idea."

Dom shook his head. "Not sure that's a good idea. They should at least be given a choice."

"Scarlet is their only living relative. You can bet your ass Wylde has already worked some magic to make her their legal guardian. Besides, you know they think Scarlet hung the moon. They'll go wherever she is. Hell, they fought like wildcats to go with her when she left with Hammer."

"He's right." Fang's deep voice penetrated the soft murmur around our meeting room. "Those girls will want to be with Scarlet. It's not a bad idea to ask them, though. Just to be sure. The last thing we want to do is make them feel like they don't have any choices. One or both of them will bolt like a wild fuckin' bronco if we do." There were more than a few chuckles around the room. Sunshine and Rainbow weren't quite on the same level as Lemon, but they were both skirting the edge of wild.

"Agreed. Now. Have Gina tell them to get packed. I'm expecting Brick to roll in here with a contingent that includes Mars and Scarlet within the hour. They'll expect the girls to be ready, and I don't intend to be more of an ass than I've already been."

"No one expects you to cave to another club in our territory, Prez," Bear snapped. "You don't think those girls need to go, fuck the lot of 'em."

"No. This is one time I'll allow it. At least, if the girls want to go. I owe it to Scarlet. After what she went through, that woman can have any fuckin' thing she wants. She needs her sisters right now. Probably more than they need her."

Byte stood. "I'll go help Gina. She had a thing for Hammer. Think it's best if she doesn't find out about it around the girls. They'll meet you guys at the entrance to the inner compound." He was the best person for the job. Sunshine and Rainbow adored the tech wiz. Probably because he kept them in the latest gaming consoles and computers. He was right to think Gina didn't need to hear about Hammer until she was away from the others. Byte would see to it she had privacy when she was told. If anyone could keep things smooth in this instance, it would be Byte. "When Scarlet gets here to pick them up, she can ask them in front of me. I'll honor their wishes and be careful of everyone's feelings."

"Good." I looked around the room, studying each of them. "We have one more thing to get out of the way." I met the gaze of each man present, really studying them. No one hurried me. It wasn't their way. We were all trained to wait patiently, no matter the circumstances. In our line of work, there was no room for mistakes. We were each other's only backup. Sometimes we didn't even have that. Each man could hold everything inside and not give anything away. Even torture would yield few results. If any. So I had to watch everyone very carefully. I'd trusted every person in the club.

Even Hammer. Even knowing the history between him and Claw and Madina. Even knowing Claw's woman had given birth to Hammer's twins. Claw had always treated the girls like his own, but now I had to be sure the threat to them was over. Also, I needed to know who in my club could be sadistic enough to contemplate hurting our children. No matter what the reason, that was as step too fucking far. "Hammer terrorized Scarlet. Beat her and threatened to harm Sunshine and Rainbow if she retaliated or left him." A couple of the men glanced at each other, showing more of a reaction than I'd expected, but more than a few simply gazed on stoically, giving nothing away. "He told her he had someone in the club keeping an eye on the girls. That one word from him and they'd suffer. I'm paraphrasing, but I took it the same way Scarlet did. Hammer had someone in Grim Road working with him to destroy Claw through his children."

"That's fucked up," Spike muttered. "Only a fuckin' coward preys on kids to get back at an enemy."

"It's worse than that," Dom said, giving me a glance. I nodded. The club needed to know. "Sunshine and Rainbow are Hammer's daughters. Claw is the one who killed Madina."

That got more than a few disbelieving grumbles.

"No fuckin' way," Spike snapped. "Not possible."

"Which event are you referring to?" Dom asked. "Because there's a couple things I had trouble with."

"Fuckin' all of it! Hammer would never disrespect a brother by movin' in on his woman. Madina and Claw had been an item for years before Hammer even patched in."

"I confirmed the first two with Hammer myself." I scrubbed a hand over my face. "Look. I know this is a real dick punch, but the fact is the only innocent parties in all this shit are Scarlet, Sunshine, and Rainbow. Hammer fucked Claw's woman. By all accounts he loved Madina. Claw and Madina had... issues. I'm not certain what they all were, but I know Madina was unhappy. I wasn't there when she told him about the babies, but I suspect she was going to leave him."

"The signs were there." Bear stroked his beard as he mused. "I remember thinking there was something going on between the two of them, but..." He shrugged. "Not my business."

"Fuck." Spike was possibly the most transparent of all of us. His work in Black Ops usually had to do with scouting a mark and planning the strike. Even though he had the training, he wasn't as experienced with deep cover as the rest of us. "I still don't see it. Hammer would have taken revenge on Claw directly. Not by going through kids to do it."

"Think about it, Spike." Falcon gripped Spike's shoulder in an effort to calm down the other man. "Claw was the VP. Hammer was a newly patched member. How's he gonna fight Claw?" He looked up at me. "What I don't understand is how Hammer could have someone ready to harm the girls if he knew they were his."

I nodded to Falcon. "Good point. When we took Hammer apart, I got the impression he was so eaten up with hate he didn't give a fuck. Claw had raised Sunshine and Rainbow as his own. Hammer knew he'd never have their loyalty and love the way Claw did. I think he distanced himself from the fact they were his daughters. He gave away more than I thought he would, and I think that was only because of what we did."

"Every man has his breaking point." Falcon nodded like he understood. "Must have been bad."

"Was." I barely suppressed a shudder. What we'd done to Hammer… Yeah. He deserved what we did and worse, but I had no idea if I could have done it by myself. If any of us could have. The men of Iron Tzars were pretty hardened and used to torture, but Hammer had been subjected to a special kind of hell. While it made my stomach roil, I still regretted none of it. "Ain't goin' over what we did so don't ask. Like I said. He wasn't in one -- or even a few -- pieces when we finished.

"So. We have a few things to discover. First, I want a rundown of Hammer's movements, Crush. I want to know where he was every second of every day in the weeks leading up to him and Scarlet leaving. You can't find a pattern or a person of interest, go back further." I gave my intel officer a hard look. "I want everything. And I mean everything. No matter how trivial you think it is."

"Maybe Hammer was fuckin' with you." Spike spoke up again. "Maybe he just wanted you to think there was a problem in the ranks."

"Wouldn't put it past him," Falcon agreed. "He's a wily son of a bitch."

"Was." I grunted. "And I get your point. But trust me when I say he was in no shape to make that kind of story convincing. All he could do was withhold information. Which he steadfastly did. Even when he was screaming. No. he had someone prepared to make good on his threat. Probably part of the reason he wanted to leave town. It gave him free rein to hurt Scarlet while distancing himself from any violence toward the girls. At least, I hope so. If not, then he was a truly evil man. And if there's one person that evil in our midst, there could be more. We're a secretive lot by nature, so this hurts in ways we've not even considered before."

"On it, Prez," Crush said softly. "I'll get Byte to help, if you're good with that."

I thought about Byte. He was younger than Crush by close to ten years and fresh out of the CIA. He'd put in his time and that time hadn't been kind to him. He'd also been on more than one mission with Hammer. "He gonna have a problem with this? I know Byte and Hammer were close."

"They weren't." Crush snorted. "Hammer was an asshole in the extreme. Byte tolerated him because he was part of the club, but I know Byte can absolutely believe this of him. I certainly do."

"Fuckin' little pissants. Both'a you," Spike muttered.

"Spike, you're out of this meeting." I had to take a stand on this if we were going to ferret out who was working with Hammer. "Listen up, people." I put as much hard authority as I could in my voice. "I know Hammer is guilty. That's not up for debate. What I'm interested in is finding out who was working with the son of a bitch. If your loyalty is to him, you need to get the fuck out." I turned to the now fuming Spike. "You're confined to quarters until further notice. I'll have food prepared and sent up by officers I trust."

"Come the fuck on, Prez! You might have had time to process this, but I don't remember a single fuckin' thing that would lead me to believe Hammer was capable of harming a kid. Not one."

"You can process it in your quarters."

"Fuck!" Spike smacked the back of the chair, tipping it over, and stormed out of the room.

"Anyone else?"

There were a few grumbles but nothing overt. I could see Crush noting every single one of them mentally, too. Crush was the more unbiased of the two, but Byte would be fine. Crush would keep him focused on the right thing. It was the way they worked. While Byte was the better investigator, Crush could keep his personal feelings out of the work. I figured it came with age.

"Good. No one is exempt from this investigation, Crush. Even me. I want to know everyone Hammer had contact with and to what extent. I absolutely will not have anyone in this club who is willing to harm a woman in our care unless there is a fuckin' good reason, or willing to harm a child for any fuckin' reason."

"Understood." Crush shook his head slightly, closing his eyes and taking a breath. I got it. He kept an eye on things most of us would prefer to be kept quiet, but this was a whole different level of spying on his brothers. It set him apart and now he was including Byte. No one blamed Crush for what he had to do. Not really. But it was still damned uncomfortable to know he knew some of the darkest secrets some of them had. He would never mention anything to anyone else, and he only talked to me if he deemed the situation a security risk. This was something else entirely, and we all knew it. Thing was, of all of us, I trusted Crush the most. He was the only one who ever willingly came to me with issues of his own. He said if he could know everyone's private business in the club, I could know his.

"Good. You two get on it. I want a detailed report every twelve hours, or anytime you find something important." I gave the room a hard stare, daring anyone to go against me.

"Don't you think that's an invasion of privacy, Prez?" The kid, Jackhammer -- yeah, wasn't touching that one -- raised a finger in the air. He had an innocent, dumb expression on his face I would have found adorably naive and laughed it off in any other circumstance. Given the situation, though, I was less than amused.

"No. You done somethin' you don't want Crush to find out?" I raised an eyebrow.

"Well, yeah, actually. Don't we all?" There were some grunted assents and some scowls thrown the kid's way. Looked like the club was solidly divided on this one.

"Tough shit." I grinned, but knew that smile didn't reach my eyes. "He's investigating me too. And yeah. I got my own fuckin' secrets. The only people who will know everything are Crush, Byte, and me. You don't like it? You can leave." I let my mask of civility drop so everyone in the meeting could see how serious and fucking furious I was. "But rest assured. I will find out who was working with Hammer, whether he's here or not. And I will annihilate them, whether or not they're still part of this club."

Having said my piece and given my orders, I left the meeting room to go to the front gate and await the Iron Tzars contingent. And… her. Because I knew there was no way Scarlet would come back to Grim Road without Lemon. I was anxious to see how Lemon dealt with this bunch. I had a feeling fireworks were about to fly. I wouldn't interfere, but I was damned sure going to enjoy the show.

Chapter Two
Lemon

I've heard that sometimes you just know when your life's about to change. As we rolled into the Grim Road compound, I got that feeling. It was a strange sense of foreboding and anticipation. And I was pretty sure I knew who it was centered around. But I didn't even like the bastard, so I chose to ignore that inner voice. My inner voice was stupid anyway.

The only fucking reason I'd come to this stupid place was to support Scarlet and to make sure her sisters, Sunshine and Rainbow, knew they had someone watching their backs. Well, other than some of the men. I suppose I trusted most of them in Iron Tzars, but I'd rather a woman had my back. So I wanted them to know I had theirs. Also, I knew this was probably going to be a special kind of hell for Scarlet. While her man, Mars, was with us, I was Scarlet's best friend. There was no way she was facing this alone.

When the two big Excursions pulled into the compound of Grim Road, a group of big, hard-looking men waved us through and two more men on bikes escorted us to what I thought was the center of the place. Scarlet had told me it was where the old ladies and children lived, though there weren't many people there. Mostly just her and her sisters and a couple of women who were steady lays of the men. I was sure Dani wouldn't want me to know about steady lays, but I wasn't a kid. Not in any meaningful way. I let Dani think she took care of me and Apple, but it was really me taking care of them.

"Stay here until I tell you two to come out." Mars was gentle when he spoke, but it was for Scarlet. The look he gave me said I better keep her in the vehicle at all costs. When I looked out of the window at the big men surrounding the truck, the very last thing I wanted to do was disobey Mars. Not because I was afraid, but because if things went south, it would be up to me to protect Scarlet.

"We're not some bunch of bastards who're gonna pounce on them, Mars." The big man who spoke was as rough as they came. He was built like a fucking mountain. Tall, muscled, but kind of soft-spoken. I thought it was probably a defense mechanism. So people underestimated him, and so he didn't seem so big. "You can let 'em out of the fuckin' cage."

"Not until I'm convinced they're safe." Brick's rough voice wasn't raised or angry. Just matter-of-fact. As vice president, he'd come with Mars in an official capacity. Also, the big man was great backup. "I swore to Scarlet we'd keep her safe, and that's what I intend to do. If you're gonna get your panties all in a twist, maybe you should go back to your fuckin' clubhouse."

The big man took one menacing step toward Brick. Brick was by no means a small man, but this guy towered over him and had to be at least half again as thickly built as Brick. Which was saying something. Brick was the largest man I'd ever met in my life. "You don't get to dictate in this club."

"Stand down, Bear."

And just like that, everything inside me went on red alert. Rocket. The president of Grim Road. He was also just a little more scary than I liked. Of all the men I'd met in Iron Tzars and the few I'd had encounters with in Grim Road last night when Hammer and Claw had died, Rocket was the one who unsettled me the most. I wouldn't say I was afraid of him exactly, just… wary. Like I needed to be on guard at all times or he'd catch me unaware and pounce. What happened then would be anyone's guess. Personally, I was going with *he loses his balls and I mount them like fucking trophies*, but who could say.

"Don't like this, Prez," Bear grumbled, but backed off a couple steps. "I get we messed up, but we don't hurt women."

"And the only thing they're concerned with is the fact we messed up." Rocket didn't sound mad or give away anything, really. In fact, seemed like he was looking forward to this. The only way I could describe him in this moment was... gleeful. The expression on his face made me decidedly uneasy.

"Something's off," Scarlet murmured. She didn't appear scared, just puzzled. "Rocket's too accepting of this whole situation."

"You think he's gonna hurt you? 'Cause I will hand him his balls this time."

"No. Rocket is many things, but he'd never intentionally harm one of us. Whatever they had going on before must have really consumed the club because the whole deal with my father and Hammer isn't something Rocket would normally have missed. He was as baffled by the whole thing as I was."

"Still not sure I trust him."

Scarlet glanced at me. "You probably shouldn't. You caught his attention and that's not necessarily a good thing."

The door to the SUV opened then, stopping further discussion. I got out before Scarlet. When she exited the vehicle, I kept my body between hers and everyone else. Mars stood in front of me, and Brick and Smoke from the second SUV were in front of Mars.

I looked around, making sure I had a handle on our surroundings. If things went south, our best bet was to get back in the truck and do our best to get the hell outta Dodge. I had no idea if the thing was bulletproof -- knowing the Iron Tzars, there was every possibility it was -- but we'd have to keep our heads down and book it as hard as we could. If I ran over someone in the process? Fuck 'em.

"Get that look off your face, girl." Rocket stepped closer to us, his gaze focused squarely on me. "We ain't gonna pounce on you. You're here to let Scarlet get anything she wants that she left behind, and to talk to Sunshine and Rainbow."

"We're here to take Sunshine and Rainbow with us," I snapped before anyone could say anything else. "Not leavin' 'em here."

"You will if they don't want to go." Rocket didn't raise his voice or even look angry. His features were mild. Reasonable, even.

"Scarlet's their guardian now. They'll go where she says." I stuck my chin up. I thought I heard Mars groan, but I didn't dare take my gaze from Rocket to make sure.

"They're old enough to make up their own minds. If they don't want to leave Grim Road, I'll look after them."

"Not on your fuckin' life." I bared my teeth at Rocket, who looked amused. Which just pissed me the fuck off. "How 'bout I wipe that smug grin off your fuckin' face?"

That got a couple chuckles from the members of Grim Road nearby.

"That one's askin' for a whoopin', Prez. You gonna teach her some manners?"

"Yep." Rocket crossed his muscled arms over his massive chest. He wore jeans and a leather cut without a shirt under it so he showed off a lot of muscle and tattooed skin. "Just not now. She ain't old enough."

"Like fuck you are." I took a step toward Rocket, fully intending to give him more of what I'd given him last night, but Mars held out his arm to prevent me from going around him.

"Just calm down, Lemon. He's baiting you."

"Lemon?" Bear barked out a laugh. "Her name's Lemon." It wasn't phrased as a question.

"You got a problem with that, fuckwit?" I ignored Mars. I knew they were baiting me. Of all of Scarlet's protectors, I was the weak link and they were testing my boundaries and how far they could push me.

"I got a problem with your mouth. Maybe there's somethin' else you could do with it."

"Bear," Rocket growled, his facial expression changing like someone had flipped a switch. "She's underage."

"Yeah?" I plowed on, ignoring Rocket. "Try it. See what body part you lose, you freak."

Bear leaned forward in my direction but didn't actually commit to taking the full step. Then he pointed at me. "Your day's comin, lil' bit."

I sneered, looking the big man up and down like a princess eyeing a filthy peasant who'd been mucking out the pig barn. "Not from you."

"Can we please get a move on?" Brick actually raised his voice. That was new. Usually, he just growled or snarled and everyone jumped to do his bidding. Well, everyone except Serelda. He never used his growly voice with her.

"Sure. Soon as the Neanderthal gets the fuck outta the way." I gave Bear a cheerful wave.

"Glad that one's leavin'," he muttered as he stepped back. "Someone needs to teach her some manners."

"I only use manners with people who earn that respect from me."

"Which is to say no one." I thought that was Smoke, but the man didn't know me that well. OK, maybe he did. 'Cause yeah. Manners were for pussies.

I was about to open a can of whoopass on Bear when the door to the inner compound opened and two younger girls walked out with suitcases in hand. A man who looked to be in his late twenties walked with them, pulling another suitcase. The girls grinned widely when they saw Scarlet and ran to her.

"Scarlet! You're home!" The girls threw themselves into Scarlet's arms, and she might have fallen on her ass if Mars hadn't moved to put an arm around her and take the brunt of their exuberance.

"Yeah, honey. I'm back."

"Byte had us pack our stuff. We going somewhere?"

Scarlet kissed the girl's forehead before pulling back to look at them both. "Yeah. You're coming back with me to Indiana." She turned to look back at Mars. "This is Mars. I'm his old lady now."

"Old lady?" One of them wrinkled her nose. "You sure about him?" She gave Mars a look like she judged him and found him lacking. "He don't look like much."

That got a snort outta Smoke. "I think that one's already got your number, Mars."

"Don't need your help, Smoke." Mars grinned, but I knew he was irritated. Though I agreed with Smoke. Whichever twin this one was had Mars pegged. He was all right I guess, but he needed someone to keep him on his toes. "I'm Mars. If it helps, your sister chose me to be her protector. We both kinda had a rough time of it, but we're better when we're together. Kinda keep each other grounded, I guess." He held out his hand to the girl.

For a moment, I thought she might refuse to take his hand, but finally, she held out her own and gripped Mars' hand. "I'm Rainbow. This is Sunshine. And if you say anything about our names, I'll hurt you."

I got that. Before Mars could open his big mouth and be a guy, I moved forward, putting my body between Rainbow and Mars. I took her hand firmly in my own. "I'm Lemon. I have a twin too. Her name's Apple."

Like I knew it would, that gave Rainbow a start before she grinned widely at me. "I think I'm gonna like you."

"Ditto, kid."

"Are you good with going with Scarlet, Rainbow?" The guy with them spoke for the first time. He wasn't overly assertive, but I got the feeling this was a test of some kind.

"Yeah, Byte," Sunshine answered. "Why wouldn't we be?" She looked genuinely puzzled.

"We just didn't want you feeling like you had to leave. If you want to stay, you can."

"Wait," Rainbow narrowed her eyes. "Ain't we comin' back later?"

"No, honey." Scarlet said with a sigh. "We're moving to Indiana to live with another club. Mars belongs to the Iron Tzars. I know you've heard Claw mention them."

"Yeah. But why do we need to stay there?"

Scarlet looked up at Mars, uncertain of how to proceed next. I could tell she didn't want to do this here, but I wasn't sure she was gonna get out of telling Sunshine and Rainbow their father was dead.

"I'll tell you everything when we get back to Indiana. It's a long story."

Rainbow nodded slowly and I knew she knew something was amiss. "Yeah. All right." She turned and raised a hand for Byte to high-five. "See you in the game."

"You can count on it, squirt." Byte gave her a grin. "You know how to find me if you guys need anything, but I'm sure Scarlet's got everything under control."

"Of course, she does." Sunshine lifted her chin. "She's Scarlet!"

Byte laughed. "Yeah. She is."

Rainbow looked around. "See you guys. Bye, Rocket."

Rocket nodded at the girls before his gaze landed squarely on me. "I'll be seein' you around, Lemon."

I snorted. "No. You won't."

He raised an eyebrow. "Wouldn't bet on that if I were you. Because you will. When you do, you'll be comin' back here. With me."

"Right." I gave him a derisive sneer. "Only if you want your balls detached from your body."

He grinned, shaking his head once as if he found my objection cute. "Challenge issued? Challenge fuckin' accepted. You got a year, little girl. Best you get ready."

"Guess I need to say the same fuckin' thing to you. 'Cause there's no way in fuckin' hell I'll ever go anywhere willingly with you, motherfucker."

Chapter Three
Lemon
Palm Beach, Florida
One year later...

"I can't believe Dani let us come to Palm Beach by ourselves for Spring Break." Apple slathered sunscreen over her pale skin. She had the biggest smile on her face and was practically vibrating with excitement. If she hadn't been my sister, I'd have punched her in the tit. No one should be that fucking happy all the time. Not that I'd change any second of this for her. I just liked bitching about it.

"Right." I had to consciously keep myself from rolling my eyes where Apple could see me. "We're all alone in the big wide world with no one to watch over us. However will we manage?" I sighed, sounding bored as I put my sunglasses on and my hands behind my head. Apple might not have spotted the men from a local MC called Salvation's Bane, and I wasn't going to point them out to her. The last thing Wylde told me before we left was that if we needed anything while we were in Florida, I was to go to anyone at Salvation's Bane. He'd even given me the phone number of Bane's tech guy, a man called Ripper. So when I'd seen the cut the men wore, I knew they were there watching over us.

I'd never admit it to a fucking soul, but I liked that situation for more than one reason. First, I knew Wylde and the Tzars had our backs, because there was no way Salvation's Bane had decided on their own to watch over a pair of random women. Second, Bane had our backs because they were helping out the Tzars. And lastly, it just felt good to know someone besides me was watching over my sister. And I would do anything to keep my sisters safe, but especially Apple. Wylde had Dani's back. While I was sure he'd do his best to protect me and Apple, his first priority would always be Dani. At least, it better be. Otherwise I'd allowed him be with my sister for nothing. While I really liked Wylde, I would kill him if he didn't.

"Bitch." Despite her words, Apple laughed and threw a handful of wet sand at me. I was stretched out on a towel in a bikini, my skin hot and damp from sweat and lying under the noon-day sun. Bliss!

"Whore." I threw a handful of sand back at her along with the word. It was our way.

This was the start of our third day in Florida. We'd come to this beach each morning at sunrise and hadn't left until the sun set each night. Which I hated. At least, the morning part. But Apple was one of those people. You know. A morning person. It was hard to believe she was my sister, let alone my twin. Morning people sucked, and my sister did not suck. She was a far better person than I was, and I didn't care to admit it.

But none of that was important. What was important was the fact that I'd seen the same guy on this beach the three days we'd been here. He'd watched the whole beach, studying everyone in the area. I'd seen his gaze briefly focusing on us more than once. The last time I'd caught his gaze and gave him what I hoped was a fucking death stare. Because if he had any thoughts of coming near my sister, I wanted him to know I'd make him wish I'd only killed him.

That had been Tuesday morning when I'd given him the stink eye. It was now Wednesday afternoon. I'd seen him a few more times since that day, but I didn't think he saw me. He still studied the beach, but I'd noticed he seemed to be focusing on children. Girls in particular. At least, that's what it looked and felt like to me. Had we been at a more crowded beach, I might have dismissed my concerns as me being a bitch who didn't trust anybody. But this was a smaller section and in a spot that was more difficult to reach than other sections. So there were many fewer people. Following this guy's gaze wasn't difficult. And he always stopped on and watched young girls.

I was half listening to Apple going on about what a beautiful day it was and how free it felt to be outside under the sun, and blah, blah, blah, when I saw him again. This time, I saw him zero in on the same girl of about seven or eight, whom he'd been watching the past two days. She was by herself at a water fountain. I wasn't sure who she was here with, but there wasn't an adult in the area. Which is when the guy made his move.

"Apple." I got to my feet and shoved my legs into my shorts.

"What's wrong?" My sister could always tell when my mood had shifted the second it did.

"Behind us next to the food truck under the canopy are two guys in black MC vests. They're from Salvation's Bane. You go to them, then shoot an S.O.S. text to Wylde. Tell those men from Bane I'm following a man who took a little girl and for one of them to come after us. You stay with the other man and Bane until Wylde sends help." I slipped on my flip flops.

"Where are you going?" Apple didn't question me. She was already snagging her shorts and phone as she looked in the direction I'd indicated.

"To try to help that girl."

Without waiting for Apple to fire off more questions, I ran through the sand across the beach as hard as I could go. I had the guy firmly in my sights, focused on him as he carried the screaming girl. He clamped a hand over her mouth as he continued to hurry off the beach and down an alleyway. I was glad I'd thought to slip on my flip-flops as I padded across the pavement. They weren't much, but were better than my bare feet.

He made it halfway down the alley when the girl managed to wiggle out of his grasp. That gave me the precious moments I needed to get within striking distance before he got hold of her again. I saw him snake a zip tie around the girl's wrists at the small of her back. He tossed her into the back of the van at the same time I leapt for him.

With a battle cry, I jumped onto his back, wrapping my arms and legs around him as tightly as I could. I had a choke hold on him, but couldn't get the leverage I needed to make him hurt. I knew I didn't need to hold on long before the member of Salvation's Bane found us. I just had to hold out a couple of minutes at most.

The girl screamed shrilly, and I could hear her sobbing occasionally. When I heard the sound of someone smacking the child just before she stopped screaming, I realized we weren't alone.

"Get this fuckin' bitch off'a me!"

Yeah. I was in trouble. Just as I felt hands grab my waist, I snapped my head forward, slamming my forehead into the guy's nose. Then I did the same to the other guy by jerking my head backward. I think I caught his chin instead of his nose and it made the back of my head sting.

"Mother fuck!" The second guy didn't let me go, but staggered backward, his beefy arms solidly around me even though I'd obviously hurt him. "Secure the girl in the van, then help me with this bitch." He squeezed his arms tighter around my slight form. It was like a python wrapping around me. Every time I breathed out, he seemed to know and adjust his hold even tighter, making it hard to breathe.

I gave a furious yell and started struggling in earnest now, knowing I had seriously bitten off more than I could chew. The guy used one hand to cover my mouth, which helped me breathe. Didn't help me get away from the big bastard.

Just as the first guy turned away from the van, I got in a good, solid kick to this guy's knee. It gave way and he fell to the ground. Amazingly, he retained his hold, but I took the opportunity to bite down on his hand with everything I had.

"Fuck!" He roared and jerked his hand away. I hoped the fuckers from Salvation's Bane did what Apple told them and one of them was headed in my direction. If not, there was no way I was going to be able to help this girl before the men got her away.

"Bitch!" The first guy aimed a kick to my middle, but managed to catch the arm of the man holding me.

"Son of a bitch!" How this guy was still holding me, I had no idea, but he held on for dear life. "Stop tryin' to kick her and get her fuckin' legs so we can toss her in the van!"

When the first guy went for my feet, I kicked out, catching him in the balls. Even with only my flip-flops on, I still got in a good blow. He grabbed himself, stumbling backward. "Fuck! Goddamn fuckin' bitch!"

The man holding me slipped a meaty arm around my neck and tightened his hold, cutting off my air but good this time. "Gave you a chance to go easy, girl. Now you're gonna go the hard way." Spots danced before my eyes and I continued to fight. I tried to yell out, but I could barely drag in a breath to keep myself conscious let alone scream. I knew someone from Bane had to be close by. I just had to hold out a few more minutes. Surely!

"She does that again, I'm gonna kill the bitch." The first guy grabbed my feet, slipping a zip tie around my ankles. He sounded pained and his breath wheezed in and out of his lungs, but he got the job done.

"Just shut up and get her hands and get another tie for her feet. Someone's coming."

That made me fight all the harder. At least, I tried to. Not being able to breathe properly took more out of me than I thought. The next thing I knew they tossed me into the back of the van. The bigger guy managed to get a zip tie looped around my ankles and pulled securely. Then he slammed the door shut. When it took off, the tires peeled out on the asphalt. I was still taking in great gulps of air and the momentum slammed me back against the shut door. I groaned, doing my best to stay conscious. Beside me, the girl whimpered, occasional sobs coming from her.

"It'll be OK," I managed to get out. "Just stay as close to me as you can, and I'll do my best to protect you."

"I'm scared," the girl whimpered.

"I know. But I promise I'll do everything I can to get us both out of this. I won't leave you." I didn't tell her we had help coming because the last thing I wanted was for her to slip up and say something. It would give away any advantage of surprise the guys from Bane had.

"What's gonna happen to us?"

I shook my head. The combination of the guy choking me nearly to death and the lick I'd taken when I'd smashed the back of my head into that same guy's chin was enough to make me dizzy. I had no idea how to answer that Goddamned question.

After a couple moments, I looked up at her terrified face. "What's your name, kid?"

"Effie." Her face was tearstained, and she looked like she had a sunburn, but otherwise didn't appear to be hurt.

I nodded. "That short for something?" I wanted to distract her while I struggled to sit up. I needed to think if I wanted to figure out how to get us out of here in case Bane couldn't find us right away. Wylde said Bane's intel guy, Ripper, was good, but I'd really feel better if I had Wylde on this. And I'd never fucking tell him I fucking thought that because it would make him more of an insufferable bastard than he already was.

"Euphemia." She said, wiping her nose on her wrist and grimacing like she thought the snot was disgusting. "It's Greek. It means 'well spoken.' So Mom said I needed to read a lot so I could live up to my name."

"Well, Euphemia is a mouthful, but I like Effie."

She ducked her head. "It's a freak name."

"It's a great name," I snapped. "Don't you let anyone tell you different. If I were you, I'd make everyone call me Euphemia just to fuck with 'em."

That got a small giggle out of the kid. She still looked scared, but she'd stopped crying at least. "My teachers at school can never say it."

"Yeah. I bet first days are hell."

"What's your name?"

I lifted my chin and gave her a cocky grin. "Lemon."

Her eyes widened. "Really?"

"Yep. I have a sister named Apple. She's the sweet sister. I'm a bit... tart."

Despite the situation, the child managed a small,

genuine laugh. "Tart means you're a little sour."

"Yep." I tried to match her smile with one of my own when I was still trying to take stock of my body. I didn't think I was injured. Just winded and a little banged up. All in all, I think I gave better than I got. "You know. Like a Lemon."

We shared a smile before the van took a sharp right turn and threw us both against the wall of the van. Effie yelped and I managed to catch her. They'd zip-tied my hands together, but in front instead of behind, so I was able to protect her a little.

"Do me a favor, Euphemia. Check my back pocket and make sure my phone is as far down my back pocket as it can be."

She nodded and I rolled over so she could push my phone farther down so it was as secure as I could make it. Considering I was wearing a bikini top and a pair of cut-off jean shorts, I was damned proud I'd even remembered the fucking phone. I had nowhere else to put it. Also, it wasn't a fancy smartphone. I'd never take one of those to the beach. Nope. This was an old ass, small-as-shit flip phone Wylde had fixed for me as a backup. Which was both good and bad. Because he'd be looking for my main phone first. I had no doubt Apple would do what she had to do so I knew it was only a matter of time before he found me. Just might take longer than I'd like because I had my back-up phone. On the other hand, it was good because it was small and fit snugly into my back pocket. So, all I had to do was hold out until Wylde sent someone for me.

"Whatever you do, don't say a word. You can cry, you can scream, you can do whatever you need to, but don't talk. The more information you give them the easier you'll make this for them."

"What are they gonna do?" Euphemia looked up at me. And yeah, I was calling her Euphemia to get her used to it because, once we were out of this shit situation, I fully intended to get her to make everyone call her Euphemia just to fuck with the people in her life. Fucking with people was the best way to show them you cared. Or that you hated them and wanted them as far away from you as possible. Either worked.

"I don't know. But whatever it is, the last thing we want to do is make it easier for them."

The van jerked to a stop, throwing us forward. Euphemia screamed but I managed to keep my body between hers and the front of the van. I heard the front doors open and close and scrambled to put the girl solidly behind me and prepared myself for a battle.

They had us. There was little I could do to escape and even if I managed, I couldn't leave Euphemia. With both our legs tied with zip ties, there was no way to do anything quickly.

I found a fire extinguisher strapped to the front corner of the back of the van and snagged it, pulling the pin and preparing myself for a battle. They'd still get me, but I wasn't going quietly.

The doors jerked open. Euphemia screamed and I let loose with the fire extinguisher. A spray of carbon dioxide gas assaulted them. The guy who'd first grabbed Euphemia fell to the ground, rubbing his eyes and wheezing. Which was my mistake. I'd aimed at the wrong threat. I might have been able to fight off that first guy, but not the second, bigger guy. I got him, but not enough to make him have too hard a time breathing. At least, not right away. I could only hope he'd inhaled enough of the shit to give him cancer or pop a lung or something. Wouldn't kill him immediately, but might make it slow and painful. And ugly. And maybe he'd even shit himself in the process.

"Mother fuck!" the first guy yelled between coughing fits. The second lunged for me, wrestling the extinguisher away from me before I could turn it around and hit him with it.

"That's all I'm takin' from you, bitch." The last thing I saw was his hand coming toward my face as he backhanded me. Then… nothing.

Chapter Four
Rocket

Talia, the woman I thought of as a daughter, was all smiles as she walked into the clubhouse hand in hand with Doc. Dr. Jude Collins had taken my ward as his old lady a couple of years ago and he'd done right by her. I couldn't remember Talia smiling as genuinely or easily as she did when either dancing or playing the piano except when she was with Doc. Or Doc's daughter, Caroline. The three of them seemed to have formed a tight family that protected both girls and put a spring in Doc's step. Still didn't mean I didn't want to wipe the smug smile off the bastard's face whenever I saw them together.

"Rocket." Doc offered his hand and I took it. "Good to see you."

Talia smiled widely and threw herself into my arms. I'd never been overly demonstrative towards her, but I knew she thought of me as her dad same as I thought of her as my daughter. I'd done my best to fill in that role a after her real father had died when she was just an infant. Talia's mother was a good woman, but she'd never gotten over her husband's death. When she died, Talia came to live with me until Doc had claimed her. I'd never admit it to another person, but she'd might have taken a little piece of my soul with her. She was a good kid. And so giving and compassionate I had to wonder how she'd managed to stay so sweet growing up in a place like Grim Road.

No. She wasn't a kid. She was a woman. And she was currently married to a man I thought of as… not a friend exactly, but close. Men in my line of work didn't have friends. At least, not if we wanted them to live.

"I've missed you, Rocket." Talia looked up at me

and I grinned down at her, leaning in to kiss her forehead.

"Missed you too, kiddo. You keepin' Doc in line?"

"Mostly."

"You should ask me if I'm keeping her in line. Woman's a holy terror when she wants to be." Doc smiled affectionately down at Talia, and it warmed my heart. Not for Doc. Bastard didn't deserve her. But Talia deserved every happiness she could have. And it was clear Doc made her happy.

"What's up?" Doc gave me a quizzical look.

"Can't I come by to visit my daughter?" No, she wasn't really my daughter, but she'd thought that for most of her life and, if I were honest, since fate had taken her real dad away from her, I wouldn't have it any other way.

Surprisingly, it was Talia who rolled her eyes and cocked her hip as she shook her head. "Dad. You never come by for just a visit. What's going on?"

I shrugged. "Not a thing. Thought I'd talk to Thorn. He helped me out of a tight spot several months ago and I wanted to return the favor."

Doc was all business then, his features going from happy and carefree to hard in the blink of an eye. "I'll send a prospect for him."

"In a minute. It's not so important I can't sit and talk with Talia for a while."

So Talia started telling me about her new studio Doc and the club had bought for her in town. It was a combination dance and music studio where she taught kids who couldn't afford lessons otherwise. She had a whole slew of students, as she put it. The glow on her face and the sparkle in her eyes told me she was happier than I ever thought she could be. Especially when she lived in the Grim Road compound.

I was about to start asking questions just to keep her talking when a young woman and one of the Salvation's Bane members ran into the common room. When I realized who the woman was, my mouth went dry and dread settled in the pit of my stomach.

"Where's Ripper?" Apple, the twin sister of the one woman I couldn't seem to get out of my head looked like she was about to have a panic attack. "I need him to talk to Wylde!"

Several Bane members emerged from various offices and rooms just off the common room. One of them was the man in question. Ripper was the Bane computer wiz and intel officer. He'd been wounded during a tour that took muscle and tissue from one leg and put shrapnel in his face. He was scarred and had a slight limp, but he was one deadly son of a bitch. Especially when someone he cared about was threatened.

"I'm Ripper," he said, not acknowledging the interruption or the fact that Apple was so distraught.

"I sent an S.O.S to Wylde and he wants to talk to you." She held out her phone to the big man with hands that trembled like a leaf in the wind. Ripper put it to his ear and spoke.

"Ripper." There was silence while someone on the other end -- presumably Wylde -- spoke to him. Ripper headed back to his office and Apple followed.

"What's goin' on, man?" Doc spoke to the guy with Apple. Lock, according to the patch on his chest.

"Her sister. She took off after a guy she saw nab a child off the beach. Poison ran after her, but he was on foot. That guy joined another guy and they took off with Lemon and another girl in a white van. No windows. No license plate. Poison got there just as they sped off. He's right behind us."

As if on cue, another man entered the clubhouse, a hard, angry expression on his face. "Don't know whether to spank that woman or give her a medal."

Ripper exited his office just as Thorn and Havoc appeared from deeper inside. "Thorn. I've got a location on Lemon's phone, but she's not in Palm Beach." He glanced at me. "She's in Riviera Beach."

"OK. Stop." I stood and joined the Bane president and vice president. "What the shit's goin' on?"

"They took Lemon," Apple sobbed. "They took her and the girl she was trying to save."

I glanced back to Poison. "You get a look at 'em?"

"Yeah. One's a big son of a bitch. The other's a bit of a runt. Both of 'em had on long sleeves, so I couldn't see any distinctive tattoos and their faces weren't marked."

"Gang?" I raised an eyebrow.

"Not sure. Possibly." Lock looked like he was ready to put his fist through a wall. Or someone's face. "Poison said she fought 'em hard but the big one got her in a choke hold and, well, you can't fight if you can't breathe."

"Goddamnit!" Something akin to panic seized me. My chest tightened and at that moment I wanted to throttle the younger woman. "What the fuck was she thinking?"

"That a little girl needed help," Apple cried. She marched up to me, poking a finger in my chest, much like Lemon might. "She did what she had to do. You better not say a fucking bad word about my sister."

This… didn't compute. "You're supposed to be the docile sister." Which must have been the exact wrong thing to say because Apple, bless her heart, slapped me full on the face. She didn't hold back either. The side of my face stung and my ear rang where she'd clapped it with her blow.

"All right, Apple," Thorn said, stepping between me and the girl. "Calm down. We'll find your sister, but she's in his territory. You might want to keep that in mind before you go beatin' up the president of Grim Road."

"He better keep in mind I might not be as big as he is, but Lemon is my sister. She's taught me things." Her words were tough, but tears spilled freely down her cheeks and she fought off sobs. Mostly.

At any other time, that might have gotten a laugh from more than one member of Bane. Hell, I might have even laughed myself. But not now. Not with Lemon in danger and Apple struggling so hard to keep it together.

"You know where she is precisely, Ripper?"

"Yeah. It's a small crackerjack house near the beach. Kind of off to itself. Far as I can tell, it's just the four of them, but I've had about two minutes to study the city camera feeds, so I could be wrong."

"Thorn, I'd appreciate it if you got your people ready in case I need backup. Ripper, do you have Crush's contact info?"

"Yeah. He and I've opened a loose dialogue." The big guy shrugged. "Nothing heavy, just keeping tabs on each other."

I didn't like that and I'd be talking with Crush later, but I had bigger problems. I didn't want anyone from Grim Road going in on this. They had a tendency to shoot first and consider the collateral damage later. Every single one of us, to the man, were black ops. Our specialty was killing. We were only sent in when there were no other options and there was a plausible explanation if more people died than were supposed to. While I trusted the men in my club… to a point… I wasn't willing to risk Lemon's safety -- or the safety of her charge -- with little to no planning. I'd be doing this myself.

"Give him the information. Tell him I said to watch. He'll know what to do from there. Keep Wylde in the loop, too." I turned to Apple. "You stay here until Wylde gives you instructions."

"Where are you going?" God, the girl sounded as belligerent and demanding as Lemon. Just without the lethal bite Lemon had.

"To get your sister."

My phone buzzed in my back pocket and I took it out, glancing at the screen. Ripper had sent details of where Lemon was being held. I knew the crappy little house. It was a place we'd had under surveillance but hadn't pounced on yet. I guess now was the time. Only I'd be doing it myself.

Shoving my phone back in my pocket, I headed out the door and to my bike. It was less than a fifteen-minute ride back to Riviera Beach but I made it in ten. I had no doubt Lemon could take care of herself. The thing that got me was that she'd protect that girl with everything in her, even if it meant sacrificing herself. I knew it like I knew my own name. That was the problem. Which meant I had to be careful going in.

I parked my bike a few blocks away from my target. If I had the timeline anywhere close, the girls had been gone right at an hour. As I approached the house, I could hear the men arguing inside. And there were definitely more than two. Their words were indistinct, but the voices were different. I thought there might be at least four if not five men in the house.

There was a thud, then a sharp yelp from one of the men. "Fuckin' bitch! I'm gonna fuckin' kill you!"

"Bring it on, you son of a bitch!"

"Fuck." I muttered the expletive. The guy meant business and so did Lemon. While I'd put her one-on-one against a man -- even a battle-seasoned one -- for a short while, there was no way she would survive four or five to one. Not waiting a moment longer, I kicked in the back door, charging the first man I saw.

Snapping his neck was easy, but I'd lost the element of surprise. Two more guys charged me, one pulling out a gun. He shot once before a third man snagged the gun from his hand.

"You want someone callin' the fuckin' cops? Kill the bastard, but do it quiet!"

"I'll kill you!" Lemon shouted as she charged the third guy. Though her hands were tied together in front of her, she'd managed to score a thick wooden stick for a weapon. Looked like a chair leg or something. She swung, but I didn't have time to see if she connected because the two other men took me down. Which was when I realized the shot the second guy had gotten off had hit my shoulder. Pain ripped through me, but I ignored it. Just like I'd been trained to do.

I fought two, then three men while Lemon swung her weapon at the fourth. With my attention divided, I took more hits than I should have. One to my wounded shoulder didn't hurt as much as I'm sure it should have -- or would once the tissue shock wore off -- but the blow to my knee put me on the floor.

There was a shrill scream and Lemon gave a brutal yell. I could hear thuds in the background and I thought she was beating the shit out of her attacker, but that could have been wishful thinking.

"Get behind me, Euphemia!" Lemon took another vicious swing at the guy in front of her. I heard the bone in his forearm snap as he held it up defensively. I made as much noise as I could, hoping to keep these three men's attention on me so Lemon could escape with her small charge, but Lemon was having none of that. The second she knew her guy was down for the count, she started in with one of the guys attacking me.

"Motherfuckers!" Her battle cry was hard to miss as she fought first one, then another of the three men attacking me. Though I fought, I wasn't nearly as effective as I normally would have been. My knee was in a bad way. I'd be lucky if I hadn't blown it out.

When I finally got to my feet, I threw myself in the general direction of the other two men Lemon had engaged. I noticed the small figure huddled behind Lemon, trying to do what Lemon asked her but afraid of getting hit. The girl still had her hands tied in front of her, but it looked like her feet were free.

"Goddamnit, Lemon! Get the kid and get the fuck outta here!"

"Shut up and fight, you asshole!" That demand in her voice really shouldn't have been a turn-on, but there it was.

"Imma kill you, bitch!" One of the guys fighting Lemon lunged in an all-out attack, backing Lemon up and with her, the girl.

With one last-ditch effort, I gave an enraged roar as I launched myself at the guy, lowering my shoulder and running him over like a linebacker. Immediately, every man in the house was on me, giving Lemon the opening she needed. Even as I fought, I could see her indecision. She very much wanted in this fight, but she also knew she couldn't protect the girl and engage these assholes at the same time. One thing about Lemon I'd noticed. She wasn't afraid to wade in where angels feared to tread. But she knew her limits. I also knew that, if she hadn't had the girl with her, trying her best to protect the child, she'd have said to hell with the consequences, doused herself in gasoline, and jumped into the fire with both feet.

"I'll send help, Rocket!" she yelled as she hurried the girl toward the door. "We'll rain hell down on this fuckin' place!"

"Go, Lemon! Get her outta here!" The last thing I needed was her coming back. I'd get out of this myself. Just like I always did.

"If you get hurt, I'll fuckin' castrate you, you bastard!" That sounded like the Lemon we all knew and loved. If I didn't know better, I'd think she was worried about me. Knowing Lemon, she just wanted me to survive so she could kill me for whatever reason she thought I needed killing. Why the fuck that made me want to smile was beyond me. All that really mattered was that Lemon was out of this fucking place away from these fucking bastards. What happened to me was of no consequence.

My only regret was not being able to enjoy Lemon and her snarky disposition more before I claimed her. But I would.

I most definitely would.

Chapter Five
Lemon

I'm not sure what I expected, but an empty street wasn't it. I wasn't sure where we were or where to go, but I'd have thought Rocket's men would have been right behind him. Instead, I gripped Euphemia's hand. And yeah, that name was getting really fucking old really fucking fast. I wasn't one to make fun of a person's name, but what the fuck had her mother been thinking?

As we navigated between houses and buildings, I tried to hurry Effie without scaring her any more than she already was. Before my sister had taken up with Iron Tzars, I'd have taken us straight to the first policeman I could find. Now, my instinct was to stay as far away from the law as we could unless it was life or death. All that aside, my first order of business was to put as much distance between us and those assholes as possible. The next thing we needed to do was find out where the fuck we were and get these fucking zip ties off my hands. Thank God I'd managed to find a sharp rock to cut our feet and Effie's hands free before the battle. Hadn't managed to get my own hands free, but at least they were zipped in front of me instead of behind my back.

"I'm scared," Effie whimpered. She clung to my arm and constantly looked around her as if expecting someone to swoop down and pluck out our eyeballs.

"I know. Me too." I wasn't really. I wasn't! But I thought it would help Effie feel better if she thought she wasn't the only one scared.

I could feel the clock ticking. How long did Rocket have before he was too weak to fight? I knew he'd been shot. I saw the blood on his shoulder going through to his back. But I'd be Goddamned if he hadn't kept on fighting. He hadn't made a sound through all that, but when he was trying to keep those asshole's attention on him, he bellowed like a fucking mad cow. And if he'd gone and gotten himself killed because of that little stunt, I'd raise him from the dead so I could fucking kill him myself. I would bet my last dollar that he'd been trained not to acknowledge pain. Either that or his tissue was in shock or some shit.

Didn't matter.

What was important was that Rocket was in trouble. And I needed to get him help. We made our way farther into the city. Took me a bit, but I figured out we were in Riviera Beach. Which… was Grim Road territory.

"Fuck," I swore under my breath.

We rounded the corner beside a brick building and I set about using the edge to saw through the zip tie around my wrists. Then I got us to a busy street and sat with our backs to the wall of a building so we could keep an eye out in front of us for any sign of those men. Pulling out my phone, I tried to remember how to use the fucking thing. Now that the immediate danger had passed, I was starting to shake. I was going to crash and I couldn't afford to do that yet.

I finally found Wylde's number and connected a call. He answered on the first ring.

"Lemon? What the fuck's goin' on? Is Apple with you?" Wylde sounded like he was about to lose his shit. Which was kinda funny since the man bragged about how he had the coolest head of the club. When he wanted to have.

"Apple should be at the Salvation's Bane compound. I told her to make those guys from Bane you had following us take her there. What happened is

I saw a guy kidnap a kid off the beach and I got her back."

"What do you mean you got her back?"

"I mean, I followed those bastards and took her back." There was a long pause. "Might have had a little help from Rocket."

"Are you safe?" He was obviously trying to hold on to what little patience he had left.

"For the moment. I've got Effie with me. She's the girl they took. We ended up in Riviera Beach. They've got Rocket now and ain't no one from Grim Road anywhere in fuckin' sight. Will Bane come help?"

"Not sure, kid. First things first. I'm sending directions to your phone to Grim Road. It will be quicker for you to go to them than trying to get a ride back to Bane."

"This crappy phone? Wylde, it barely sends text messages."

"Yeah, it'll be pretty basic, but if you squint just right, you should be able to get an idea where you're going. All you really have to do is get close to their compound. They'll find you."

"Sounds like a great bunch'a guys, there, Wylde. Did Rocket not tell them he was going into a fight? Why ain't they already at that fuckin' house killin' some punkass motherfuckers? Are they little bitches?"

"For Christ's sake, Lemon. Don't go 'round sayin' shit like that in Grim Road territory. You'll hurt their feelings."

I started to lay into Wylde and tell him to take their hurt feelings and shove them up his ass when a thought occurred to me. "You're on the phone with one of 'em. Ain't cha'?"

I could practically see Wylde grinning with glee. "Why, Lemon. Why ever would you think that?"

"'Cause that's just the kinda asshole you are. Where are they? I need someone to protect Effie while I go back to help Rocket."

"Just stay put, honey. They're comin' to you."

"You're a bastard, Wylde."

"Yeah, but you still love me."

Smug bastard. I might kinda sorta maybe just a little bit love him. But I'd never tell him that. "No, I don't. Dani might, but me and Apple tolerate you at best."

I stayed on the phone with Wylde until two men pulled up in a big Bronco. Effie seemed to understand what was happening and looked up at me trustingly. Another pulled up behind them on a bike. Immediately, I handed Effie off to the two Grim Road members and, surprisingly, she didn't protest. Then I sprinted to the guy on the bike.

"We've got to go help Rocket. I can take you to him."

"Let's get you and the kid back to the compound, and we'll figure out how best to help Rocket."

I looked at the guy's cut. Apparently, this was Falcon. I'd only met a very few of the Grim Road men, and he wasn't one of them. "I realize you don't fully appreciate the situation, but when I left Rocket, he'd been shot, his knee had buckled, and he was fighting three men with one only unconscious. Not dead. They will kill him if they haven't already." I tried to block that out. The mere thought of those bastards killing Rocket made me more furious than I wanted to admit. And maybe, just a touch, sad. No. That was anger. Pure and simple. The man was an asshole at best, an accomplice in Scarlet's torture at worst.

"I'm sure it seemed worse than it actually was, lil' bit. You let us take care of this." I stood there with my mouth open. Not because I couldn't believe he'd basically said the equivalent of "Don't worry your pretty little head. Let the big men take care of this," but because I knew there was no point arguing. And I wanted him off that fucking bike. As I knew he would, Falcon dismounted the bike and came around to lead me back to the Bronco. The second I was between him and the Harley, I jumped on it, kicked Falcon in the balls when he tried to grab the handlebars, started the big hog, put it in gear, and took the fuck off.

Fuck a buncha bullshit pissing matches. I was going to get Rocket. He'd come for me; I'd damned well come for him. And Goddamnit, he better not be dead. Or I'd kill him.

I approached the house, not bothering to slow down or quiet the engine. I wanted them to fucking know I was coming for them. Instead of slowing down, I aimed the front tire for the door and hit the gas. Right before it hit, I jumped, rolling to the ground as the bike broke through the door.

There were shouts and a grunt. I hoped Rocket hadn't been too close. I'd left him on the other side of the small house, which is why I chose this side door instead of the front door. OK, so I hadn't really thought about it. You know. Until now.

The second I was on my feet I ran through the splintered door. The front tire was on one guy's chest, the bike on its side. He heaved and shoved it off him, but there was a trickle of blood coming from his mouth and a bloody bubble coming from his nose. My guess was he had some internal damage. But I'm not a doctor or anything. Just... duh!

I heard Rocket yell from the other side of the house and breathed a sigh of relief strong enough to make my knees weak. Why it mattered that he was OK

I wasn't about to examine too closely. He was an asshole in the extreme and a dumbass asshole to boot. The way I saw it, it was partly Rocket's fault Scarlet had been hurt so badly. He'd somehow overlooked the fact his vice president was a pussy too scared for his big secret to come out to protect his daughter from a fucking monster. I got that Scarlet said she wanted to go with Hammer initially, but I wasn't ready to let Rocket completely off the hook. He knew what Claw had been capable of, and he knew Hammer had every reason to want to hurt Claw any way he could. So by allowing Claw to approve Hammer taking his daughter away from the protection of Grim Road, Rocket was as guilty as Claw was.

When he gave another shout, I grabbed the big knife on the kitchen table, laying it against my forearm as I stalked through the living room where three men were shaking off the initial shock of the motorcycle bursting through their side door. It looked like they'd been in the process of working Rocket over. His face was a bit worse for wear, but he was on his feet and giving back better than he was getting.

I fought my way past one of the guys, making a deep slice across the back of his thigh as I went. He went down with a sharp yelp and I stopped to stab him three times in quick succession in the neck. With that initial kill, blood arcing over my shirt, the full impact of what I'd just done hit me. I didn't care that I'd been the one to kill that asshole. Anyone who could kidnap a child deserved whatever he got. What horrified me the most was that I'd done it in Grim Road's territory. Anything I did they couldn't clean up could and probably would fall back on them.

I met Rocket's gaze as he snagged a knife from the boot of the guy next to him and made a swipe up, catching the guy's femoral artery if the blood instantly soaking his jeans was any indication. Then he stabbed him twice in the neck before doing much the same to the last guy.

We stared at each other for several long moments. I had this overwhelming urge to run straight into Rocket's arms and take from him what I'd dreamed about taking for months now. I wanted to with everything in my being. But I was not about to make the first move. He could damn well chase after me because I absolutely would not make a move on him first. That was assuming I didn't kill him. Which was a pretty big Goddamned "if".

"What the fuck were you thinking!" I yelled at him, uncaring if anyone else saw or heard our little tiff. I mean, we were both covered in blood. I was pretty sure my dressing him down would be the last thing any witness would be concerned about. "If you hadn't tried to play the fuckin' hero, I could have taken out another of these assholes and you could have taken the other two. Even if you had been shot."

"I was trying to give you a way to get the kid out without either of you getting killed." He didn't sound any less angry than I felt. "Ever think you don't have to play the fuckin' hero, Lemon? I promise you, I'm more than capable of taking care of myself. Now, what'd you do with the girl?"

"I finally found a few of your club. You know. The ones who didn't follow you when you came to get me. They were on the other side of fucking town! Wylde had to send them to find me, and they had no intention of coming after you! Then that asshole, Falcon, tried to get me to calmly go back to the compound so they could decide what to do about helping you. Like he didn't already know you were coming here and what the situation was. And that it wasn't a given they were going to help you out either. What kind of fuckin' bullshit is that?" I was talking a mile a minute and asking questions I had no business asking. Also, I didn't want to know about his stinking club. Any MC who would leave their fucking president hanging out to dry wasn't an MC I wanted to be anywhere near. Granted, Iron Tzars was the only club I had any real experience with, but they were a true brotherhood. They had each other's backs. To the death. The way it should be.

"Will you shut up? Who rode Falcon's bike through the door?"

"That'd be me. Problem?" I raised an eyebrow.

"Not with me, honey. Falcon, on the other hand..."

As he spoke, the man in question stomped through the door and straight to his bike. He looked like he was ready to throttle someone. Probably Rocket. 'Cause Rocket had been bad.

"You don't spank her ass, I will, Rocket. She fuckin' wrecked my bike!"

"Don't be a pussy," I snapped. "It's just a fuckin' bike. If you can't fix it, bring it to the Tzars. If I can't fix it, Clutch can." No way I could fix his bike, but he didn't need to know that.

"Christ, Rocket. How has someone not killed her in her sleep yet?"

"'Cause I don't sleep, asshole."

Falcon bared his teeth at me. I flipped him off. Yeah. We were gonna be besties. Not.

"Back the fuck off, Falcon. I'll get the club to buy you a brand-new fuckin' bike if it'll soothe your delicate sensibilities."

That got a snort from me. "I was right to have

pegged you as a pussy. You're totally a fuckin' pussy."

"Knock it off, Lemon. Know when to stop." Rocket sounded like every inch the MC president then. Which was to say scary as fuck. Like your dad might if he caught you sneaking out of the house to go screw your boyfriend. Too bad I didn't give a fuck. He didn't scare me. Besides, I was pretty sure I could take him on a good day.

"I'll stop when he stops being a pussy."

"Rocket, woman or not, I ain't takin' this kinda shit."

Before I could say anything, Rocket wrapped one arm around my middle and clamped the other hand over my mouth. "Not a word. We'll talk later. Right now, you shut the fuck up and do what I say. We've got to get scarce and let the boys do their job." I turned my head as much as I could to meet Falcon's furious gaze with one of my own. Yeah. I didn't need to say anything to get my point across. Me and pigeon nuts here were gonna have it out sooner rather than later. And, yeah. That would've sounded way better out loud than it did in my head.

Chapter Six
Rocket

I was hard as a motherfucker. Lemon... That woman... That fucking woman...

Fuck!

I'd known for a long fucking time I was going to hell, but here was the proof. Lemon had gone toe to toe with Falcon, one of the fiercest men I knew, and hadn't backed down one fucking inch. Maybe she didn't know what a badass he was, but I honestly don't think she really cared. This was Lemon. Unfiltered and in your face. Had I not started feeling every single injury these assholes had dealt out to me, I'd have taken her over my knee and spanked her in front of God and everyone. Just to show she was mine. Then again, it might get my balls removed. Didn't matter. I loved living dangerously.

"Get on outta here, Rocket." Ringo, my enforcer, stepped into the house, looking the small space up and down, eyeballing the damage as he did. "I'll get a cleaning crew out here to take care of everything."

"I don't want so much as a fuckin' pebble that doesn't belong still here when this place is cleaned. Get Scrubb."

"On it, Prez." Ringo left to get started as I kicked the front tire of Falcon's downed bike.

"Should be fine."

Falcon glared at me, his face hard and a very unflattering shade of red under his beard. Lemon mumbled, but I still had my hand clamped over her mouth. When she stuck her tongue out and licked my hand, my first instinct was to pull away and wipe my hand down my jeans, but that was exactly what she wanted. Instead, I gave her a hard stare.

So she bit me.

"Goddamnit, Lemon!" I did jerk my hand away that time.

She stepped away from me, then turned and shoved me backward.

Falcon snorted. "Who the fuck cut her loose, anyway? She'll probably wreck the whole fuckin' club before she's done."

Lemon just shrugged, looking about as concerned as that old cartoon kitten sitting on a bulldog's back. "I mean, it's possible. Seems like you guys need a good swift kick in the balls. What better way to do that than through your bikes?"

Falcon actually growled and took a step forward, his fists clenching and unclenching at his sides. "You're about two seconds from gettin' an ass whuppin', woman. Rocket won't do it, I got no fuckin' problem. Figure you owe me my pound of flesh for demolishing my bike."

"Sweet Baby Jesus in the manger," Lemon muttered. "I didn't demolish your fuckin' bike. It's fine. Might need a new wheel on the front or something's all. This club needs whippin' into shape, Rocket. Is it full of pussies or is it just this clown?"

"Lemon --"

"No, Rocket." She turned to face me, stabbing a finger in my chest none too gently. "They weren't coming after you. They were going back to their 'clubhouse' to talk about it." She made air quotes. She looked back at Falcon and gave him a derisive snort. "So, yeah. I can see some changes need to be made."

"Go to the fuckin' truck, Lemon." I made a step, then barely suppressed a wince. I did clamp a hand over my side. Which is when my shoulder screamed at me. 'Cause, you know, I'd been shot. I still tried to ignore it because the only way Lemon would have me was if I was a strong man. Right now, she probably didn't see me as strong. At least, not in body.

"You go to the truck. You're the one who's shot!"

I saw it then. That vulnerability Lemon never showed anyone. The fact that I'd been shot bothered her more than she was willing to admit. Or, likely, than she wanted me to know.

"And you got kidnapped. And beaten," I countered.

"How about you both go to the fuckin' truck and let me get started on this fuckin' cleanup before the turn of the next fuckin' century?"

"Wow. Someone woke up cranky. Did you not get your full nap in?" I really thought Falcon was going to turn her over his knee. He actually took a threatening step forward, but Lemon didn't back down. Instead, she met his gaze with her own steely one and took her own step forward, tilting her head to the side. "Come on, then. Give it your best shot. You get one."

Falcon narrowed his eyes. "You're playin' with fire, woman."

"And you're not nearly as intimidating as you think you are." She put her shoulders back and lifted her chin. The sun filtered through a window in the house and fell over her face, highlighting a reddish bruise darkening her cheek. Lemon hadn't said anything about hurting, but I knew she'd taken more than a few hits. Especially during the fight when she'd used Falcon's bike as a battering ram. "We'll have it out. You and me."

Yeah. That was it for me. Despite the pain settling in after the adrenaline started to wear off, my cock -- which had been at attention since the end of the fight -- felt like it had absorbed every single drop of blood in my fucking body. I ached with the need to claim this fierce, brash woman in front of the entire world so everyone would know she was mine and mine alone.

"I ain't sure what you got goin' on with Rocket, but you need to learn some respect for this club. And I hope and pray to every deity I can imagine that you ain't stayin' at Grim. You need to get your ass back to the Iron Tzars. Sting might tolerate shit like this in his outfit, but Grim Road? We don't."

"No. You just leave your president to fend for himself after I told you he'd been shot." She tilted her head, obviously goading Falcon. "You gunnin' for his position?"

"Stop it, Lemon. You're taking up valuable time we might not have. Get your ass in the fucking cage." As amusing as it was to watch Lemon run circles around Falcon, now wasn't the time. Also, if anyone was going to spar with Lemon, it would be me.

"You and I are going to have to come to an understanding, Rocket." She was back to poking me in the chest. "You've got some serious issues in your club. I'm guessing every single fuckin' one of them have to do with either secrets or trust. I'm going to help you with this one, but your men are gonna have to understand that I will never defer to them simply because they're members of this club."

"You're puttin' yourself in a pretty high position there, princess." Falcon just couldn't resist. He thought he was going to get the last word with Lemon, but I had news for the man. His best bet would be to bite his tongue and let her say whatever she wanted. She would anyway, and he'd be left feeling like he'd been skinned alive.

She snorted. "Why wouldn't I? If I'm going to be Rocket's old lady, I'm definitely going to have my say and I will be respected above anyone else. Even Rocket. Why? Because I'm a Goddamned lady. It's right there in the fucking name. So yeah. Maybe I am a princess. Get fuckin' used to it."

Yeah. That shut Falcon up. Shut me up, too.

"Now. Getting back to the conversation before. If I'm making the move from Iron Tzars to Grim Road, it's not going to be a step down. We will get this club in order and working like a fuckin' team so incidents like today won't happen again. There's gonna have to be some fuckin' changes if I'm staying, Rocket. Non-negotiable. Clear?" When I didn't say anything, Lemon nodded crisply. "Good."

She tossed her head, her long ponytail brushing the string wrapped around her back where her bikini top fastened, and sashayed her sweet ass outside. Which was when I fully appreciated what the woman was wearing. Which was to say, not fucking much. That was when I fully noticed the blood she had all over her, that she didn't acknowledge at all. She didn't try to wipe her face or her hands. It was like this was her way of owning the shit. She'd killed and she didn't give a rat's ass who knew it.

As I watched while Bear helped her into the truck, I had to adjust myself. The blood in my body must have truly all headed south because there was no way this was my life right now.

"What. The. Fuck. Just. Happened?"

"Old lady?" Falcon looked and sounded like he thought he might have heard wrong and like he might follow Lemon outside and throttle her. Because he absolutely wouldn't be aiming that look at me.

I started to deny it, to tell Falcon Lemon was

fucking with him, then stopped and tilted my head. "You got a problem with that?"

"Oh, come on, Rocket!" I thought maybe Lemon had broken Falcon. Pretty sure the other man was getting ready to snap. "You can't take that hellion as your woman. What is she? Fourteen?"

"She's eighteen, and I'll do what the fuck I want. It's my life. I'll take whatever woman I want to be my old lady and you won't make a single fuckin' comment."

"The men ain't gonna like this."

"What? That Lemon's mine? Or that she'll put them in their place if she thinks they need it?"

"Have you even fucked her yet?"

Couldn't let that one go. I swung a haymaker at Falcon, catching him in the chin. He didn't go down, but he staggered back a couple of steps. "That's the only warning you get, Falcon. Talk about Lemon that way again, I'll kill you."

"Jesus Christ, Rocket! You better know what the fuck you're doin'."

"I can honestly say I've never been more sure in my fuckin' life."

I followed Lemon to the cage and climbed in beside her. Knox, our road captain, started the truck and sped off. She sat silently, still a bloody mess. I was sure she was uncomfortable as the blood dried on her skin, but she didn't complain or wipe at her skin, or acknowledge the situation in any way. Instead, she kept her gaze fixed out the window.

I placed my hand gently over hers. She turned her arm and laced her fingers with mine. There was a slight tremor running through her I almost missed. Had I not been holding her hand I doubt I'd have noticed. Could be she was chilled in the air conditioning, but I didn't think so.

"You're safe, Lemon."

She whipped her head around to look at me, her brows knit together in anger. "Of course, I'm safe," she snapped. "But you could have fuckin' been killed, Rocket. You were shot. And I saw that guy get a solid kick to your knee. It was four on one. And these pissants were gonna just leave you there?"

I blinked at her. She was constantly keeping me off-balance. "You... were worried about me?"

"Of course, I was fuckin' worried, Rocket! I told you. I'm your old lady. How do you think I'd feel if you died, huh?"

Knox, the bastard, let out a bark of laughter before coughing to cover it up.

"We'll talk about that later. Let's get home and we'll get you cleaned up and go check on your little charge."

Lemon grunted but otherwise said nothing. She went back to staring at the moving scenery until we pulled into the Grim Road compound. Falcon must have complained to the entire club because I was sure every single member in the compound had come out to greet us. Or, more accurately, watch the fireworks. Sure enough, as I climbed out of the truck, I saw Wolf and Crush pull chairs out into the parking lot and set a big-ass cooler between them. Crush opened it and pulled out a couple of beers, handing one to Wolf before popping the top and clinking the necks together.

"Rocket!" A decidedly female voice cut through the low murmur of male voices. As a rule, club whores were regulated to a certain space within the compound. Like our families had their own separate area, we kept the club whores contained in *their* separate area. Not only did it keep the peace, but it kept them from putting their noses where they didn't belong. Apparently, that wasn't the case tonight. On the heels of the first woman, several others emerged from the party room. I wanted to pull my hair out. I'd bet my last dollar this had been Falcon's doing. All of it.

The woman -- she called herself Plush -- jumped into my arms. I had to catch her to keep from stumbling backward. I wasn't stupid enough to keep holding her, though. I immediately shoved her away from me, keeping my hands on her only long enough to make sure she didn't land on her ass in the gravel.

Lemon chose that moment to exit the truck. She'd climbed out of my side instead of her side, so my body was between her and the woman. When she stepped around me, it was with an eerie grace and slow, deliberate movements. Even in the fading light, she looked like a sight from a horror film. Her expression was completely blank, but her gaze was fixed on Plush. Lemon took one slow step at a time toward the other woman, letting her hips sway with each step, proving to everyone watching she was just as sexy as any club whore. More so, because she was also covered in blood, proving the violence she was capable of. In her Daisy Dukes and bikini top, she was every biker's wet dream come true.

And yeah. I was so fucking fucked it wasn't fucking funny.

"Touch my man again, and I'll bury you somewhere neither Google nor Siri will know where the fuck you are."

Plush backed away. She looked like she wasn't sure whether this was a big joke or if Lemon was some kind of serial killer.

"Fuck. Me." Dom scrubbed a hand over his

mouth, taking one slow step backward before stopping himself and standing his ground. "That's fuckin' creepy."

"Honey, you ain't seen creepy yet." Lemon continued past him and into the party room. I was so mesmerized by her retreating form that all I could do was watch. The woman had an ass that didn't fuckin' quit. She was slender but had curves like a back country road and legs that went on for fucking miles. "After I get cleaned up and Rocket and I have our little discussion, I'll show you creepy."

"Prez," Dom said, his gaze on Lemon's retreating form was as horrified as I'm sure mine was lust-filled. "Please tell me Falcon was shittin' me when he said you took an old lady. And if he wasn't shittin' me, please tell me that ain't her."

"You gotta admit" -- I shook my head -- "she's a president's old lady."

"No fuckin' doubt there. A word of advice?"

"Yeah?"

"My grandma always told me you should never go to bed mad. I have a feeling that's going to be especially true of that one."

"No fuckin' doubt, Dom. No fuckin' doubt."

Chapter Seven
Lemon

I'd known there was a likelihood I'd have to deal with club whores. It was why I didn't immediately find a way to wash all the blood off my face and body. I knew it would be creepy as fuck and wanted to make a positive impression. Mission accomplished.

Now, though, I wanted a shower. Yesterday.

I had no idea whose room I was in, but I found the first unlocked door with a full bathroom near it and ducked inside, stripping as I went. I had no other clothes but I simply to God could not stand the sticky, coppery, mess on me one fucking second longer. I wasn't a girlie girl. I didn't care about getting dirty. But, despite my actions earlier, I'd never really been a violent person. I mean, I fucked up people sometimes if they needed fucking up, but this was violence on a whole other level.

I turned on the shower to let the water heat and caught a glimpse of myself in the mirror. Yeah. I looked like I belonged in a horror film. A wave of nausea hit me with the subtlety of a battering ram to my stomach. I stumbled to the toilet and vomited over and over. I closed my eyes to keep from seeing whatever I puked up because I could just imagine it being bright red blood spilling into the toilet. I was literally covered in it, so my mind was working overtime, kicking my imagination into high gear.

When the vomiting stopped, I weakly grabbed at the handle of the toilet. Another hand beat me to it. Before I could even see who was in the bathroom with me, I fell back on my ass, slumping against the wall. Sweat coated my skin, making the dried blood look that much worse. To make matters worse, I was as naked as the day I was born.

"Come on, old lady. Let's get you in the shower." Rocket bent and lifted me into his arms. He was still fully dressed but got in the shower with me, holding me as the water sluiced over my body.

I shivered, closing my eyes again and burying my face in Rocket's chest. Blood trickled from my skin to the shower floor, turning the white surface a reddish brown. The sight made me queasy again.

Rocket held me close with one hand and picked up a bottle of shower gel with the other, squeezing it over me before gently rubbing my back, neck, and shoulders. I knew I should probably be embarrassed that I was naked while he was fully clothed, but it was what it was. I couldn't stay in bloody clothes. He chose to be here. So if my nakedness bothered him, he'd have to get over it.

With gentle hands, Rocket urged my head back so my hair was under the spray. He washed my hair as thoroughly as he had my upper body, carefully getting all the blood off me before urging me back onto the wooden bench. Then he washed my legs. I was sure he got a good look at my pussy, but he didn't acknowledge that view, nor did his hands stray into forbidden territory. Closest he got was when he washed under the cheeks of my ass. But to be fair, the cut-off jean shorts I'd worn were short enough to show the underside of my ass, so I probably had blood everywhere he touched.

"Crashing?"

I shivered. "Nope." I was totally crashing.

Rocket caught my chin with his fingers and tilted my head back so I had to look up at him. "You've been yelling at me for not communicating with my club, and you laid down some pretty tall ultimatums earlier. So

I'm going to give you one now. Don't ever lie to me. Not for any reason. You get me?"

I wanted to nod, to surrender to his wishes but I was never overly fond of the word surrender. "I'm fine, Rocket. I just hate blood, all right?"

"OK. I believe that. At least the part about you hating blood. But you're not fine."

"I admit, this whole day has been a bit extreme, but I'll make it through. I just needed the blood off."

"Good. Then I helped. Now. About being my old lady."

Before I could suppress my feelings, a stab of doubt and vulnerability swept through me. I wasn't sure I kept it off my face entirely. If this man knew I had a hopeless crush on him, the jig was up. If he thought I was just being annoying and plowing ahead like I always did, I might be able to worm my way into his life and prove to him I could be an asset before he figured out I cared more for him than he did for me.

Maybe.

* * *

Rocket

I sucked in a breath, unable to keep the excitement at bay. This was the first time since I'd met her over a year ago that I saw what I thought was the true Lemon. Sure, she was tough as nails, but I was getting close to peeling back the layers underneath and finding the real Lemon. And I was pretty sure she was just as caring and compassionate as her sister, but I'd never tell a soul.

Needle scratch… Back to reality. She threw me the sass. "Well, you need an old lady. Not sure I'll keep you, but for now, you're stuck with me. I meant it when I said your club has some serious issues. It's now my job to help you fix this."

"You're right. But we'll get back to that. First things first. I ain't takin' an old lady I ain't kissed. So, if you're serious about this, you're gonna have to kiss me."

She rolled her eyes. "Fine. But remember, you asked for this."

Lemon grabbed my beard and pulled me down to her. Her kiss was uncharacteristically tentative. The normally take-charge, no-holds-barred, brash as hell, vulgar, wonderful woman wasn't as experienced as she wanted everyone to believe. I didn't mean sexually so much as worldly wise. Though, I'd bet my left testicle she didn't have a whole lot of experience sexually either.

Instead of taking over, I let her kiss me at her own pace. Just to see what she'd do. Her little tongue darted out to lap at my bottom lip and I groaned, unable to help myself. How long had I dreamed about having her in my arms like this? Because my arms had closed around her the second her lips met mine. It was only a matter of time before I took over and found out exactly how far I could push her.

Then she sucked in a breath and pulled back. I put a hand to the side of her face, darkening with a reddish-purple bruise where that fucker had hit her. Though my shoulder and ribs screamed, I'd still have taken this as far as I could have before she put a stop to it. If she put a stop to it. I was willing to bet I could take her and make her mine. If she'd been up to it.

We were both breathing hard. I didn't loosen my hold on her, but leaned in to rest my forehead against hers. "There. Much better. Now you can be my old lady."

She snorted. "Like you had a choice."

"Like I had a choice." There was no way to keep the amusement out of my voice. "Come on. Let's get dressed and we'll have that discussion you're so hell-bent on having."

For long moments, Lemon looked up into my face. Searching. Finally, she did something I didn't expect. Lemon -- my beautiful, strong Lemon -- dissolved into tears.

* * *

Lemon

I was such a fucking idiot. When had I let my guard down enough to fall apart in front of Rocket? He needed to get to a doctor and let them see to his shoulder.

"We n-need t-to get y-your sh-shoulder taken c-care of." I tried my hardest but couldn't keep the hitch out of my voice.

"Yeah, we do, honey, but I'll do it later. Right now, I need to take care of you."

"Me? You're the one who got shot!" I pulled back and traced the wound with my fingers, shuddering as I did. "What if the bullet's still in there? What if it gets infected? What if your arm falls off and you get gangrene and die!" Yeah, that escalated quickly, but I couldn't seem to help it. "And your ribs? What if you popped a lung? What if you're bleeding internally? You'll drown in your own blood!" I pushed away from him, stepping out of the shower and snagging a towel. "That's it. You're going to the ER. We'll figure out what to tell them later."

"Lemon, stop." His big, rough hand landed on my shoulder, and he turned me back around gently to face him. "I'll get Bullet to look at me later."

"Bullet?" The mundane thought that Bullet could

not be the name of their club doctor or safety person or whatever was enough to pull me out of my embarrassing meltdown.

"Yep. Safety officer slash doctor."

"You have a doctor named Bullet." Iron Tzars' doc was named Stitches, but that was different. Stitches was good people.

"Sure do." He grinned down at me, so I scowled back at him.

"I don't trust a doc named Bullet. He might put one in your other shoulder."

Rocket barked out a laugh before scooping me up and setting me on the vanity. He then grabbed a towel and dried himself off before helping me finish.

"Come on. I'll get Bullet to come to us. He can check us both out."

"Ain't no doc named Bullet touchin' me."

"Maybe not, but you will let him check you over. As my old lady, it's my responsibility to make sure you're not seriously harmed and to take care of you. You will let me do my job. Hear me?"

I rolled my eyes. "Fine. I need clothes and a hairbrush. That'll go a long way toward taking care of me."

Rocket grinned. "There. That wasn't so hard, was it?" He reached over and snagged his phone off the vanity beside me, shooting off a text. I took the time to really appreciate his magnificent body as he did.

Tattooed skin played over muscles as he moved. His ink was intricate, with pictures of bikes and machines mixed with barbed wire and tribal etchings. Each piece told a story, and I found myself drawn to the sight of him with a renewed sense of desire.

As Rocket peeled off his wet clothes and reached for a dry pair of jeans, I couldn't help but notice the torn and frayed seams that spoke of long use. Probably his favorite pair, if I had to guess. It was clear that he had been through a lot, both physically and emotionally, and yet he still stood before me with an unshakable sense of strength.

"You know, I've always been drawn to the rough-and-tumble kind of guy." I reached out and placed a hand on his chest, bringing his attention back to me. "That you?"

"Nope. But I'm deadly. Deadly trumps rough and tumble any day." He grinned at me and the last of the fear and grief I'd been feeling melted away. And yeah. I could admit, at least to myself, that I'd been afraid Rocket would die. I'd actually felt a sharp sense of grief I hadn't fully acknowledged until the moment I'd lost my shit.

He brushed a thumb gently over my bruised cheek. It didn't hurt that badly, but I liked that it seemed to bother him. Maybe he felt something for me too. "This hurt?"

I shrugged. "A little. Not too bad."

A satisfied grunt told me I'd said the right thing. "Good. You didn't lie. From this moment forward, we don't lie to each other, Lemon. Not about anything. If you're hurting -- physically or emotionally -- I need to know. You've thrown down the gauntlet by telling me you're gonna be my old lady so you can fix my club. Now I'm picking it up. You will help me. But the only way we accomplish everything we need to is if we're honest with each other. No matter how hard it is. There are no secrets between us."

Did I imagine he winced at that last? Time to push him a little.

"Really. So you'll tell me everything?"

"If that's what you need, then yes. Just be careful

what you ask because I will tell you. If you can't handle what I tell you, you don't ask."

"How about if you warn me before you answer if it's something too bad?"

Rocket nodded slowly. "I think that's the best way to approach it."

"Good." I crossed my arms over my chest to hold the towel in place better. There was a knock at the door across the room. I didn't even know whose room I was in.

"That'll be either Bullet or someone bringing you some clothes." He gave me a stern look. "Stay here. I'll be right back."

Rocket exited the bathroom, and naturally I followed him. He must have missed that I was on his six because he marched to the door and yanked it open.

"Someone ask for a fuckin' house call?" A big, burly man with a cranky expression pushed past Rocket but stopped short when he saw me wrapped in only a wet towel. "Wow. So the rumor's true. You got yourself a woman."

Rocket sighed heavily and turned to me. "Didn't I tell you to stay in the bathroom?"

I shrugged. "Not sure. Might have messed up my hearing listening to all Falcon's bitchin' and moanin' over his bike."

Bullet raised an eyebrow, but didn't comment. Instead, he tossed me a bag of frozen peas. "Hold that to your face for a while. It'll help with the swellin' and kinda numb the pain. You hurt anywhere else?"

I wanted to tell him no, but one look at Rocket's uncompromising features and I sighed. "My ribs kinda hurt. A little. Not much." Bullet reached for my towel, but I backed up a step. "Touch it, you die. I'm fine." I meant it too. No way I was letting that man see me naked. Doctor or not.

"How about you put on some clothes, then let him look." Rocket tossed me two garments and jerked his head back to the bathroom. "Which is why I wanted you to stay put." He shook his head slightly. "Gonna have to work on you following instructions."

"Might want to work on world peace too while you're at it," I shot over my shoulder. "Or maybe capturing a unicorn. Either would be easier tasks."

"Don't I fuckin' know it." Rocket muttered his response like he was all put out and shit, but I heard the humor in his voice. He liked my sass. He just didn't want to admit it.

Chapter Eight
Rocket

"That'un's gonna be a handful." Bullet didn't look up as he examined my shoulder from both sides. "Looks like the bullet tore straight through. I'd like to get an X-ray to make sure there ain't fragments. Don't want it gettin' infected." He tossed me a bottle of pills. "Antibiotics. One pill twice a day until they're gone." He took out some peroxide and was cleaning the wound when Lemon exited the bathroom. Dressed in my big shirt and a pair of gym shorts.

Sexy. As. Fuck.

She must have seen my satisfied smirk because she scowled at me. "These your idea of clothes? They're a mile too big."

"Yep. But they're comfortable. And, more importantly, they're mine."

"Oh. Well, OK then." She flopped down in a chair and watched intently while Bullet worked on my shoulder.

"You could use some staples, but bleedin's stopped. Up to you."

"Just put a bandage on it. I'll keep it clean. It'll make a nice scar."

"And we all know scars are sexy," Lemon added, never taking her eyes from Bullet's hands. She looked like she was just waiting to pounce on the other man if I flinched. Which... yeah. Cute as hell, if unnecessary. I'd be lying if I said it bothered me that she was so possessive and protective. I could tell the sight of my wound worried her though, and I doubt it was the blood and gore that upset her. Her face grew tight, and I could see the fragile hold she had on her control.

"Yeah?" I raised an eyebrow at her. "Try gettin' a

wound bad enough for it to scar you and see what happens." I had to do something to help her without embarrassing her.

She snorted. "You're Neanderthal enough for a battle scar to turn you on. Remember that whole being honest with each other shit you spouted earlier?"

"Yeah. You still get hurt at your own peril. 'Cause, once you've healed, I'll spank your ass, then you'll wish you hadn't tested me."

"If you two are done with the foreplay, I'd really like to finish up here." Bullet finished with the bandage on the back side of my shoulder before going to Lemon. He stood over her, his arms crossed over his chest. "Now. Lift your shirt and let me see your side."

Lemon stood and pulled up her shirt, holding it out of the way but with an arm clamped firmly over her breasts so she didn't flash Bullet. I was happier about that than I wanted to admit. While I hadn't taken much time to admire her naked body when we were in the shower, I knew she had small, perfect breasts with delicate, pale pink nipples. They were mine to look at. Not Bullet's.

The bruising on her skin was a mottled red and purple. It took up almost her whole side and there was no way she wasn't hurting.

"You need an X-ray too."

"Why? If my ribs are broken, there's not much to do. Just, you know, breathe so I don't get pneumonia or whatever."

"You could have a punctured lung."

"I'll let you know if I have trouble breathing." She lifted her chin stubbornly.

"Rocket's gotta have one. Ain't like you won't be with him anyway."

"She'll get one," I answered for her. When she

opened her mouth to protest, I leveled a look at her that I hoped said it didn't matter how much she protested, this was happening. So instead of losing an argument in front of Bullet, she'd do better to keep her mouth shut. Didn't mean I didn't expect her to give me hell later. Just meant I was trying to keep her from losing face.

"Good. I'll call a buddy and set something up for later tonight. It's not an emergency, and we want to keep this off the record. Either of you need painkillers?"

"She will," I said at the same time Lemon answered, "He does."

Bullet glanced from one of us to the other. "Both it is." He pulled out another bottle from his bag and tossed it to Rocket. "No more than two every six hours for her. You can take a couple every four hours."

"Got it." I snagged the flip-flops Bullet had brought for Lemon. They were probably a little big, but beggars couldn't be choosers. They'd work.

"Now," Bullet said as he pulled off his cut and folded it neatly before draping it over the back of a chair. "If the two of you don't mind, I'd like my room back. Been a pisser of a day and I still need to make arrangements for those X-rays."

"We were just leaving." I snagged Lemon's hand. "Sorry 'bout the mess in the bathroom."

"Just as long as you didn't leave any spunk. Don't fuck in my area, Rocket."

"Fucker."

I tried to pull Lemon along after me, but she paused just long enough to say, "I think I might like you after all, Bullet."

I took her from the main compound to my home in the family area. The only person other than me who'd ever been inside my house was Talia. I'd never brought a woman here for any reason. It was my sanctuary. The place I could always go to and know no one would bother me if I didn't want them to. Even the men of Grim Road would never come inside unless I invited them. I wasn't inviting them.

I ushered Lemon inside my home and something I hadn't realized was restless settled inside me. Lemon was here. In my domain. Mine to do with as I pleased.

Except my shoulder was starting to fucking hurt.

I groaned as I shut and locked the door. "Give Wylde a call. I'm sure he'd like to hear from you."

"Fuck." Lemon collapsed onto the sofa in a heap, closing her eyes. "Yeah. Need to do that."

When she didn't move, the corner of my lips twitched. "Want me to do it?"

"Nope. I got this."

"Do you even have your phone?"

"Nope. Was in my shorts pocket and I have no idea where they even are. Probably in the trash by now."

I chuckled and took out my phone. I aimed to snap a pic, but Lemon seemed to sense what I was doing and hefted the bird up, if a bit weakly. I sent the pic to Wylde who responded back with a rolling-on-the-floor-laughing emoji. Yeah. The man knew her and knew that middle finger meant she was good.

"Want to go to bed?" I kicked off my shoes before walking through the small house to toss my shirt in the bathroom. My jeans followed and I started to march back to the living room only to remember I was naked. Much as I loved the thought of taking her to bed now, any bed-taking would only involve sleep. I didn't think either of us were up for it. Yet.

I found a pair of clean gym shorts and slung

them on before going back to the living room. I hadn't waited for her answer before, and she hadn't given one. Which meant she was dead where she sat.

As I stood beside the couch, I studied Lemon. Really studied her. I already knew she was sassy and more full of life than any person I'd ever met. I'd expected her take-charge attitude. The snark was a given. But the way she'd dealt with the members of my club, the club girls, her sisters, and her young charge -- who we needed to check on -- and the men who'd kidnapped them were all surprises. I'm not sure if I expected her to back down -- especially with regard to Falcon -- or what exactly, but to have her take on all those challenges and win wasn't something I'd been prepared to handle. For the first time since I met Lemon, I wondered if maybe I was the one in over my head. And that was damned hard to admit even to myself.

I was about to pick her up and carry her to bed when she spoke. "If you want to have sex, I'll try. Not sure how much I can manage."

"Right. I don't think either of us are in any kind of shape to fuck."

She didn't move and her face was still relaxed. Her eyes closed. "Didn't say we had to fuck. Damned sure ain't up for that. But we can have sex. As long as you do all the work. I can be on top if you need me to, but you'll still have to do most of the work. I'll just straddle your hips and lay there."

I laughed then, even though it hurt like a mother bitch. "You are somethin' else, princess."

She frowned then, still not opening her eyes or moving. "That's not goin' away anytime soon. Is it?"

"Nope." I leaned in to scoop her up off the couch. She was completely limp in my arms, her head resting against my shoulder as I carried her to my bed. Even though I had no intention of making her mine yet, my cock tented my shorts at full attention. I think I had been hard the entire day since I'd first laid eyes on her. "We'll get a couple hours sleep, then we'll meet Bullet for those images. After that, we'll call and check on your little friend."

Instantly, Lemon was wide awake. "Effie! I promised her I wouldn't leave her!" She wiggled, trying to get down. "Your men brought her to the compound. Where is she? I've got to bring her back here with us."

"Stop struggling, princess. You ain't gettin' down." She did stop and looked up at me like a furious little pixie. "And before you go layin' down the law, Gina has her. She's a sweet girl, if a bit shy and withdrawn. Especially since Hammer…" I swallowed what I was about to say. The last thing I wanted to do right now was dredge up the past.

"Why would Hammer's demise affect her?" I could see the calculating look in Lemon's eyes. She was putting things together quickly.

"She had a thing for Hammer. Was pretty withdrawn before he left with Scarlet, but she's gotten worse since his death. Hardly ever leaves her house. Byte checks in on her most days. If he's not with her I'll be surprised."

Then Lemon asked a question I hadn't been expecting. "Did you ever flush out the rat in your club?"

I sat on the bed with Lemon in my lap, my brows narrowing as I tried to see where she was going with this. "No. Crush and Byte have been working on it off and on for over a year. Since right before you came with Scarlet to pick up Sunshine and Rainbow. We'd kinda came to the conclusion Hammer was fuckin' with her."

"Are you sure? I mean, really sure? If this Gina wanted Hammer, maybe she'll want revenge like he did."

That pulled me up short. Surely to fucking God I wasn't that fucking stupid. "No. No way. It's not in her nature to even think about harming a child, let alone threaten or, God forbid, carry through."

"That's what I thought." Lemon wiggled until she got out of my lap. I was so dumbfounded, I let her. "Take me to Effie. I want to see her and I want to talk to this Gina."

I sighed. "The only reason you're gettin' your way this time is because I believe you have a good reason to be concerned. I think you're wrong, but I'm willing to concede we hadn't considered her as an actual suspect."

"Why not?" The woman was determined. I couldn't blame her. Scarlet was Lemon's best friend. It was because of Lemon's interference that Scarlet made it out of her situation alive. Lemon had proven many times over that she took friendship seriously.

"Like I said, it's just not the way Gina is."

"Whatever," Lemon muttered as she shoved her feet into her flops. "Come on. Take me to Effie."

Chapter Nine
Lemon

The visit with Effie went surprisingly well. I wasn't sure what I was expecting, but the subdued young woman patiently looking after Effie wasn't it. When we first got there, a man not much older than me opened the door. Rocket called him Byte. He didn't talk much.

"Lemon!" Effie bolted from the couch and threw herself into my arms. I caught her, hugging her back, if a bit awkwardly. I wasn't a hugger.

"Hey there." I tried to put her down, but the kid wrapped her legs around my waist to go with her arms around my neck. She wasn't getting down any time soon. "You OK?"

"Yes. I'm OK."

"Good. That's good."

"Gina made me cheeseburgers. I ate three, and she didn't mind!" The kid sounded so excited I couldn't help but laugh. She reminded me of a younger version of Apple in a way, though I hadn't been around her long enough yet to really know.

"Three? Where the fuck'd you put em?" I poked at her thin belly, trying to distract her from me dropping the F bomb. If I was gonna be 'round her much, I'd have to watch that. Maybe. Fuck it. It was a fucking word. "There ain't room in there for three cheeseburgers."

Effie giggled as I tickled her lightly. "Are you taking me home with you now?" She looked up at me with big, trust-filled eyes. Like she fully expected that's what would happen.

"Well, I thought you'd want to go home. You know. Back to your mom who says you need to read."

The second I mentioned Effie going to her mom, the girl's face fell, and I knew I'd said the wrong thing.

"Uh, why don't you go back to Gina, Effie," Byte said. "She's still got half the story to go."

"But I wanna stay with Lemon." Effie wrapped her thin arms around me once more. Tightened her legs too.

"How about this," Byte said, meeting my gaze warily. "I need to talk to Rocket and Lemon. I'll bring her back to you when we're done. OK?"

Effie wrapped her arms tighter and whimpered. "I want Lemon."

"Hey." I turned my back so I faced away from Gina and moved away from Byte. At this point, I didn't trust anyone. Well, except maybe Rocket. And that was a hard maybe.

"Look at me, Euphemia." When her attention was focused solely on me, I spoke softly, for her ears only. "Did anyone here hurt you?"

"No." She whispered. "But I think something's wrong with Gina. I think she's afraid of Byte." Effie glanced around behind me. "But I like Byte. He's nice."

"OK. I have to talk to Byte and Rocket, but we'll do it here. I'll be just outside, then I'll come back and get you. Can you let me do that?" She nodded. "Good. Go on back to Gina and let her finish reading your story. I'll be just outside the front door. I'll even stand in front of the window so you can see me."

"All right." She gave me one more hug, then climbed down and went back to Gina. Gina looked nervous, glancing from Rocket to Byte several times before her gaze darted back to me briefly. She shuddered slightly, then ducked her head and began reading softly to Effie.

I gave Rocket a hard look and jerked my head

toward the front door. No doubt he'd heard mine and Effie's conversation. He nodded and Byte followed Rocket out the door. I shut the door behind us and positioned myself in front of the window. I waved my fingers, knowing Effie would be watching. Then I turned to face the two men.

"So. Gina had a crush on Hammer."

Byte glanced at Rocket who nodded. He didn't play off my concerns to Byte, only gave Byte the go ahead to speak his mind.

"She did. But she's clean. She didn't do anything to betray the club, and she certainly didn't harm those girls." Byte shook his head. "She's got something going on, which is why I'm here. But she wouldn't harm a kid. Lost her own when she was just thirteen. She almost died too. But that girl does everything she can for kids of all ages and socioeconomic backgrounds. Said the ones with rich families often have the roughest time. Especially the girls. But since Hammer left with Scarlet, she's… changed."

"How?" Rocket growled the word, taking a threatening step toward the younger man.

"She never leaves this house, Rocket. Ever. Not to go to the grocery store. Not to shop or go to a party. She doesn't even go to the back yard or sit on the porch. She's holed up here and I can't figure out why."

"What does Crush say?"

Byte shrugged. "He can't find anything either. She had no hidden accounts. She gets no phone calls. She has no friends come to visit. Not even the other club whores come to see her. She's effectively a prisoner in this house and I have no idea why."

"Have you asked her?" It was the obvious question, but I knew no one had. I also thought I knew why. Same as no one came to help Rocket, even when they knew he was in trouble.

"No." Byte looked at his feet and shuffled around a little. "Not my business."

There were so many things wrong with that statement, but now wasn't the time. I needed that conversation with Rocket before I took on everything else. It was a good fucking thing I'd come along; otherwise, this club would end in disaster. Soon.

"OK. So, Effie needs to get back to her mother, but I have a feeling there's something wrong there."

"Yeah," Byte said, looking relieved to change the subject. "Her mother's dead. Just a few days. Kid saw her get hit by a car. From what I can find it was a hit and run, but I'm still digging. I haven't found her father yet, but I think he's..." Byte cleared his throat looking nervously at Rocket. "Military."

"Embedded?"

"Yeah. You could say that. Might have something to do with... uh... you know." Byte and Rocket shared a look. It was the look that said, *we've got secrets we need to keep from the outsider*. Still, I bit my tongue and said nothing. I'd unload on Rocket later. While I might berate him when I thought he needed it and give him shit continually, I'd never truly undercut him in front of his club. Not like that needed to happen in this instance. While I intended to fight at Rocket's side any time he had to fight, I'd never disrespect him or go against him in public. One battle at a time though. Because, no matter what, I intended to be a good old lady to him. Even if we parted ways afterward.

"Does she have other relatives besides her mother?" This was something that had to be decided now. Rocket was surprisingly quiet. He didn't offer input, but he watched me intently. Well, if he didn't want to participate in any meaningful way, he didn't get to bitch when it didn't go the way he wanted.

"No. Her mother's parents are dead, and there are no living relatives on her mother's side. They've been living here by themselves since Effie was born. As far as I can tell, Effie's mother, Mary, had no close friends. No intimate relationships. No job. She had a modest inheritance she got when her father passed, but it was enough for her to be able to live off the interest while Effie was little. It looked like she'd planned on going to work soon, but hadn't, deciding to wait a while longer. They didn't have a whole lot, but they had a roof over their heads and food in their bellies."

"Why didn't the state take Effie in?"

"They couldn't find her. The girl was scared and ran, then hid. She's been living on the beach ever since. Cops 'er still lookin', but not very hard. A nobody's child with the only person who cared about her dead? There's other things for the state of Florida to spend time and effort on. With no one making any noise, finding her isn't a priority."

"Fuckin' pricks," I muttered. "So Effie has nowhere to go." That was the bottom line as I saw it.

"Correct."

"Rocket, it's time we have this conversation."

"You gonna leave Effie with Gina?"

"Of course not!" I snapped. "She's coming with us. We'll talk after she goes to sleep. Quietly."

"That's what I thought." Rocket chuckled. "Go get your girl. I'm tired and in pain. I'm sure you are too. Let's go home." He didn't look like he was in pain, but my ribs were screaming. I'd never admit it, but I'd really like to have one of those painkillers Bullet left us.

"Good." I gave a curt nod before stalking back inside the house. Again, Effie immediately ran to me.

"Ready to go, sport?"

"Where we going?" The girl looked at me with such trust, I had to wonder how she'd processed her mother's death. She'd need help there too, but that was above my pay grade. We'd figure it out. "I'm taking you with me and Rocket. We're going to his house and staying there."

"You're staying with me. Right?"

"Yeah, honey. Me and Rocket got things to talk about, but we'll wait until you go to sleep. We won't leave the house."

"You promise?" Her chin quivered, but I could see how worried she was.

"I promise. You're staying with me and Rocket. As long as you want."

"Can I stay with you forever?"

I thought about that. I couldn't promise her forever with Rocket. That was a day by day thing. Maybe even hour by hour. "I can promise you can stay with me. No matter what."

"Doesn't Rocket like me?" She looked forlorn. Defeated. That look tore at my heart, ripping it to shreds.

"Rocket doesn't know you. But he doesn't matter. It's you and me. If he wants to be with us, that's his choice." Which was good advice to myself. I knew Rocket saw me as an amusement. Hell, he was probably just sitting back waiting to see what deficiencies I thought his club had and what I thought would be the best way to fix them so he could laugh at me and tell me how naive I was. That thought hurt as much as it infuriated me.

"OK. As long as you promise I can stay with you."

"I promise." And I'd make that stick. Even if I

had to go back to the Iron Tzars. Of course, if that happened my heart really would be in tatters. Because the idea that I was really Rocket's old lady had taken hold in my heart, and I knew that's what I wanted.

All of that depended on the conversation we were going to have, though. After all, there weren't many MC presidents who were capable of letting a woman tell them why his club sucked ass. I didn't know these men like he did. All I knew was there appeared to be little cooperation when it counted. The lack of finding out what the relationship between Gina and Hammer had been was just another example of that. Falcon's refusal to go after his president when he knew Rocket was in trouble was another.

I might not persuade Rocket things needed to change, but I was going to try. Because I could see something in Grim Road even Iron Tzars didn't see. There was something about these men that made me think there wasn't anything they couldn't accomplish. But before all that, they had to work together. They had to trust each other, and they had to value the club and each other more than their secrets.

Yeah. Time to go find that fucking unicorn.

Chapter Ten
Rocket

I could tell Lemon was expecting a fight. I could practically hear her going over all her points and arguments she'd come at me with in her head as we made the short drive back home.

Home...

She'd been in my house less than an hour and already I thought of it as a home rather than a simple house. It was partially for that reason that I'd give her whatever she wanted. I know she saw Grim Road as a broken club, a place not of brotherhood but of secrets and lies. I couldn't even say she was wrong. What she hadn't yet realized was that we weren't like other clubs. There were members of this group who would be shot on sight if it were found out they existed for what they might know. Well, she was about to learn. And I was eager to see the fireworks.

Once inside, I showed the girls where Effie's room would be. There were only two bedrooms in the house -- which I mentioned for Lemon's benefit -- and Effie seemed excited to have her own room. I'd have to take both of them somewhere to get a few essentials tomorrow, but for now, a few of the prospects had rounded up some shit like toiletries and such.

While Lemon got Effie settled, I fixed a quick supper, though after three burgers, I doubted Effie would be too hungry. Spaghetti was a quick, easy meal to make. By the time I was done, the girls had wandered back to the kitchen.

Effie clapped her hands in joy. "I love spaghetti! Thank you so much, Rocket!"

"You're welcome, honey." I patted the top of her head as she smiled up at me.

Supper was surprisingly easy. Effie didn't mention anything about the kidnapping or her mother, and Lemon was her usual snarky self. The two of them ganged up on me something horrible. I loved every second of it. By the time we were finished eating, Effie was drooping. All of us had had a long day, but Effie had to be exhausted.

"Come on, you little hellion," I said to Effie. "Let Lemon help you clean up for bed."

"Will you let me and Lemon stay here with you forever, Rocket?"

The question caught me off guard, but before I had a chance to think about it, I smiled. "Absolutely. In fact, I'm going to insist on it. This is your home. Lemon's too."

"So when I wake up in the morning, you'll both still be here?"

"I promise neither of us will leave unless we tell you where we're going and when we'll be back. And we won't leave you alone. As for tomorrow…" I gave her what I hoped was a reassuring smile. "We'll both be here when you wake up."

She grinned and let out a long breath, I was sure she'd been holding it until I answered. Lemon put her to bed and held her hand until she fell asleep. By that time, Lemon was herself nearly asleep.

"Come on, little mama."

"Ain't no mama," she groused. I gently extracted Effie's hand from hers and lifted Lemon into my arms. She laid her head on my shoulder.

"Sure you are. And a good one, too, if the way you treat Effie is any indication."

"Shut up."

I chuckled as I carried her to our bedroom. "We need to talk, but I think it's gonna have to wait until tomorrow."

She grunted but didn't move in my arms. I laid her on the bed, slipping her shoes off her feet. I pulled off my shirt but kept my shorts on, then crawled into bed beside her. I thought she might protest, but she simply turned into me and snuggled against my side. She situated herself with her head on my shoulder and one arm thrown over my chest.

As I sifted my fingers through her hair, I was struck at how right this felt. Sure, I was sexually attracted to Lemon to hell and back, but just having her next to me filled something in my life I hadn't realized I'd been missing.

I dozed off and on, not really wanting to go to sleep but not wanting to leave Lemon either. When she finally stirred, it was just after midnight. She stretched and rubbed against me like a contented cat.

"Hey there." I brushed my lips over the top of her head.

"Hey." Her voice was rough from sleep. If I'd thought she'd be shy about us being in bed together, I'd have been wrong. Just like everything else about Lemon, this was a surprise. "What time is it?"

"Little after midnight."

She stretched, draping her body more fully on top of me. One thigh was over mine and she snuggled her face into my neck and inhaled.

"You smell good."

I chuckled. "You smell good yourself."

"Guess you're used to sleeping with a woman, huh?" Lemon was fishing and I could hear the uncertainty in her voice. Despite how assertive she normally was, I knew Lemon had little experience outside of her immediate family with close personal relationships. Anyone with her personality would. She was raw and unfiltered and so fucking protective not many people could handle her brand of affection. She'd reluctantly let Wylde into her circle, but probably only because he was so much like her. Even if he was her sister's man, if Wylde had been anyone other than who he was, Lemon would never have accepted him as solidly as she did. He would never have been the one she called when she needed help or was in trouble.

Now, she was in bed with a man she barely knew. She'd proclaimed herself my old lady and had even sealed the deal with a kiss. I wondered if she'd thought beyond that kiss. Had she been any woman other than Lemon, I'd have said she knew exactly what she was doing. Instead, I got the feeling she was just doing what felt good. It was a side of her I hadn't seen yet but was enjoying the shit out of.

"Nope. Never slept with a woman. Have I fucked women? Sure. More than my fair share. But I don't sleep with them."

She froze before rising up and bracing herself on my chest. "Are you fuckin' with me?"

I grinned. "Nope."

"Then why… Wait. You didn't want to sleep on the couch." She deflated a little and started to pull away. Which wouldn't do.

"Stop, Lemon." I wrapped my arms around her and pulled her against me. It didn't feel right, so I urged her to lie fully on top of me, one of her legs on each side of my hips. "There. Better."

"Rocket --"

"Nope. You're going to listen to me. I don't sleep with women. But you're not just any woman, Lemon. You're my old lady. Remember?"

She sighed. "You know you don't have to

pretend. I know you don't… that is, I'm a lot to handle. I know I am."

"You are at that. Do you hear me complaining?"

She cocked her head, studying me. "No, but your club's gonna hate me. Falcon already does. Besides, I only said that so I could get you to listen to me and see how wrong it is for them to abandon you when you're in trouble."

"There are things I need you to understand before that conversation. But I'm not ready for that yet."

"You're not?"

"We have unfinished business between us first."

"What's that?"

I threaded my fingers through her hair gently and brought her down for a kiss. At first, she stiffened, but it didn't take long for her to sigh and melt against me. Where I'd let her control things last time, now I led her where I wanted us to go together.

As our lips moved in sync, the tension between us dissipated, replaced by a fiery passion that ignited from deep within. Lemon's body molded perfectly against mine, fitting like a missing puzzle piece. Her breath mingled with mine, creating a symphony of desire that echoed through the room.

Our bodies intertwined, moving with a raw need that had been simmering beneath the surface for over a year. We hadn't interacted much until the last day, but I'd seen her. I'd watched her watch me. It had been an erotic mind game, one I'd both enjoyed and come to hate because there was no way I could act on my lust and no way I could get her out of my head.

I deepened the kiss, a collision of passion and desire that left no room for doubt or hesitation. Lemon surrendered herself to the rhythm I set, her little mewling whimpers mingling with my low growl as we shared this intimate dance.

As gently as I could, I rolled us until Lemon was beneath my bigger body. She sighed, her arms going around my neck.

"So fuckin' sweet." The words were ripped from me, my need to let her know how much I wanted this paramount. Lemon would never admit it if she were scared or nervous. That wasn't the way she worked. She'd plow ahead and damn the consequences if she wanted it badly enough. It was my job to make sure she was never scared of being intimate with me. If she was a little nervous? Well, nervousness built anticipation.

"Rocket…" Her breathy moan was the sweetest music. She grew braver, her hands roaming over my bare back and shoulders. She arched her neck so I could kiss my way down her jaw to her neck, then her collarbone just above the neckline of her shirt.

"I want this shirt off, Lemon. Your shorts too. I want to taste every fuckin' inch of you."

That got a sharp cry from her and I grinned. Of course, Lemon loved dirty talk. I chuckled even as I ran my hands up her sides under her shirt. She quickly helped me pull it up and over her head. I kissed her again, praising her for doing as I wished.

The room was consumed by an intoxicating energy as I trailed my lips along Lemon's newly exposed skin. Each touch ignited a fiery desire within me, pushing me further into the depths of a lust that threatened to overwhelm me. Her body quivered beneath mine, her soft gasps fueling the fire that raged between us.

I could feel the heat radiating off Lemon's body as I continued to trail my lips along her soft skin. Her curves fit perfectly into the contours of my body. It was as if we were two halves of a whole, destined to come together in this moment. It was just as I expected sex between us to be. Fiery and passionate.

The more I touched her, the more animated she became, arching against me to rub her nipples over my hair-roughened chest. I scooted down her body until I was able to suck one puckered nipple between my lips. Her sharp cry echoed in the room and I quickly put a hand over her mouth to silence her.

"Hush, baby. We don't want Effie to wake up."

"Oh, God! The door."

"Don't worry." I chuckled. "I locked it behind me when I brought you in here."

"More." Her demand was more a breathy sigh, one I was only too happy to comply with.

I began a slow and deliberate dance of caresses and kisses, teasing her sensitive flesh with feather-light touches and nips that sent shivers cascading through her body. I traced the delicate lines of her belly button with my tongue, dipping inside to taste the salty-sweet sweat that had erupted over her body.

She gasped, her body tense. I whispered into her ear, "You want this, don't you? You want my hands on you, Lemon?"

She nodded her head in quick little jerks. I gently eased down her body, her curves undulating beneath my hands and lips, trailing my fingers over her, my mouth and tongue over all that delicious skin. Lemon writhed under me, even as I held her still to kiss the bruising over her torso where she'd been kicked.

My shoulder ached like a mother, but there was no way I was missing this. I'd take the pain with a smile and a fucking princess wave if I could just enjoy this encounter with Lemon to a spectacular conclusion.

As I made my way down her body, I took my time, wanting to savor every second we had. I didn't want this moment to end. Lemon's breathing was erratic, her body bucking against me as if she couldn't contain the passion that flowed through her.

Her eyes were shining, mirroring my own desire, as I slowly pulled her shorts over her hips and down her legs before tossing them on the floor. I hadn't provided her with panties yet and I wasn't sure I was going to. I like the idea of having access to her anytime I wanted it. And I would most definitely be doing this with her again.

She shoved her hips up, revealing her wet folds, inviting me in. My fingers delved between her lips, spreading the juices I found there. Denying myself a taste wasn't even an option.

I stuck my fingers in my mouth once. Then repeated the whole process, playing with her outer lips before thrusting two fingers inside her once more and licking them clean.

"Fuckin' sweet as fuckin' honey." My voice was a husky rasp. And really. I'd never tasted anything as wonderful as Lemon's sweet pussy. It was more than the physical experience and the fact that she ate up the attention I was happy to lavish on her. There was no artifice, no ultimate goal for her. She'd already declared herself my old lady. While I suppose I could pat her on the head, tell her she was cute, then move on, I knew I'd never leave her. Or let her leave me. She had no reason to pretend to enjoy this. And, really, this was Lemon. She never did anything she didn't want to, nor would she continue doing something she'd started if she decided it wasn't for her.

With a groan, I dipped my head to her pussy and took a long, slow, satisfying lick from her opening to her clit. The second I did, Lemon… went wild.

"Fuck! Rocket!" she screamed, and I had to lunge up to cover her mouth with my hand.

"Shh… You don't want to wake Effie. She'll want you to stay with her and we'll have to stop."

"I'm sorry! I'm sorry!" Her voice was muffled behind my hand, and she gripped my thick wrist with her much smaller hand and held it tightly over her mouth. The next time I licked at her clit, she clung to me, screaming into my hand with a ferocious, muffled roar. It made me feel ten fucking feet tall.

Before she'd finished coming, I moved up her body, wedging my hips between her legs. I let her come down by kissing her over and over, wanting her sane but still on the verge of out of control.

"That's it, woman. Give me all of you. Your screams. Your pleasure. Your pain. My… woman…"

I had no idea what nonsense I was spouting, but I knew I meant every fucking word.

As I kissed Lemon gently, her breathing began to slow down and her body relaxed under mine. Her eyes met mine, and I could see a mix of love, lust, and a strange sort of vulnerability that I had never seen before. I didn't let her thoughts linger too long, instead, I held her gaze and told her what I expected of her.

"You're my woman, Lemon. From this point forward." My cock kissed her entrance and she squirmed, trying to get closer. She nibbled her bottom lip and her brow furrowed. I knew she was with me but still reaching for the pleasure she knew I was going to continue. "Hold still," I snapped.

"No," she bit out. "I want you inside me."

"And I'm gonna be. Listen to me first."

Her eyes were wide, blue pools, glazed with lust as she looked up into mine. She was trembling as she lay beneath me and sweat glistened on her forehead and upper lip. "Please, Rocket. I-I need…"

I kissed her again, thrusting my tongue into her mouth. She opened willingly, meeting my thrust with one of her own.

"Now, listen to me, Lemon. Really listen." When she gave a small nod, still clinging to my gaze with her own, I slid the tip of my cock inside her and stopped. "This is it, Lemon. You claimed me and that claim is gonna stand. You're my old lady. There is no going back."

"I don't understand. I figured you'd kick me out once I helped you or when you got tired of me."

I barked out a laugh. "Honey, first of all, there is no fuckin' way I could possibly get tired of you. You will run circles around me like no other woman ever could. Because you're you. Second, honey… We'll talk about the club later, but you have to understand what Grim Road is before you can understand that this is who we are. The way we operate. You can't change us because it's ingrained in us to keep secrets. Even from each other."

"You're wrong," she said, reaching up to stroke my beard with her delicate hand. "You can change. You have to. Otherwise, someone in this club you love will die and you could have prevented it. Then, because you're you" -- she grinned up at me, throwing my words back at me -- "you'll regret it. Horribly."

Then she gripped my ass and pulled me farther inside her. I saw the wince and felt her sharp inhalation. And I knew I'd just taken her virginity. Or, rather, she'd given her virginity knowing exactly what she was doing.

"Fuck, woman." I shuddered as I felt her heartbeat around my dick. "Fuck!"

She whimpered but didn't let go of my hips. Instead, she pushed back slightly before pulling me back, essentially fucking me at her own pace. The second she became comfortable, when her face was flushed with only pleasure instead of pain or any discomfort, I settled my full weight on her and took over.

Lemon sighed, wrapping her arms around my neck and pulling me down to kiss her. Her little tongue tangled with mine for a long time. I continued to move slowly until I felt her heartbeat quicken and her breath hitch as the pleasure slowly began to build back to a fever pitch.

I broke the kiss, my gaze locked on hers. "You ready for this, Lemon? This is real. You're in deeper than you know."

She nodded, her eyes seeming to glow with determination.

"I mean it. No more secrets, no more hiding. We're in this together. You will know my every secret and possibly secrets of other members of the club I know. We're a team."

"That's all I wanted, Rocket," she said softly. "Since the moment I first saw you. I wanted you to be mine, but..." her voice hitched. This was a side of Lemon she didn't let anyone see. I doubted if either of her sisters had seen this vulnerable, unsure side of her. Lemon was larger than life. She wasn't a woman who showed her belly to anyone for any reason. Yet, she was doing exactly what she demanded of me. She was giving me the honest truth. The truth about how she felt and what she wanted. Her dreams. Her fears.

"Tell me, honey." I stroked her cheek tenderly, brushing a kiss over her chin. "Tell me what's wrong."

"I don't see how a man like you could want

someone like me."

I barked out a laugh. "Baby. Why in the world would you think that?"

"I'm too young, for one thing." Then her features hardened. "But I'm not waiting any longer. And I'm not giving up on having you."

"Baby, you have me. That's not something you've gotta worry about."

"I don't…" She winced, shaking her head slightly. "You're my first fuck buddy," she said with more strength that I thought she had at the moment. I knew it hurt her to phrase it that way but I thought she might have done it to sound like she could give a damn when she'd just admitted how badly and how long she'd wanted me.

"OK, stop." I flexed my hips so that I was inside her as far as I could go. "I don't know what you think this is, but one thing we are not is fuck buddies. You're my woman. How many times do I have to say it before you believe it?" I trailed kisses over her neck and chin before meeting her lips with mine again. "You're the one who claimed me. Why is it so hard to believe I've claimed you right back and that I'm holding you to your claim? This is what you've gotten yourself into. You've got to live with me. For the rest of our lives."

"You can't know that." Her voice was no more than a whisper, but she wanted exactly what I'd described with every fiber of her being. I could see it on her face as clearly as if she'd admitted it out loud.

"I can." I put as much force in my voice as I could. I absolutely needed her to know I meant every word I said. "Now. Are you gonna argue with me or are you gonna come on my cock?"

My words seemed to flip a switch inside her. She did indeed come, her eyes wide with shock as her pussy squeezed my dick in a vicious grip. I caught her surprised cries with my kiss, relishing how her untried body willingly gave me what I wanted.

Lemon was a fighter, but in this, she surrendered. Which told me she trusted me. And that was something I would forever treasure and never take for granted.

Chapter Eleven
Lemon

This is the place I'd wanted to be for over a year. Since the first time I'd had time to observe Rocket and how he conducted himself. I still had questions he was going to have to answer, but I wanted this time before we got down to the serious conversation I knew had to follow. I was also very aware that he was inside me. Without a condom. And I wasn't broken up about it.

After the orgasm pulsing through me began to ebb, Rocket started to move again. This time with more vigor. He'd been giving to me, and now he was taking his own pleasure. I was eager to see what he looked like when his own orgasm overtook him.

His eyes locked on mine as he began to pick up the pace. He plunged deeper into me, pulling my hips closer to him with each thrust. I could feel his heart pounding against me, and his breath coming in short bursts. His body tensed, and I could feel his thrusts becoming more erratic. He leaned forward, his lips brushing against mine in more heated kisses. His hips moved faster and harder, and I could feel his cock pulsing inside me. I wrapped my legs around him, urging him on, eager for him to come inside me and solidify this thing between us.

I knew there was a battle ahead, one I absolutely had to win. Not because I cared about this fucking club. As far as I was concerned, Grim Road could suck ass and swallow. But I would not lose Rocket because his club refused to back him up. It was my obsession with this man, something I wasn't quite ready to call love but knew was damned close, that drove me to do everything I could to protect him. Even if it was from his brothers. Especially if it was from his brothers.

With a deep groan, Rocket held himself as deeply inside me as he could go and came. Pulse after pulse of hot seed seared me inside. Cleansed the last drop of blood in my heart that tried to hold out from falling completely under his spell. I knew I had to be all in for this to work, but I was afraid he'd take me over completely. That I'd be a shell of the woman I'd fought so hard to be.

The room was filled with an intense warmth as the smell of our lovemaking hung in the air. I savored the moment, the tender caress of his skin against mine. Finally, after what felt like an eternity, Rocket pulled away and rolled off me. He scooped me up and carried me to the bathroom where he cleaned us both. Neither of us spoke, as if he were putting off the coming talk as much as I wanted to. I knew the conversation to come next wouldn't be pleasant, but it was past time.

It seemed like everything around us was conspiring to keep us from talking about the elephant in the room. Time passed like a serpent slithering through the grass, and my heart became more and more entwined with Rocket's even as I wasn't sure I could handle being in his world. The club, Grim Road, was a shadowy presence that cast long, ominous fingers over our lives.

OK, that was a bit of a melodramatic description, but I was good and pissed at every motherfucker in this place. Even Rocket, though I could now admit there was no way to deny myself being with him as long as I could.

When he'd cleansed us both, he braced his hands on the vanity beside my hips. "What the fuck am I gonna do with you, Lemon?"

I stiffened and felt the blood rise to my face.

"You don't have to do anything with me," I

snapped, shoving at his shoulders. "Move, you bastard." I tried to ignore the way my heart gave a painful jerk.

"For Christ's sake, Lemon." He chuckled. "Stop assuming the worst of me. I'm not rejecting you, and I never will."

"Then what did you mean?"

"Honey, you have me." He stood, bringing my hands to his chest and holding them there. "I knew the first time I saw you. You stood by Scarlet, holding her hand and refusing to leave her side when Claw killed himself. Even when Mars took her away, you stood in her stead. You did it because you knew she couldn't. That is courage and loyalty. I didn't even admit it to myself at the time, but the truth is, I wanted that loyalty you showed Scarlet for myself, and I wanted it from you, Lemon. You."

He pulled me closer to the edge of the counter, one arm around my back, one between us, guiding his cock back inside me. I gasped and clung to him even though I felt like I should be strong and push him away. Heaven help me, I couldn't do it.

We'd just made love. I was feeling the effects of post-orgasmic let down, yet he was expertly building me up again with little effort.

"Don't hurt me, Rocket," I blurted out. A small sob escaped before I could stop it. "Please."

"Hush, baby." He whispered his command as he caught my mouth in a hungry kiss. As the emotional turmoil between us raged like a tempest, he whispered, "You're safe with me," and I believed it was the truth. I just wasn't sure he was ready to hear what I had to say. If he rejected my observations, if he refused to see how wrong things were that his club could leave him to fend for himself even knowing he was wounded, I wasn't sure what I'd do.

Then he reached between us and found my clit with his thumb, and I let the pleasure he created in his wake have me. My head fell back on my shoulders and Rocket found my skin with his lips. He sucked gently, leaving little stinging kisses in his wake. The slight pain in such a sensitive area tipped me over the edge.

With a shuddering cry, I came in his arms. Rocket moved inside me in short snaps, his breathing as ragged as mine. It wasn't long before he came inside me again. Part of me rejoiced while another part, once again, reminded me how in over my head I was.

He rested his forehead against mine as we both caught our breath. I was gratified to realize he was sweating with exertion as hard as I was.

Rocket kissed me again, this time, with tender feeling, coaxing me to take comfort. It was a kiss to heal, not to arouse. It felt like a new beginning. Like everything I'd experienced with this man had been leading to this point. Most of my life, I'd used my snarky personality to keep everyone in my life off-balance. The snark now deserted me. All I had was my belief in Rocket and hope that I could get him to understand the truth as I saw it. And how dangerous it was for everyone.

Again, Rocket cleaned us both before lifting me and taking me back into the bedroom. He tossed me a shirt, and he slung on a pair of jeans, then indicated I should sit at a table in the corner of the room. It was big enough for two people with chairs on either side so that we faced each other. I laced my fingers and twisted them nervously as I rested my forearms on the smooth surface.

Rocket reached out and covered my hands with his bigger ones and smiled at me. "Don't look so nervous, honey. I'm here to listen to you. We're going to listen to each other. So I'm going to start so you understand how and why Grim Road is different from Iron Tzars or any other MC you've been around. When I'm done, I'm going to listen to your concerns." Rocket looked as serious as the situation called for. It was a little unnerving when I was still reeling from my first sexual encounter. But this was the life I'd signed up for. I could do this. In a way, I'd been training most of my life for this.

I took a breath and squared my shoulders, meeting Rocket's gaze with a steady one of my own. Rocket nodded slowly before giving me a small smile.

"Good. I knew you were up for this." He squeezed my hands once before sitting back and scrubbing a hand over his face. When he looked at me again, it was as an equal. I knew in my heart what he was about to tell me would change my outlook on everything in my life I wanted to build here. I only hoped I could handle it because I had no intention of leaving Rocket without a fierce fight.

Then he began. "Grim Road was created to be a safe place for soldiers who" -- he seemed to search for the right words -- "aren't supposed to still be alive. Or at the very best need to stay hidden. Sure, we go out in the community when we have to, but we try to be as self-sufficient as we can. This whole place is over six hundred acres of government land in the middle of a designated wildlife reserve."

I frowned, doing my best to concentrate on what he was about to tell me when I was starting to feel the effects of the day. My face and ribs hurt, but instead of wanting a pain pill or an ice pack, I embraced the pain, using it to keep me in the here and now. The last thing I needed to do was get lost in the memory of what we'd just shared. This was too important. "If it's a wildlife reserve, how can you build structures and live here?"

"That's a bit more complicated." He smiled, but it was self-deprecating. "When Grim Road was first formed several decades ago, our president, who was a high-ranking military official, negotiated this land off Riviera Beach for us. It's cordoned off with fences and barbed wire in places. No one is allowed in the area ten miles square around us. While we have a house in town we keep manned at all times and use to do business, this is our home. We keep to ourselves and are as self-sufficient as we can be. We have greenhouses, gardens, and animals we raise for food."

"Still seems like it would be hard to keep secret from locals."

"It is. But anyone living around the reserve thinks we're some kind of doomsday cult or something. They leave us alone because they think we're crazy, and we stay out of everyone's way and keep a low profile."

"OK. I'll buy that." I narrowed my gaze at him. "Why?" It was a demand more than it was a question, and I saw the way Rocket's lips twitched. Like he wanted like hell to smile but didn't dare. Which was good because I'd have hated to have to punch him in the taint.

"Because every single man in this MC is or has been Black Ops. There are men here who'd have a price on their head if the current administration knew they were alive, what they'd done, and what they knew. No one here knows everything about everyone here." He shrugged. "Except maybe Crush, but he's more close-lipped than Byte -- and that's saying something."

"Black Ops. As in soldiers who run missions not

sanctioned by the government?"

"Eh, sometimes. Sometimes it's a faction within the government, usually the executive branch, when they don't want the American people to know anything about it. Sometimes it's CIA or FBI. Most of us here did our bit in the service. A few still take on jobs as part of paramilitary operations, but we all work alone or in very small groups, and we never talk about it with anyone."

I was silent for a moment, absorbing what he'd said. "So, by telling me, you're breaking some kind of unspoken code?"

"Somewhat. But I also happen to believe that partners shouldn't keep secrets from each other. That trust extended to me and Claw because he was vice president of Grim. He chose to keep his secrets buried deep and to lie to me when he sent Scarlet away. I'm trusting you with this because I expect you to trust me with your secrets." He shook his head. "I'm not a hypocrite. Also, I want you to understand why my club acted like they did yesterday. Why they would sacrifice me if they didn't think they could get us all away clean."

Everything inside me rebelled at the thought of the fucking club "sacrificing" Rocket to preserve themselves. It was exactly opposite of what I'd learned since Danica had taken up with Wylde. Instead of saying anything, though, I took a breath and let it out. Then another. Rocket nodded his head slowly and gave me a small smile, as if he realized I understood what he was saying and disagreed strongly, but was waiting for him to continue.

I shook my head slightly. "What to address first," I muttered.

Rocket chuckled and reached for my hands

again. "Take your time, Lemon. We're in no hurry now. The only thing we have to interrupt us is Effie if she wakes up too soon. If she does, I'll get Gina or Byte to come entertain her until we're done."

"Aaaaand you had to go and bring up another situation." I lowered my head to the table and thumped it a couple of times.

"Welcome to the inner workings of an MC, honey. This the life you want?"

I snapped my head up and glared at him. "No. I want a life where we fuck like mad and ride motorcycles, then get high as balls and all the other things you read about and see on TV and shit!"

That got a belly laugh from Rocket. It should have irritated me, but instead it steadied me. He stroked my hands with his thumbs and squeezed gently. "Honey, we can do that all you want too. But you had specific goals in mind when you came to me. Now we're working through them. I'm just tellin' you why it might be a challenge."

"If you're trying to discourage me, it's not going to work."

"Good. Let's begin." He raised an imperious eyebrow and I snorted.

"That look's gonna get you an eye put out."

"Just one more reason I'm growing to love you, Lemon. You'll never let me get away with anything."

It felt like he'd punched me in the gut. I wanted to jerk my hands away from him, but his tightened around mine like he could read my fucking mind. I had to take a couple of deep breaths before I spoke next.

"You said no lying. We never lie to each other."

"So I did. What's your point?"

"You don't love me. You're not going to make

me believe you love me. Not yet."

"Why? Don't you love me?"

"NO!" I did jerk my hands away then. Because I might love him.

Instantly, his face hardened, then he scowled at me. "No. Lying. Especially not about this, Lemon."

"Why not?" I spat. "You just did."

"How do you figure that?"

"You do not love me, Rocket. We've known each other less than a fuckin' day! Fuck!" I stood so quickly I knocked the chair over as I paced across the room. I had to put some distance between us before I fucking cried again.

Rocket didn't immediately refute my words which only made that need to fucking cry that much worse. The tightness in my throat made me feel like I was choking. And maybe I was. Choking on emotions I desperately wanted to deny because I knew with all my heart he was right. I did love him. I hadn't seen him much over the last year or so, but when I had I'd been so drawn to him my imagination had taken over, and I'd built this wonderful fiction around us.

He moved in behind me, wrapping his arms tightly around me. His breath fanned over my cheek, making me shiver. We stood like that for a long time before he spoke.

"I'm many things, Lemon. I've done bad shit in my life. Still do. Always will. But I will never, for any reason, lie to you. But you're right. I did lie. I'm not growing to love you. I'm already there. Have been since you insisted on staying through Hammer's torture." He chuckled. "Fuck. There were so many things that led me to that moment. I think you might have had me when you bashed your head in to my fuckin' nose."

I sighed, leaning into him. "I'd say that wasn't one of my finer moments, but I'd be lying. And I don't want to lie to you."

He whispered next to my ear. "I think it was your best moment."

There was no help for it. I turned in his arms and threw my arms around his neck. Tears tried to fall, but I held them back. Mostly.

Almost mostly.

Rocket held me, those strong arms of his wrapped so tightly around me I could barely breathe. And I wouldn't have it any other way.

We stood there for long moments. I wanted to go back to bed and learn more about the sex he'd shown me earlier, but we had shit to fix. It started now, and I absolutely would see this through.

Chapter Twelve
Rocket

Yeah, I was fucked. How many times had I thought that very same thing with regard to Lemon? It was the fucking truth. This woman had me wrapped around her little finger. She might not realize it, yet, but when she did I was in serious danger of losing my reputation as a badass motherfucker. Maybe even my man card. Because my men would absolutely find out. Hell, no one could see how I looked at this woman and not know. The only question was, did I really care who knew? Because the answer to that was a resounding and big ol' hell no.

I let her compose herself. No way was I stupid enough to acknowledge I felt her tears on my bare chest. I'd been on the receiving end of Lemon's fury more than once and had no desire to repeat the experience.

OK, so that was a Goddamned lie. Any show of aggression by her got me hard and ready to fuck her. Just thinking about that first time I'd witnessed Lemon in all her furious glory had my cock stirring. And that was after coming my brains out twice already.

When she was ready, she pushed me away and sniffed, wiping her nose on the back of her arm before lifting her chin. "OK. Let's get to this."

That was my Lemon. Ready to take on anything she needed to. I got why she thought the club was broken or dysfunctional. In a way, I thought that might have been why I'd forged ahead with ties to Salvation's Bane and Iron Tzars. The Tzars had men I'd served with, other members of Grim had served with, and now had one of our own daughters. Bane had my own daughter. True, Talia wasn't mine by birth, but I'd raised her from a young teen and she was a daughter of my heart.

We sat and Lemon cleared her throat. "So. First problem. You."

That surprised me. "You have doubts about me?"

She met my gaze unwaveringly and took another little piece of my heart when she did. Whatever she was about to say next wasn't something she was going to let me off the hook easily with.

"How much did you know about Scarlet?" It wasn't a question so much as a demand.

"All I knew was what I told you and Scarlet a year ago."

"Yeah. That the club was in danger or some shit and you thought it safer. If that's the truth, why not send her sisters with her?"

I knew this was coming. These were questions I'd been asking myself since the shit had hit the fan. "The strict truth is that I had doubts Hammer could keep all three safe. The rest of it is, Hammer taking Scarlet away was one less person I thought I had to worry about."

She frowned, clearly not expecting me to be so brutally honest. "Look, Lemon. I'm not proud of my actions regarding Claw, Hammer, and Scarlet. There are so many things I should have done that I didn't. My only excuse is that I'd stretched myself too thin."

"Which wouldn't have happened if your club had been on the same page." She didn't sound angry, just like she was trying to drive her point home. "Was there ever any indication Hammer was as twisted inside as he was?" Again, there was no anger. She was looking for answers to questions she needed to take action. I knew the feeling well because I often did it myself when trying to solve a difficult problem.

I thought about that question. Really thought about it. "No. Looking back, maybe there were small signs I should have paid attention to better, but nothing overt. I knew how he felt about Claw. He told me soon after Claw killed Madina. But he made me a promise he'd back off until he could control his anger. Even took some time away from the compound for beach house duty. There are always three brothers there, so he was never alone."

"The house in town."

"Yes. Crush kept tabs on him covertly, making sure he wasn't planning anything outside the club. He stayed there six months before he said he was ready to come back to the club. By that time, Claw had been sent on a mission to North Korea. It was another six months before the two saw each other again."

She started. "North Korea?"

I grinned. "Told you. Black Ops."

"Sweet Jesus." She scrubbed a hand over her mouth. Yeah. She understood the full impact of my disclosure. I was all in with her. Now, she had to be all in with me. She must have come to that last conclusion a little late because it took her a second before she glared at me. "Don't think I don't know what you did there." She tapped her temple. "I'm on to you, buddy."

"It's one more tie to weave us together. I will continually drop little things like that just to keep you on your toes." I held my grin for a moment before letting it fall. "You do know information like that is only ever to be discussed between the two of us, right? Never say anything even in front of the members of this club. Even to the person in question."

"You said before Crush knew everything."

"He does. No one but the two of us knows he

does. Hell, who am I kidding? He doesn't tell me everything. Just about eighty percent or so."

"Why." Again, it was a demand.

"Crush is our... safeguard, for lack of a better word. There's not much he can do for a member if things go to shit, but he can keep blowback from coming to the club."

She stood again, pacing back and forth. "See, that's the problem. He should be able to help one of your brothers out if things go to shit on a mission. All of you should. Especially in your own city."

I frowned. "Lemon, no one can know about us. Or about this compound."

"The government knows," she countered.

I nodded. "Maybe," I conceded, "but the more time goes by, fewer in government remember. Administrations change. Agency heads change. Paperwork gets buried. For teams like us, paperwork never existed."

"Aren't you afraid someone will find the place? I mean, just because it's off-limits doesn't mean people don't wander in. For that matter, there have to be scientists who wander through."

"Not in this area. When it was set up by the land owners, it was to allow no one in. Let nature take its course. While there is a huge area around us, we are in the very center. We keep things small, only using what we need to be self-sustaining, and we never hunt outside our area, and only small game like squirrels and raccoons."

She nodded, my answer apparently making sense to her. "OK, so back to Hammer and Gina. They were an item?"

I frowned. "To be honest, I'm not sure. I thought they were, but then Claw said Hammer and Scarlet wanted to be together."

"Well, obviously that went south. I know you don't think Gina could have been Hammer's plant, but what if she was?"

"So, we need to talk to Gina."

"No." She shook her head. "We don't need to do anything. I need to talk to Gina. One on one."

"You can talk to her, but you'll do it with me and Crush present."

"She might not talk with the two of you around. It's obvious she's scared of Byte. Why would she not be afraid of Crush too?"

"OK, then I'll be with you." Lemon pursed her lips and I knew she was going to try to argue. "Stop right there, sour puss. Me being with you when you question Gina is non-negotiable."

As I hoped, she scowled. I had to smother my grin. "Sour puss? I thought we were past that."

That grin tugged its way free. "Still fits."

If I lived to be a hundred, Lemon's beautiful chuckle would always warm my heart. Like it did now. "Point taken. So, we talk to Gina. If Byte is right and she hasn't left her house in months, she'll feel safer there."

"Good. On to the next thing."

"Falcon is on my shit list."

"Really. Never would have guessed. Guessing you're on his too."

"For refusing to come after you when I told him you'd been shot, he deserved what he got."

"There's a reason for that, Lemon."

"Yeah, yeah. If they couldn't contain the damage the whole club could be outed. You said that before." She stuck up her chin. "Not buying it."

"Lemon --"

"No! The men of Grim Road are your brothers. Right?"

"Yes. They are."

"Brothers are family and family always protects family."

"He was. By not going after me he was protecting the rest of his family."

"So you guys use Spock logic."

I tilted my head. "Aren't you a little young to know what that means?"

"Dude. It's Spock."

"Yeah, well, the needs of the many outweigh the needs of the few."

"You realize he also said the needs of the few outweigh the needs of the many. Right? Same fuckin' movie."

"What's your point, Lemon."

"The point is, when your family is in danger, you protect them. The bigger family was safe, and there were enough Grim members with Falcon they could have contained the damage."

"Falcon isn't an officer."

"So he can't make decisions for the club. Is that where you were going?"

I grinned. "You know me so well." It was an answer to her question. Not an observation.

"Right. Should a' known. Fuckwit isn't smart enough to make decisions for himself." Before I could comment she plowed on. "We'll come back to that, but we'll do it with the rest of the club present."

"Whatever you say. Next."

"Just to recap. You admit you were stretched too thin to realize you should have questioned Hammer's motives and actually talked to Scarlet after you sent her off."

"I will probably never forgive myself for my negligence in that matter. Being busy isn't a reason for not doing right by Scarlet. Especially when I didn't insist on speaking to her after she left. I also should have trusted my brothers to keep everyone safe inside the compound. I trusted them to keep Sunshine and Rainbow safe here. I should have kept Scarlet here as well. My only defense is that I thought anywhere would have been safer than this compound. But I wasn't sending the women or girls away without protection, and I thought Scarlet wanted to be with Hammer. Claw told me she did."

"I guess that's not a mistake you'll be making again anytime soon. Or ever, really."

"I'm not, as you say, a fuckwit. I learn from my mistakes. Especially one as big as that one was."

"So now, we need to go see Gina."

"It's close to three a.m. I doubt she's awake."

"So, first thing in the morning, then."

I grinned. "So we've got time."

Her smile was simply to God glorious. "Oh, yeah. We've got time. And I know just what I want to do with that time."

"I hope it involves getting naked again."

"It does. Only, I have one request."

"Anything."

She picked at the collar of my shirt she wore. "I'm gonna need some clothes that actually fit. Much as I like wearing your clothes, I can't look like a kid playing dress-up when I take it to the rest of the club."

"I suppose that would take some of the sting out of whatever you decide to say."

"Can't have that. So, I need a couple of T-shirts and jeans. And maybe some motorcycle boots, 'cause old ladies need to look the part. Speaking of which."

Her expression hardened again. "Where's my fuckin' vest?"

I barked out a laugh before wincing and glancing toward the room where I hoped Effie was still asleep. "Honey, you got here less than twenty-four hours ago. I can't pull a property cut outta my ass."

"How long?"

"It's being made. You'll have it tomorrow before we call church."

She poked me in the chest none too gently. "I better. I don't want to go in there without something to prove what I am, but I will. And if any one of those motherfuckers challenge me, I will bust a motherfucker up."

"All right," I grunted, bending to scoop her up. "You've done it now."

"Rocket, what are you doing?" She didn't struggle but looked appropriately put out.

"Takin' you back to bed. You gave me a hard-on and I need to fill your pussy with more cum."

She jerked back, looking at me with a surprised mien. "Oh. Well, then." She pointed to the bedroom. "Carry on."

Chapter Thirteen
Lemon

It was later than I intended to get up when Rocket finally roused me out of bed. To be fair, he'd kept me up all night. First the sex, then our talk. Then more sex. And I might have woken him a couple more times for sex. What can I say? When it's good, it's good.

Effie was all smiles and curiosity, but I could see the forced cheerfulness on her little face. Kid would need all kinds of therapy and getting it would be an issue since I'd decided we both needed to effectively fall off the grid. Like, forever. I'd get Wylde on that. Crush might be able to do it, but I wasn't counting on him until I knew more about him. He might not have done anything overt, but he was still on my shit list. I had the feeling he knew way the fuck more than even Rocket thought he did. I also thought he could have kept closer tabs on Scarlet. But one thing at a time.

"I'll have Crush give Gina a heads-up we're coming."

"NO!" I jumped up from bed and snagged the T-shirt Rocket had kept pulling off me last night. I'd given up trying to keep it on and just tossed it over a chair after the third round. "Don't do that."

He gave me a puzzled look. "Why not? She'll want to be prepared for us."

"Exactly." I gave him a curt nod and marched out of the bedroom to the kitchen. I was fucking starving.

Opening the fridge, I found a pound of bacon and tossed it to the counter. Pulling out a big cookie sheet, I lined it with the bacon while the oven was heating. Once it was all laid out and in the oven, I hurried to the shower.

"What'er you doin', sour puss?"

I looked over my shoulder as Rocket's face split into a cocky grin. "Fixin' to mop the floor with your smug ass." I pointed at him. "Do not call me sour puss in front of anyone. You do, I'll start callin' you dumbshit."

He leaned in and kissed me. If Effie hadn't been awake I'd have dragged him into the shower with me. But she was. Beside, someone had to keep an eye on breakfast.

"Timer's set for twenty minutes. I ain't out, check on the bacon. If it's not just this side of burned, do not touch it."

"Burnt bacon." He chuckled. "I like it."

"I don't care if you like it or not. You touch it before it's done, you die. *Capice*?"

He raised his hands in surrender before heading back down the hall. "Understood, sour puss."

"Don't call me that!" My ire was met with his deep laugh. I made a face behind his back.

"I saw that."

"Did not." He pointed to a nearby mirror and I realized he probably had seen me. He hadn't lied. "Fine. Point taken."

I hurried through the shower. I was sore as a mother, but not from the sex we'd shared the night before. OK, I was sore from that, but not like I was from the beating I'd taken when I'd rescued Effie. And yeah. I'd given up trying to call her Euphemia even in my head, because poor kid. We'd have to come up with a road name for her. If we were going to vanish off the grid, we could totally do that. Might help her feel like she fit in.

Rocket had set some real clothes out for me on

our bed and, yes, my property cut was there. I grinned. Apple was gonna be so jealous.

I reached for my phone to snap a pic for her, only to remember I didn't have one. Which is when I remembered that Dani and Apple would be worried. Wylde too but fuck him. He was a grown-ass man.

I sighed. No. I'd never tell a soul, but I loved Wylde as much as I did Apple and Dani. I didn't want him to worry.

When I made it to the kitchen, I was fully dressed and sporting my new vest, skintight jeans, a white tank top that showed my belly, and fucking fabulous motorcycle boots. I found Effie and Rocket chatting and eating eggs and toast with their bacon. Along with strawberry jam. I ruffled Effie's hair before picking up a piece of bacon from Rocket's plate and studying it. It was crispy but there was still a speck or two of brown on it.

"You get a pass this time 'cause you're new, but it needed another three or four minutes."

"Woman, it's burnt to a crisp. Any more burned and it'd be ash."

I blinked at him. "What's your point?"

Effie giggled and scooped a forkful of egg through her jam and shoved it into her mouth. "I think it's delicious." For emphasis, she picked up a piece and popped it into her mouth.

"Don't go takin' his side, you little imp. We girls gotta stick together."

"What about Gina?" Effie looked up at me, her eyes wide. "Shouldn't we stick with her too?"

"I'm going to fix that as soon as we finish breakfast," I said. I avoided looking at Rocket because I knew he was probably grinning. I also knew that out of the mouth of babes…

"I like Gina. She read me my favorite story three times and never once complained."

"She did, huh?"

"Uh-huh. Are we going back to Gina's house?"

"Yeah. We are. But. You have to promise to do what I tell you to. If I tell you to go with Byte, I want you to do it. I promise it won't be long."

She nodded eagerly. "I like Byte." Then she frowned. "But Gina doesn't. Maybe I'll just stay with you. That way Byte doesn't scare Gina." She grinned and I knew I was being played. How did I know? Because it was exactly something I'd say. Besides, it was the perfect excuse I needed for me to get Gina one on one and away from the guys in the club. So, in a way, Effie had helped me play Rocket. I was good with that.

"Right. Awesome idea, kid." I held out my hand for a high five. Which Effie gave me eagerly.

I ushered Effie out the door with Rocket right behind me. "Did that just fuckin' happen?"

I looked up at him innocently. "What? Effie was looking out for Gina. It's good for kids to understand and know how to protect the feelings of others. I'm so proud of her for realizing Gina was uncomfortable around Byte and since Effie doesn't know anyone else in the compound, I know you don't want someone else looking after her. That might scare her and Effie has to be fragile after everything that's happened." I barely stopped to take a breath, wanting to cover all the bases before Rocket could come up with an alternate plan.

"I'm so fucked," he muttered before snagging my hand. "Come on, sour puss. And before you get all pissed off, you earned the nickname after this stunt." I'd have been worried if he really looked angry that I'd managed to get around him, but he didn't. If anything, his eyes twinkled with amusement. Almost like he was pleased I'd worked out a way to get what I wanted without defying him.

"Yep." I didn't look at him, letting him lead me to the big F-150 in the driveway. His bike was in the garage. Typical.

It was a short drive to the little house where Gina lived. Effie chatted the entire way, preventing Rocket from saying much about what was about to happen. Which was what I wanted so I kept a running dialogue going with the kid. She and I were going to be epic around here. I could already tell.

We pulled into Gina's driveway and I saw her peeking out the front window behind the curtain. Yeah. Nothing fishy there.

"Come on, squirt," I said. To Effie. Not Rocket. Though calling him squirt made me want to giggle. There were so many different ways that could be implied and I was cataloging every single one of them for use if he ever called me sour puss in front of anyone. I'd forgive him for doing it at the Iron Tzars' barn a year ago but my benevolence only went so far. As I hoped, Rocket gave me the side eye. Yeah. He knew me. "Game, set, and match."

"Little witch," he growled, but there was no real heat in it. If anything, I thought he might be more amused than before. Yeah. Maybe he did get me.

Effie ran ahead and knocked on the door. Gina opened it a crack and tried for a smile, but I could see she'd been crying.

"Effie, give Gina a hug and thank her for the hamburgers and reading your favorite story three times in a row," Rocket said, ruffling the girl's hair. "Then me and you'll stay out here and let Lemon and Gina have some time to gossip."

"Gina!" Effie launched herself at the other woman and hugged her as fiercely as she'd hugged me when I showed up here the first time. It was clear Gina had made a positive impression on little Effie. Which was good since I'd decided Gina was probably innocent. I knew she was complicit in some way, but I'd bet my last cunt hair she was just as much a victim as Scarlet had been. "Thank you for all the things! You're really cool!"

"Thanks, Euphemia. I'm glad I made you smile."

Effie smile broadened. "You called me Euphemia! You remembered!"

"Of course, I remembered. It was important to you." Gina glanced at me nervously before ducking her head again. Her chin quivered and a tear trickled down her cheek before she brought her wrist up and caught it. This situation was devolving rather quickly.

"Come on, Effie," Rocket said. "We'll be outside when you're ready, Lemon." Rocket spoke softly and stayed close to the door. Even still, Gina flinched when he spoke.

Effie saw Gina's distress and, bless her heart, looked like she didn't know what to do. She took Gina's hand in hers and waited until Gina met her gaze. "Don't worry. Lemon will make it all better." Fuck me. No pressure there. Especially when I'd first thought Gina had been the hold out in the club. The one who was supposed to carry out Hammer's instructions to harm Sunshine and Rainbow.

Once we were alone, I leveled a look on Gina. "Have a seat."

"Has Rocket come to… to kill me?" I could barely hear her. It was obvious she was terrified but resigned.

I took a deep breath. "That depends." I gestured

to the couch. "Let's sit and talk. You tell me what happened. I'll decide what to do next."

She started and met my gaze with a shocked one of her own. "You? Rocket's the president. He won't do what you say."

"He will totally do what I say." That came out harsher than I intended, but Goddamnit, this woman was making me have a fucking feeling! "I'm his old lady. Do you honestly think I'd be in here right now instead of him if he didn't trust my judgment?" I was surprised at how easily those words came out. And how much I believed them.

"No," she said softly. Then sighed. "It was me," she said. "I was the one Hammer had in the compound who was supposed to hurt Shine and Rain if Scarlet didn't do what he said." She started sobbing then. "It was me. It was me."

"Fuck." I wasn't sure what to do other than let her cry it out. When I reached out to hold her hand -- 'cause I'm not a complete bitch... most of the time -- she threw herself at me, wrapping her arms around my waist as she lay against me, sobbing uncontrollably.

Rocket looked through the screen-door window and raised an eyebrow at me. I shook my head, and he nodded before continuing on with whatever he and Effie were doing.

I patted Gina's head awkwardly. I didn't want to let my guard down. Not yet. Jury was still out as to how much of an act this was.

It took her a while to calm down, but she was trembling and sweating. There was no doubt she was having a visceral reaction to something. So now, I had to get to the bottom of everything.

"OK. Come on. Sit up and tell me what's going on." I put as much command in my voice as I could and not sound angry. I had to be neutral here. If she was playing me, I was not going to miss it. But if she was as much a victim as I thought she might be, I didn't want to punish her.

She blinked. "I just told you! Hammer had me here ready to hurt Shine and Rain. I know the men know. Crush and Byte. And if they know Rocket knows. So don't drag it out. Just get it over with."

"What do you think's going to happen here?"

"Probably the same thing that happened to Hammer. I know he's dead. Byte told me. He also said he knew what happened. Said he was looking into it thoroughly, but that I'd best make my peace sooner rather than later."

"Fine. Byte's digging. I was told you had a thing for Hammer. That true?"

"No. Not really." She sniffed. I handed her a tissue 'cause she was getting ready to use her arm again and that's just gross. "I mean, I did have a thing for him. Until he took me on." She looked down at her hands. "I thought he was the kind of man I wanted. Good-looking. Rough. More than a little arrogant, but I kind of liked that about him."

"What happened?"

"The first night we were together, he... hurt me. You know. During sex. I didn't like it, but he just laughed and continued."

I didn't want to know. "What'd he do?" Fuck, my mouth!

She shrugged. "Tied me up. Gagged me. Whipped me. I couldn't move the next day. Couldn't lay on my back for days afterward. He humiliated me every chance he got. In front of any of his brothers who came over. He liked oral sex when they were here. And he liked to pass me around."

"I take it that wasn't something you wanted." It wasn't a question.

"I know that's what club whores do sometimes, but I didn't come here to be a club whore. I left that life behind to be here with Hammer. Once I got here, he told me I couldn't leave because this was a secret place. That if I tried to leave, the club would kill me. After they all took a turn at me before I died." I actually saw the gooseflesh pop up on her arms, the stress of reliving the conversation making her sweat.

"I take it you'd have done what he wanted you to. Hurt the girls. Because he would have hurt you worse." I was careful how I phrased my question. Demand. Whatever. I tried to put sympathy into my voice, like I could understand that she'd made that decision. I wanted her to give me the truth because if she lied and I found out about it, I'd have to kill her. And I wasn't altogether sure I could do it now.

She started crying again but shook her head vigorously. "NO! That's the problem! There's no way I could have hurt those girls! Not even to save myself. I've been waiting over a year for Byte or Crush to bring Rocket or Claw here to… to…" She shuddered. "I don't want to die, but I couldn't hurt children to save myself. What kind of person would that make me?"

"OK. It's all right." I tried to reassure her. "I believe you. But you understand I've got to check with Crush."

"I know." She sniffed, her voice sounding small and forlorn.

"I can't promise everything will be all right, but I can promise you that no one is gonna torture you. Not if you didn't actually do anything. I've been with Sunshine and Rainbow since Scarlet and Mars came to pick them up over a year ago. Granted, I didn't spend much time with them, but they weren't mistreated. That much I know. They never mentioned your name either."

"I tried to stay as far away from them as I could. I knew I couldn't hurt them, but I wasn't sure Hammer didn't have someone else in the compound watching them."

"Why didn't you tell Rocket or Claw, or anyone?"

"Claw was gone. I didn't find out he was dead until Byte came for the girls. It was one of the few days I was watching them. I only did it when I had to because, if someone did hurt them, I didn't want anyone to think it was me. That was when Byte told me he knew Hammer had me watching the girls and that Hammer expected me to hurt them if he gave the word." She dabbed at her puffy, bloodshot eyes and wiped her red, runny nose. Her whole face was blotchy. Very unflattering. Girl wasn't a pretty crier. Which might have been one of the reasons I believed her. You could never trust a pretty crier. "I'd only been here a few weeks before Hammer left with Scarlet. The only men I'd met were the men he brought home. The ones he shared me with."

"Any of them hurt you? You know. Like Hammer did."

She shook her head. "No. I got the feeling they thought I was there willingly. Which, I kind of was. Just not to be passed around like a piece of meat." She scrubbed her arms like she was trying to get clean. Fury unfurled inside me and I actually pressed my hand over my chest to ease the ache.

"OK. Will you trust me, Gina?"

She shrugged. "Do I have a choice?"

Chapter Fourteen
Rocket

I knew the second she walked out of the house Lemon was in a snit. This wasn't going to end well for someone, and I was really, really hoping it wasn't me. She plastered on a smile and went straight to Effie.

"Hey, squirt. Gonna need you to stay with Gina for a while. That OK?"

"Sure! Maybe she'll make cheeseburgers again!" Effie jumped into Lemon's arms and hugged her tightly before going inside the house. Lemon followed her and returned a minute or so later. She headed straight for me, her shoulders back and the most determined look on her face I'd ever seen.

"Yeah. Someone's gettin' their balls busted."

"You're damned right, they are. Call fuckin' church."

I didn't answer her. We got in the truck and I took us to a barn on the southern edge of the property we occupied.

"Why do I get the fuckin' feelin' this ain't fuckin' church, Rocket?" Yeah. She was good and fucking pissed. "We got shit to get fuckin' straight. Startin' with what the fuck really happened to Gina after she got here."

"I'm gonna call church, sour puss. But first you're gonna tell me what's got you in such a foul mood."

Then she told me everything about her conversation with Gina. By the time she'd finished, I was nearly as angry as Lemon was. I couldn't show it. Not yet. I knew once I lost the tight control I had on my emotions bad things were going to happen.

"You're right." I had to give her this. Because she

was right. "We keep too damned many secrets from each other."

"Rocket, I'm an outsider. I'm eighteen years old, a fuckin' kid compared to you guys. But I'm tellin' you right now. You cannot have a club like this and not pull your shit together. This is a perfect example of why you can keep secrets from the outside world, even your old ladies, but you cannot keep secrets from each other."

"Not arguing with you, woman." I knew my response came out angry. I also knew Lemon wouldn't take it personally. In fact, I thought she'd appreciate I was upset over something that had happened and had been very preventable. I pulled out my phone and shot a text off to Crush, telling him to call church. I wanted every single motherfucking man in this club to meet at the barn in fifteen minutes. Anyone not here could expect a slow, painful death when I found them. This shit ended today. Right this Goddamned second. I told him to be prepared for him and Byte to tell everyone everything he knew about Hammer and Gina and the woman's involvement in keeping Scarlet under control by threatening her sisters. "Fuck!"

Unable to take the confines of the truck any longer, I stormed out, slamming the door shut and stalking inside the barn. There was something very similar to this very structure at Iron Tzars. It was where I'd watched and participated in completely destroying Hammer's body. While he was still alive. That incident had taken far less time than it should have. Now, I had to wonder if there were going to be more men I had to take apart in much the same way.

"Rocket." Lemon marched up to me. When I turned to tell her to go back to the truck, she snagged my beard and pulled me down for a scorching kiss.

Immediately, I bunched her hair in my fist, angling her head where I wanted it to better dominate her. Anger and aggression overrode good sense and I forgot she was relatively new to sex. Lemon didn't push me away, though. In fact, she fought me for dominance. Yeah. Not fucking happening.

I shoved her against the wall and spun her around. She still wore my property patch on her vest. It wasn't until this very moment I realized I'd expected her to renounce my claim on her, her claim on me, and demand to be taken back to Evansville. Or that she'd dispense with the pleasantries and just wreak havoc on this place. Realistically, she didn't have a chance of doing that. But I'd bet the entire Goddamned world she'd put several of us out of our fucking miseries before the others took her down.

Given everything she'd told me, I should have asked her permission. Made sure she wanted me to fuck her. But I couldn't. She'd initiated this. If she wanted to stop it, she knew how.

"Get your Goddamned pants unfastened, Lemon," I growled. "Now. Or I'm rippin' 'em off you."

It was the only permission I was capable of asking. I needed to be inside her like I needed to fucking breathe! Lemon was my only anchor in a turbulent sea. The only person in the motherfucking world capable of keeping me from destroying this whole fucking place.

She unfastened her jeans and shoved them off her hips so they were around her thighs. With her boots on there was no way to get them off any farther. And they were fucking skintight. When I'd first seen her in them, I'd fucking adored her in them. Now I wasn't sure I could stay sane if I couldn't get them down far enough to fuck her.

Then I noticed something. "You fuckin' little bitch." I whispered the words more in awe than the anger my words implied.

She looked over her shoulder and bared her teeth at me. "What? Never seen a woman go commando before?"

"You Goddamned fuckin' little bitch. You're tryin' to push me over the edge. Aren't you?" I jerked down my fly and pulled out my impossibly hard cock. With shaking hands, I gripped one of her hips and guided my dick inside her with the other. Once the tip kissed her entrance, I shoved home. Hard.

Lemon cried out, bracing her hands on the wooden wall of the barn while I gripped her hips hard enough to bruise and fucked her harder than I'd ever fucked a woman in my life. She pushed back against me just as hard, her screams echoing as we came together in all the rage and violence we felt. After the events she'd revealed, I wasn't sure I didn't deserve the same fate as Hammer. Because I'd allowed this to happen. I'd agreed to let everyone keep their secrets. I'd agreed it had been best for the greater club that we never draw attention to ourselves.

"Me," I bit out. "It all comes down to my decisions." My voice shook with the force of my thrusts. I had to be hurting her, but Lemon didn't push me away or protest. She took what I had to give and tried to give back as good as she was getting.

"Shut up!" she shouted. "Fuck me, Rocket. And when you fuck me, you're not allowed to think about anything or anyone but me. You fuckin' understand?"

"Don't fuckin' order me around, Goddamnit! I'll do what I fuckin' please! That means I'll fuck you into oblivion if that's what I fuckin' want to do." I couldn't stop the alpha male rising up inside me, taking his mate out of grief, pain, and anger. I needed to lose myself in her body, even for this little while. Even if it was the last time she let me find the solace I needed.

"Then fuckin' do it, you bastard!" she screamed at me, bracing herself as I rode her hard. Flesh slapped against flesh. Her cries pierced the air alongside my harsh grunts. Every time we came together, I got more and more aggressive.

I smacked her ass. Hard. She yelped but promptly ordered, "Do it again! Do it harder, Rocket!" So I did. Barely a stream of sunlight filtered down through a hole in the roof, but it seemed to shine right on the cheek I'd abused. My handprints stood out red and angry, but Lemon didn't seem to mind. In fact, the rougher I got, the more Lemon responded.

Finally, when I couldn't take another second, I wrapped one arm around Lemon's waist and found her clit with my fingers. The moment I touched her, her pussy gripped my cock like a vise. Her scream sounded painful, but her pussy told another story. She milked my cock until I exploded deep inside her.

I wrapped my arms around her so tightly I was afraid she might not be able to breathe, but I couldn't let up. I needed her to anchor me. To keep me from going insane.

When we finally stilled, I wasn't sure how much longer I was going to be able to stand. I braced myself against the wall with Lemon mashed between me and the hard surface. My breathing was harsh and ragged. I still felt the need to punch something, but I no longer thought I'd lose my ever-loving shit.

"You good?" Her voice was husky and rough. No wonder. I was sure they'd heard her screams all the way at the main compound.

"I think that's supposed to be my line."

"Yeah, well, maybe someone needs to take care of you from time to time. Since I'm your old lady, I guess that'll have to be me."

Just like that, the band around my chest loosened. It didn't go away, but it was enough I could think straight again. At least, I could for the moment. How long things stayed that way depended entirely on what Crush and Byte had to tell me.

I helped her pull her pants up. I was sure she'd be uncomfortable, but I could hear hogs pulling up to the barn and there was no way anyone was seeing Lemon in any state of undress if I could help it. Once she was covered, I tucked my dick back inside my pants and put myself between Lemon and where I knew the men would enter in case she needed to adjust any of her clothing.

One by one, the members of Grim Road filed into the barn. All of them looked ready to do battle, and I had to wonder if I'd be killing any of them tonight. Or if they'd try to kill me.

"What's goin' on, Prez?" Bear's gaze quartered the area, looking for threats. In all of Grim, I trusted Bear the most. He and I had served together on more than one operation. The man knew more about me than even Crush did. I probably knew more about him too. That was the moment what Lemon had been trying to do finally clicked into place inside my fucking dumbass brain.

I turned slightly to catch Lemon's gaze. "I get it now. I understand."

"Good. Now what?"

Instead of answering her, I faced the incoming crew and stood silently until the last member was in the barn. There were thirty-four men altogether. Unless someone was on a mission, everyone stayed in the compound. Some stayed to themselves, others tended to mingle in the main clubhouse. But no one ever stayed anywhere but in the compound.

When the last men entered and the door was closed, I began.

"We've got a huge fuckin' problem." That got everyone's attention. Bear crossed his arms over his chest and leveled his gaze on me, giving me his full and undivided attention. Several of the others did too, but more than a few gazes shifted anywhere but at me. "Crush. Tell me what you know about Hammer and Gina."

The man glanced at his brother and, surprisingly, it was Byte who answered. "She was a runaway. Lived on the street from the time she was fifteen until Hammer picked her up a year and a half ago. She was nineteen then. Hooking to have a roof over her head, such as it was. From what I found out, she'd been prostituting herself since she left home. It was the only way she had enough money to eat."

Lemon's hand went to the back pocket of my jeans, curling there to hang on before she asked the next question. "What about her relationship with Hammer?"

Byte shook his head slightly, obviously uncomfortable and not liking what he was about to say. "He wasn't good to her, Lemon. He smacked her around a lot. Never anything serious, but it wasn't consensual." Byte closed his eyes and opened his mouth to speak again, but nothing came out. He tried again. Still nothing.

Finally Crush, put a hand on his shoulder and continued for his brother. "When Hammer invited some of you guys over to share Gina, it wasn't something she wanted. He forced her to do what he told her to through pain and manipulation."

That got some uncomfortable murmurings. I heard the random "fuck" a couple of times.

"Are you serious?" Leather stepped forward, looking from Crush to me and back. "Are you saying we raped that girl?"

Byte dropped his head while Crush answered Leather. "Yeah, man. I'm afraid so."

"So that's why Byte warned us off." I recognized the voice as Rattler. He was a newer member but hard working and always willing to help if someone needed it. It was hard to believe the man had a violent bone in his body, but he was most definitely a seasoned warrior.

"Yes," Byte managed to get out.

Rattler stepped in the space between me and Lemon and the rest of the club, his head up. "I'll accept whatever punishment you deem fit. Give Gina all my personal effects. There's more than enough money for her to start a new life away from here if she wants." The pain on the man's face was obvious. It was hard to reconcile the gentle soul he usually presented with the deadly man I knew he had to be.

"I'm not finished," I said, raising a hand. "This isn't your fault, Rattler. Unless she specifically told you no, or gave you a reason to believe she didn't want to be in that situation. You can't read minds. Did she?"

Rattler shook his head. "No. But I should have known."

"And how could you have? Just because Hammer offered to share her?" I was angry, but not at any man who'd been led to believe Gina was good with what he did to her. "We've all had women we've shared from time to time. Some of you've had steady lays who relished being passed around. Unless some of you continued fucking that girl when she indicated she didn't want to, that's not why I called you here. Having said that, Crush, do you or Byte know of anyone who knowingly raped Gina?"

This time, Byte answered immediately. "No, Rocket. No one intentionally raped her, and after I quietly warned everyone off, no one touched her again. But by that time, Hammer had left with Scarlet, so she was safe."

"If she didn't want to be here, once she found out Hammer was dead, why didn't she just leave?" Piston's question was valid. The older man didn't speak much, but when he did everyone paid attention.

"Because Hammer told her this place was secret," Lemon answered. "He said if she tried to leave, the men in the club would kill her. You know. After they'd finished with her." The barn was completely silent as the men processed this.

"So, what you're saying..." Bear shifted his position, bringing focus back to him. It was a move he did when he thought I might make a move on someone and he wanted to give me the best chance he could. "Is that we've kept a woman prisoner for over a year?"

"That's what I'm saying."

He gave a deep sigh. "This is gonna be complicated."

"I'll take care of Gina." Lemon moved to stand more fully beside me. Like we were partners in the club instead of just in the bedroom. Which we were. It was time the rest of Grim Road recognized it too. "If that's taken care of?" She raised an eyebrow at Crush who nodded. "The real problem here is this whole situation could have been prevented." She let that statement linger, piquing the curiosity of everyone around. "If you'd just talked to each other."

"Not following." Bear narrowed his gaze at her.

"She means we keep too many secrets from each other."

"Crush knows every-fucking-thing," Falcon said from the back. "Who else needs to know?"

"Well," Lemon drawled. I winced because this was going to be epic. It was like watching a train barreling down the track, blaring its horn for the stupid motherfucker who drove his car onto the track when the light was clearly flashing yellow only to have it stall. There was going to be carnage and there was nothing you could do about it. All you could hope for was that said stupid motherfucker had enough sense to abandon his vehicle and run like hell. That... wasn't Falcon. "If Claw hadn't been so obsessed with keeping his secret, Scarlet would never have been abused the way she was. If Byte had felt comfortable bringing Hammer's secret to Rocket, Gina might have been spared pain and humiliation. How many incidents have happened in this club that might have been prevented if you knew even the most fundamental things about each other?"

"Girl, you've got no idea what you're talking about." I'd give it to Falcon. He wasn't one to quit while he was ahead. Well, he wasn't ahead. But sometimes it's best to know when you're beaten and throw in the proverbial towel.

"Oh, really?" Lemon drawled. "How about the fact that you left Rocket to his fate when he came to mine and Effie's aid?"

"Told you, girl. We don't risk the entire club for one person. I didn't want to leave Rocket, but I didn't have a choice."

"Until I took the choice away from you. We made a huge-ass mess, then you called in peeps to clean the place. Anyone figured out what happened? Come running to the compound gate accusing Grim Road of murder? Wanting to raze this place to the fucking ground?" When Falcon merely lifted his chin, Lemon continued. "You guys are a fuckin' family. Fuckin' act like it! And you." She moved to stand in front of Falcon and poked him in the chest with her finger. "If you ever leave any of your brothers shot and bleeding in a place not a hundred feet from where you're standing, I will fuckin' bury you."

"I'm makin' changes to Grim Road," I said, picking up where Lemon stopped. Mainly because I liked Falcon. I didn't want him to lose his balls. "From now on, we have each other's backs. No matter what. We always choose the missions we go on. None of us are under contract because the shit we do isn't officially sanctioned. We all know the risks. From now on, we run this club like we would a paramilitary business. All requests for our services will go through Crush. He will bring them to me and the vice president. We will decide which ones are worthy and which ones are shit. We'll also decide which shit missions are important enough for us to risk our lives to complete them. Once that decision is made, we will assign teams to do them. And we will always have each other's backs. No fuckin' matter what."

"That leaves only one question." Bear looked amused, but that couldn't be right. Bear didn't get amused as far as I knew. He was always stoic and all business.

"Yeah?"

"Who's gonna be vice president? Claw's been dead over a year and we've never discussed it.

"I wasn't ready," I admitted. "Claw was my friend. He wasn't the man I thought he was, but he'd had my back more than a few times. We've never operated like the usual MC, so the vacancy hasn't been a problem. Until now."

"So? Who'd you have in mind?"

"Actually, Bear, I thought you might be up for the job."

Bear chuckled. "No fuckin' way, Rocket. Not me." He shook his head. "How about we give you some ideas. Let the club work it out." He spread his hands to indicate everyone in the barn. "You said we should work together more, to have each other's backs. Well, I think it should start now."

I nodded. "I like this idea. Seems the perfect way to start things fresh."

"Good." Bear grinned. "Then I nominate Lemon."

* * *

Lemon

I blinked a couple times and replayed Bear's words back in my head. Then frowned and stuck a finger in my ear to dislodge wherever had stuck there because there was no fucking way I'd heard him right.

"A simple yes or no vote will do," Bear continued. Assents went around the barn, and I knew I was in trouble. "Those in favor?" A solid "Aye" went up around the barn. "Those opposed?" Dead. Fucking. Silence. Bear stepped forward and held out a vest. To me. "Seems we've got ourselves a new vice president."

I looked around with my mouth open. I was surprised I didn't catch a few flies. "What the fuck just happened?"

Rocket burst out laughing even as he wrapped me up in a bear hug. "Not sure, sour puss, but I think you just got elected vice president. Unanimously."

"What if I don't want it!" I could feel panic taking hold. "I'm not qualified --"

"I'd say you're more qualified than anyone else in this club to be at our president's side." Dom was our sergeant at arms and a good man. He grinned as he stuck out his hand to me. "Rocket is a natural leader. You're a natural at reading people. You're young, but you have an insight few people I've ever met can claim." He pointed to the vest I'd taken from Bear reflexively. "Crush and Byte have been keeping us informed of the conversations you and Rocket have had since you've been here. We all know your concerns, and we agree with you."

"So now, you agree not to keep secrets." I threw my hands up in the air. "Someone's gettin' an ass beatin'."

Rocket, the prick, snorted a laugh. "You can't have it both ways, honey."

"Sour puss is more accurate," Falcon grumbled. "But I agree with Bear."

I turned to peg Rocket with a look I hoped would burn a hole through his insides and melt his internal organs. "When we get home, I'm gonna cut off your balls."

"This isn't my doing," he said, with a grin. "Though I can't say I'm opposed. I think we'll be a good fit and work well together."

"I'm not talkin' about that. I've decided I'll make a great vice president. Might make an even better president. You know. After I garrote you with your own intestines." More than one brother laughed. I wasn't sure if it was at Rocket's expense or mine. It better be Rocket's. "I'm talking about that nickname. I warned you."

He pulled me in for a kiss. I tried to push him

away, but he was just too strong. So I let him kiss me. Might have kissed him back, but probably not.

When he lifted his head, I was breathing heavily, but tried to keep a scowl firmly in place. "I'm sorry, Lemon. It slipped out before I could stop myself."

"Ain't promisin' any of us'll use it," Bear said with a grin. "But I can promise you we'll only use it with affection. We're serious about this." His expression sobered. "We need you, Lemon. We've lived our lives in the shadows for far too long. You bring sunshine and spice to Grim Road. You'll keep us focused on what's important. And that ain't our secrets. It's each other. This club. Grim Road. We're a family. It's time we started acting like it."

One by one, each member of Grim Road shook my hand before leaving the barn. When it was just me and Rocket, I looked at the vest Bear had given me. On the back it had Rocket's property patch. Just like the one I currently had on. But the front had my name on one side, vice president on the other.

"This is serious. No one is making fun of me."

"Honey, they wouldn't dare. Not only do they know I'd kill them, they're more afraid of what you'd do if they did."

"Well," I said, shrugging out of the vest I had on and putting on the new one. "I guess I could give it a try. If it doesn't suit me, I can always try being president."

"Yeah, baby. Not happenin'."

I grinned up at him. "Challenge issued. Challenge fucking accepted."

Lemon (Grim Road MC 2)
A Bones MC Romance
Marteeka Karland

Lemon: I'm settling in at Grim Road in my role as vice president. The men test me, but it's all in good fun. I think I enjoy it as much as they do. Then, out of nowhere, things go horribly sideways. I realize how much weaker I am physically than everyone else in the club. That weakness can be a horrible liability. Yeah. Things are going great. Until they aren't. I may have bitten off more than I can chew…

Rocket: My little sourpuss is a force to be reckoned with. She takes everything dished out to her and gives it back in spades. She's my VP, but she's also my old lady. Sometimes, I need to take care of her. More importantly, she has to let me. That fact is never more apparent than when a small team of roughnecks think she's a woman from another club. They soon find out the error of their ways, but at what cost to Lemon? It's time for the president of Grim Road MC to take charge. And there's gonna be hell to pay.

Chapter One
Lemon

I made it a whole month at Grim Road MC before Falcon threatened to cut off my dick and feed it to me. I think he forgot I was a girl or something because I'm as docile as they come. Yep. Passive even!

OK. I'm lying. I liked busting Falcon's balls just 'cause I could. The guys had made me vice president of Grim Road right after Rocket brought me to the compound. Since then, we've all been working on our trust issues. And by "we," I mean the men of Grim. I get that they all have secrets. I get that everyone has things they don't want anyone else to know. Even then, you tell your family. Because it's your family who would always have your back. Grim Road is family. Rocket's family. My family.

Except for Falcon. But he was a work in progress.

"I swear to God, Rocket. If you don't do something about that little hellion, I may shoot her."

"Now, Falcon. You know it's not nice to threaten to shoot your vice president." I loved taunting him.

"Next time Rocket calls church, I'm askin' for your fuckin' patch."

I sighed, trying to fight back a smile before I ruined my indifference. "Are you still sore about your bike? 'Cause it was totally for a good cause. Saved Rocket's life."

"You know what the fuck this is about, woman!" Falcon's hair was wild and sticking out all over the damned place. Looked like he'd been trying to pull his hair out by the roots. Over and over. And over.

"I even had the thing fixed for you. Only took a couple weeks in the body shop, and they assured me it would be good as new. Not a scratch to be seen."

"You had them paint it pink!" He had his arms out like he was going to lunge and choke me to death the second he got the chance, but I wasn't worried. First, Falcon was all bark and no bite. At least he was with me. Remember the family part? Second, he knew Rocket would feed him to the sharks in very small pieces if he even looked at me cross-eyed. "Not only did you crash my fuckin' bike through a door *intentionally*, you disrespected it even more by painting it *pink*!" He practically roared the last word. And I was pretty sure there was spit flying from his lips. Which was just gross. Fucker.

"Tell you what. I'll apologize to your bike. I'll even volunteer to ride beside you when you take her for a test drive."

"No way in fuck I'm ridin' that abomination in public. I'm surprised Knox let the fuckin' thing in the compound at all."

Knox chose that moment to enter the common room. "Knox didn't know what was gonna roll out of that Goddamned trailer or he *wouldn't* have let it in," he commented.

I grinned, looking over my shoulder at Knox and popped my gum like a bimbo. "Hey, Knox. Havin' a good afternoon?"

"Was until that fuckin' bike showed up."

"Awesome! Now. Forget all that. It's not important."

"*Not important*? How the fuck is you having my bike painted fuckin' *pink* not fuckin' important?" Yeah. Falcon was in a bit of a snit. But fuck him. If he wanted to be the best patched member of Grim Road -- after me, of course -- he needed to learn that there was a method to my madness. And there was one very huge wrong in this place that needed to be righted. I figured one month was long enough for everyone involved to start their penance.

"Because it was sacrificed for the greater good. This is one of those times, Falcon."

"What the everlovin' Christ are you talking about, Lemon?" Falcon sounded equal parts pissed and resigned.

"I'm talking about Gina."

That got everyone's attention. And quit the bitching.

"She good?" Falcon was immediately sober, all his anger at me evaporating in the space of a word.

"She's learning to be. In case you hadn't noticed, she's been leaving her house more and more. Had supper in the common room last night."

"Yeah. I noticed." Falcon glanced at Leather, who ducked his head, shaking it slightly as if he wanted to deny what had happened. "A few of us made sure she had what she needed." Falcon gave a sigh. "I apologized, too. Took several tries before she finally opened her door. Not that I blame her. She say why she ain't left? Surely she knows she can. Right?"

"She knows." Rocket leaned back on the couch where we sat. He draped an arm over my shoulder, and I snuggled against him shamelessly. Not only did it feel good to have his arm around me, but it reinforced my claim to any club girls in the building. "This is her home now. I promised to keep her safe, even from men inside my own club."

"So she trusts you," Falcon nodded. "I guess that's something."

I snorted. "Nah. She don't trust Rocket." My man gave me the side eye, but flashed a cocky grin too. Like he was proud of me. But, honestly, what man with me wouldn't be proud, right? "She trusts *me*."

When Falcon looked to Rocket to confirm, Rocket just smirked. "She ain't lyin', my friend. Gina believes in Lemon. Believes Lemon can keep her safe. Ain't gonna lie and say I'm not disappointed a woman under the club's protection doesn't fully trust me, but I suppose that's just one of many reasons I have Lemon in my life."

"Damned straight, baby." I leaned in and brushed a kiss over Rocket's lower lip. "See me, love me, motherfuckers." That got a laugh from everyone, including Falcon.

"Seems like you've got that situation under control."

"I totally do, Falcon. Which is why I had your Harley painted pink."

"Not… seeing how the two go together." Poor Falcon. He was really having a hard time. He seemed to have even forgotten he was supposed to be pissed about the paint job on his bike.

This was why I liked keeping him off-balance. It was so much fucking fun to watch. I knew I shouldn't enjoy myself at Falcon's expense. This was actually serious stuff. But, honestly, I couldn't help myself. "Because, Gina happens to be fond of the color pink. In fact, she told me that, if she knew how to ride a motorcycle, she'd save everything she could to buy her a pink bike. Now, me personally?" I shook my head. "Don't see the appeal. However, if Gina likes it, I think we all owe her way the fuck more than one stupid pink motorcycle." I pointed at Falcon. "You ever want to graduate to officer's training camp?"

"Officer… what?" Falcon jerked his head back like I'd slapped him. Which, I mean, I won't lie and say I didn't want to. Not because he deserved it, but because *he* thought he deserved it. And I just plain thought beating up on Falcon was fucking fun.

But, not in this instance. Much. "Well, yeah. You don't think every officer in this club will be around forever, do you? Or even want to stay an officer? There will be a time when your services may be needed in that capacity, though why, I'm not sure. You're just as big a dumb fuck today as you were the day I met you." I looked him up and down like I was judging him and finding him lacking. "Gonna take longer than I first thought with this one," I muttered.

Falcon took a threatening step toward me, but Rocket growled at him. The younger man glanced from me to Rocket before slinking back that fucking threatening step. "One of these days, Lemon…"

I smirked. "Yep. One of these days I'll hand you your balls, and you'll probably just stand there wondering what the fuck just happened. You know. Like you're doing right now."

"Christ."

"Pretty sure Christ had little to do with it," Leather muttered. "Satan? Yeah. Possibly."

I waved them both away. "Satan has a restraining order out on me. He had nothing to do with it either."

Knox barked out a laugh before moving from the doorway. "Give it up, guys. You're never gonna get one over on that woman."

"Whose bright idea was it to make her vice president anyway?" Falcon was back to looking all surly again.

"That'd be me." Bear, the second biggest man I'd ever seen in my life moved into the room, crossing from the back to the front in his even, confident gate. He didn't pause but passed by Falcon and smacked him on the back of the head before heading out the front door to the parking lot.

"Ow, Bear! What the fuck?" Falcon looked ready to do murder, but I wanted to laugh. God, I loved it here! There was so much glorious mayhem! And, being vice president, I got to cause as much as I wanted and no one said anything. Occasionally, Rocket would pull me back, but most of the time, he let nature take its course.

"Best get on your bike and go find Gina. Give her a few rides, make her comfortable with everyone here, and maybe Lemon will let you paint your bike black again," advised Bear.

"Finally!" I threw up my hands in exasperation. "Someone who understands." I looked up at Rocket. "You should make *him* your vice president. Oh, wait…"

Falcon mumbled, but Leather actually nodded his head, his face relaxing a little, and I knew he got it. "We should all take a turn, Falcon. I know it's your bike and all, but if she likes pink Harleys, then I think we should all take her ridin'. Show her we'll do anything to earn her trust."

I tilted my head at Leather. "You just went up several notches in my esteem. Maybe we can put you in charge of sensitivity training."

"Lemon," Rocket sighed. "They're doing what you wanted. Let them work it out."

"They don't seem to be able to, though Leather got the right idea. Kudos to you!" I grinned at Leather. "See if you can get the other dumbasses who don't want to admit they did anything wrong to fall in line. You do, I'll give you a cookie."

Surprisingly, Leather chuckled. "Yes, madam vice president." He sketched me a two-finger salute and sauntered outside. Falcon gave a dramatic sigh and followed.

Rocket leaned down to murmur next to my ear. "He's not a bad guy, you know."

"Yep. I know. I just like fuckin' with him. Besides, Gina needs this. And I think the guys do too."

"They do. I'm glad you recognize that. Of course, I'm pretty sure none of them would have voted you in as VP if they hadn't known you'd have good instincts with us."

"How'm I doin'?" I gave him a cheeky grin. But... yeah. I was ashamed to admit how much his answer meant to me. When Bear first nominated me for the position I thought he'd lost his mind. Then I thought they were all just fucking with me. It might seem like I was all bluster and it was all a big game to me, but I wanted to succeed at my role here. I wanted to help these guys learn to trust each other with things they'd spent their whole adult lives holding close to the vest, so to speak, and be the asset to Rocket he needed in a mate. I honestly didn't care if I was VP or not. I *did* care that what happened with Scarlet and Gina never happened to anyone in Grim Road ever again.

Honestly, I'd been the one to tell the guys what had really happened. I'd seen their expressions and watched as every single one of them tried to process it in the days following. I included the guys in that tragedy. They didn't need to have that situation happen to them again either. I wasn't sure any of them had even looked at a club whore since then and, while I tried to stay out of the girls' business, it wasn't healthy for the women either.

Rocket smiled down at me with affection and pride. "Brilliantly, baby. Absolutely fuckin' brilliantly." He leaned down and took my lips in a searing kiss. I fucking loved the way he kissed and touched me. And the way he fucked me. He could be sweet and tender, but he could also be rough. Brutal even. Always, I loved every blistering second of it.

"Get a room, you two." Ringo, the club's enforcer, scrubbed a hand over his face as he plopped down in a chair across from us. "You're always goin' at it. It's disgustingly mushy."

"You're just jealous you don't have an awesome woman like me." I grinned brightly at him before crawling onto Rocket's lap and straddling his hips, my back to Ringo.

"Honey, I like you," Ringo said with a chuckle, "No disrespect to men or events of the past, but if I had a woman like you, I'd probably just put a bullet in my Goddamned head and put myself out of my misery."

"That was cold, man," Spike muttered as he entered the room. He'd been in his share of trouble lately, but he'd come around. Mostly.

I looked over my shoulder at Ringo, raising an eyebrow. The other man raised his hands in surrender. "I said I meant no disrespect."

"Yet you still managed to." I'd learned through the grapevine that Ringo and Claw had been tight. Claw, Scarlet's father, had killed himself after learning how badly he'd misjudged Hammer. Scarlet had paid the price for Claw's inattention and it was more than the former VP could take. He had, indeed, put a bullet in his own head.

"That'll do," Rocket said, taking over the situation. "It's done. Have a care next time, Ringo. We ain't pussies, but there are some things you just don't say. Claw hadn't taken care of what should have been precious to him, but he was still Grim."

"I'm just saying what every other man in this

club thinks. Lemon may be VP, but she's a fuckin' handful."

"That I am. And I own the shit. You're a bastard. You need to own *your* shit." I made my voice as hard as Rocket could at times. "The only reason I know the truth about Claw was because I was there the night he killed himself. I also know what he put Scarlet through. Scarlet, however, is my best friend. She has regrets about that night that I try to convince her she shouldn't, but the fact remains Claw was her father. Until Hammer took over her life, Claw treated Scarlet decently. I have no idea if Claw truly loved Scarlet or not, but I know she loved him. So shut your fuckin' mouth." I didn't list a consequence because the thought of my displeasure should be enough for any motherfucker. I could -- and would -- make his life a living fucking nightmare if necessary.

"Bitch," Ringo muttered as he stood to leave. The second he did, Rocket shoved me off his lap -- carefully -- and stood to stalk toward the other man. Two strides later, Ringo was on the floor while Rocket pounded the fucking shit outta him.

I knew I should intervene. I *knew* I should. It wasn't that he'd called me a bitch -- sticks and stones may break my bones and all -- but the fact was he couldn't seem to keep his fucking mouth shut. Unlike Falcon, he wasn't trying to one-up me. He was trying to justify his stupidity. He deserved what Rocket was giving him for what he'd said in reference to Claw's suicide. He deserved more for not backing off.

Scarlet lived at the Iron Tzars compound along with Apple, my twin, but we all FaceTimed when we could. Her being in Indiana and me being in Florida made for some serious long-distance issues. I missed Scarlet and Apple more than I ever thought I could miss someone. But if Scarlet'd been here and Ringo had said something like he had and hurt her feelings? Yeah. I'd have to kill the bastard, and I didn't much want to do that. It wasn't that I was squeamish. I'd watched them torture Hammer, and that had been the most brutal thing I'd ever imagined. It was because the men and women of Grim Road MC were family. Ringo was that asshat older brother you wanted to pound into the ground, but who no one else better touch. Having to kill your own family was never a fun thing. No matter how much they fucking deserved it.

Rocket pounded the other man. With each hit, Ringo grunted. I think Ringo tried to either fight back or fend off Rocket a couple of times, but the president of Grim Road was merciless. Rocket didn't give him the chance to fight back. He continued to beat Ringo until the other man quit fighting back altogether. The sound of Rocket's fist meeting Ringo's face was like a wet, sickening combination of a smack and a thud. When Rocket finally stepped away, Ringo was unconscious and there was blood everywhere, including splattered all over my man's arms and T-shirt. Maybe it made me a little deranged, but the violence Rocket dished out on my behalf turned me the fuck on.

"Take that little puke somewhere he can recover. Have Bullet check on him. No pain killers, even if Bullet thinks it's safe for him to have them. He gets to suffer for callin' my woman a bitch."

Mace, who'd been sitting at the bar, scrubbed a hand over the back of his neck. "Rocket, she kind of *is* a bitch. It's her gimmick. And yeah, like she said, she owns the shit." When Rocket's head snapped around to the other man, Mace hastily added. "I'm just sayin' it's part of her charm and the reason we all felt like she was the right person for the VP position."

"It's fine, Rocket. Mace is right, and you know it same as I do. I've never claimed to be anything but." I grinned at my man. Rocket was as protective as they came, and it was sweet as fuck. Though I'd never tell him that. He'd take it as an insult. Though, saying he was sweet might get me fucked hard enough that I would never think he was sweet again…

"Not the point. You're my woman before you're vice president of this club. Anyone disrespects you does so at their own peril. And that's not counting what I know you'll do to them later."

"Exactly!" I grinned. "Don't worry. Ringo'll get his."

"He already did," Rocket said, reaching for me. He wrapped his big arms around me and lifted. I'd have to wrap my legs around his waist, or he was going to carry me with my feet dangling in the air. So I twined my arms and legs around him while he carried me from the room. I had a feeling I was about to get laid. And I wasn't at all broken up about it.

Chapter Two
Rocket

Did I *need* to beat the fuck outta Ringo? Probably not. Lemon could take care of herself in any verbal confrontation. If someone truly did hurt her feelings or physically harm her, I'd kill them. But Ringo was a dick and I needed to hand him his ass occasionally just to assert my dominance. Since Lemon was smaller and not as skilled a fighter, I stepped in. Didn't mean she wasn't every bit as dominant as any of the guys here, just meant she was physically weaker. Of course, she was wily and sneaky, which made up for her lack of physical strength. I had no doubt, at some point in the next few weeks, just as the bigger man had forgotten the whole confrontation, he'd find Nair in his shampoo or some kind of funky hair dye in his beard oil or whatever. A shrinking violet Lemon was not.

I hauled her ass up to our bedroom with every intention of fucking her the rest of the night. Given the way she was now sucking on my neck, I was pretty sure she knew it too.

"You better hurry if you don't want me to start shedding clothes," she whispered, a siren in my ear. "Watchin' you go all postal on my behalf made me horny as fuck."

"Woman…" I tried to get my words to come out as a threat, one that said she'd better *not* start shedding clothes before we were in private, but I was afraid it came out a lusty growl instead.

She rubbed herself over my cock where she'd wrapped her legs around me, practically fucking me. When I finally stumbled into our room, she whipped off her shirt and started working on mine.

I whirled her around, slamming her against the

wall and fusing my mouth to hers. She welcomed me with a wicked flick of her tongue. I was absolutely her first lover, but the woman had fast become unlike any woman I'd ever had. She embraced fucking with the passion and curiosity of someone newly introduced to sex, but who took to it better than any seasoned club whore I'd ever fucked. She was abandoned in taking her pleasure and wasn't ashamed to tell me what she needed or shy about letting me know what she wanted. She was dominant but craved being dominated. I was more than happy to accommodate her.

She had a firm grip with her legs around my waist, still grinding her pussy over my cock with every heartbeat. My hand shot to her throat, pinning her head against the wall. Lemon grinned at me with a maniacal gleam in her eyes.

"What's a girl gotta do to get fucked around here, hm?"

"Beautiful little bitch."

She gave me a cocky grin. "So I've been told. Fuck me or piss off, Rocket." Her demand was sin and seduction. The dominant in me wanted to deny her just so she didn't get her way. The other part of me wanted desperately to give her what she wanted just to feel that tight pussy squeeze the life out of my cock as she came.

"I give the orders, Lemon," I snapped, my face so close to hers I could smell her sweet breath. "Not you. I'm the president. You follow me."

"In bed it's survival of the fittest." Oh, the little bitch was going to challenge me. My already hard cock got impossibly harder. It took every ounce of self-control I had not to come in my pants. By God, when I came, I was going to fill her cunt with my cum, not my pants.

I tightened my grip on her throat, stopping just shy of cutting off her air, and bared my teeth at her. "I'm way the fuck stronger than you, woman. I will take what I want. When I want."

"Then do it!" Eyes wide and more than a little wild-looking, she hissed her words at me. "Fucking do it!"

I shoved away from her only to grip her hips and spin her around. She gave a startled cry but didn't fight me when I shoved her jeans down as far as I could. Her motorcycle boots made it difficult to do more, but all I needed was access to her pussy.

Looping one arm around her neck, I freed my cock before swiping my fingers through her folds. Just as I suspected, she was drenched. She gave a sharp exclamation, and her sex quivered, already on the edge of orgasm.

"Don't you fuckin' come," I snapped. "You don't get to fuckin' come 'til I say so, you hear me?"

"Rocket!" She gasped even as she pushed her hips back, begging me to fuck her.

"I said no!" I tightened my grip on my arm around her throat. Her hands stayed firmly on the wall as she lifted her head, giving me better access to her. A female submitting to her mate. "You will hold on to your pleasure. You'll let me fuck you until I've had my fill. And you will not fuckin' come until I give you permission." I gave her a little shake even as I shoved my cock as far inside her as I could.

Lemon screamed and sweat erupted over her skin. "Fuck!"

"Fuckin' right, I'm gonna fuck you." My voice was harsh, and I began a hard, driving rhythm. Our flesh slapped together loudly in the room. I was sure everyone in the immediate vicinity could hear both of our shouts. I gripped her hip with one hand while my arm was still curled around her neck, holding her passive for my use of her body.

I thrust harder into her, my balls slapping against her flesh. The sound of our bodies colliding filled the room, mingling with Lemon's cries and my grunts and growls.

Sweat trickled down her face as I continued to fuck her relentlessly, her moans growing louder with each thrust. I couldn't help but feel an overwhelming sense of power, my dominance over this woman now rivaled only by the raw pleasure she was providing me.

Every single time we fucked this hard, every time she made me fight her for dominance, I knew I'd made the right choice in a woman. She was perfect for me. We fed off each other in more ways than just sex. Sometimes, I felt like she was the other half of my soul. Lemon might be several years younger than me, but she'd lived a life where she did her best to take care of everyone around her. First and foremost, this woman was a protector. Didn't mean she didn't need protecting from time to time. Luckily, I was up for the job.

"Is this what you want?" I bit out beside her ear, never missing a beat. "You need a good fuckin', woman?"

She didn't answer but I doubt she could with my arm around her neck. Her hands were still flat on the wall which meant she was good with what I was doing to her. Had she been uncomfortable or felt threatened, Lemon wouldn't hesitate to fight me in earnest. In that conflict, I wasn't entirely sure who'd win. Though I was the seasoned warrior, there was every possibility

Lemon would still kick my ass. Mainly because I knew I could never hurt her intentionally while she didn't have the same qualms about me if she thought I deserved it.

She grunted, never taking her hands from the wall while I railed her from behind. When I let go of her neck, she actually groaned, leaving her neck exposed to me.

I grabbed her arms and pinned them to her body as I shoved her against the wall and pounded into her. She couldn't move, my hold on her absolute. All Lemon could do was what I told her to. And I'd given her an order not to come. I knew she needed to. I could feel her pussy pulsing around my dick like mad.

"You're gonna come in a moment, Lemon. Come around my cock and milk my cum. I'm gonna put it inside you, and you're gonna fuckin' take it!" I knew I sounded like a cliche and more than a little deranged, but I also knew my woman loved me this way.

"Yes!" She screamed her response. "Fuckin' come inside me! I want it all!"

"Now, Lemon! Right… fuckin'… now!"

With a brutal yell, I emptied my balls inside her. Lemon screamed and screamed, her legs giving out as she came with an intensity I'd never seen from her before. She was a lusty one, my woman, but this was a new high. One I intended to repeat as often as I could.

We stood there for long moments. It was hard to catch my breath and I struggled to stand, but I did both. For Lemon. She'd gone limp in my arms, and I marveled at how completely she'd surrendered to me. Continued to surrender to me.

"Rocket…" Her eyes were closed, but there was a very satisfied smile on her face. I knew I'd pleased her, and I was almost embarrassed to admit how much pleasure and pride I got from that knowledge.

"Yeah, baby." I kissed the side of her neck. "You good?"

"Better than good." Her voice sounded dreamy. Like she was on the verge of drifting off. She was like a little kitten, limp in my arms. Completely trusting I'd support her.

"I know you probably want to go check on Gina, but I think you should give the guys at least one afternoon to fumble their way through this. She has your number. Right?"

"Yeah. She'll use it if she feels threatened. Might anyway just to get my opinion. She does, I'll tell her it was my idea, but the choice is hers."

"That's my woman." I kissed her neck again, licking the sweat coating her skin just because I could.

"Let's clean up, then we can rest for a while. It's a couple hours 'til dinner. We can doze. When we wake up, I'll fuck you again."

She giggled. My sweet Lemon actually giggled. And yeah, I realized the oxymoron applied on more than one level. "Only if you promise. That was fuckin' amazing."

"Insatiable little wench."

"Well, that's what you get when you have a hot, young piece of pussy to satisfy. Spoiler alert! It's hard to keep me satisfied. I mean, you *are* so much older than me -- eek!"

I dug my fingers into her side, tickling until she flailed in my arms. "You sayin' I'm an old man?"

"Well, compared to me? Yeah."

When I continued to tickle her, she let loose with peals of laughter, squirming in my arms with her feet dangling in the air. I needed to get her boots and pants off so I could clean her. Then maybe spread her out on

my bed and eat her until she was screaming again.
> Yeah. I think I could do that.
> I loved my life…

Chapter Three
Lemon

"You settling in better?"

Gina smiled and nodded her head slightly. "Yeah. The guys have been really great. They check on me every day and never..." She trailed off, her smile fading. Her eyes glistened with unshed tears but she sniffed a couple times, cleared her throat, then looked up at me again, smiling. "They're all really nice to me. I'm sure they'd scowl if they heard me say so, but it's the truth." Gina reached out and squeezed my hand briefly before letting go and folding her hands onto her lap. "I know it's all your doing. I appreciate it."

"Pffft. They're all Alpha males. I seriously doubt they do anything they don't want to."

For the first time since I'd found out how hurt and terrified Gina had been of the men in the club, even as she couldn't leave because she had no place else to go, the other woman gave me a wry grin, looking more like the woman I thought she was. "Really? You telling me they'll *willingly* take me on rides through town on a pink Harley because they want to?"

I grinned. "OK. You got me there." We shared an amused moment before I continued. "Honestly, I think they all enjoy it." I waved my hand dismissively. "Not the pink Harley thing. Spending time with you. In a platonic way. I doubt any one of them have thought of a woman as other than a sexual object since they were twelve. They like you."

"I know they're trying to make things up to me. While I appreciate it, it's not necessary. I know they were unaware of... you know. The situation."

"That doesn't lessen the trauma to you, or the

guilt to them." I reached over and covered both her hands with one of mine and squeezed. "You may not realize it, but even though they're all morally gray, they're not bad men. They have their lines they won't cross. All of them consider what they did to you as not only crossing the line, but obliterating it. If they'd known you were fucking them against your will, they'd never have allowed anyone to touch you. And that bastard, Hammer, would have been dead long before he finally was."

"How'd he die?" Gina winced as she asked her question. Then she shook her head before swallowing and looking up at me, her expression equal parts relief and pain.

How the fuck to answer *that* question? How to tell her the man she'd once thought she loved had been systematically and surgically taken apart piece by piece? While he was conscious. And made to watch through an overhead mirror. I still had nightmares about it and I hadn't been close to him.

"Gina, do you really want to know the answer to that? I'll tell you if you insist, but I really think you might want to just accept he's dead and leave it at that."

She stared at me for long moments before nodding her head slowly. "Yeah. I can see in your eyes that maybe I don't want to know."

"Just know it was sufficiently brutal and that, while he didn't suffer everything you did, he suffered. Very fuckin' much."

Two tears overflowed her eyes and spilled down her cheeks before Gina swiped them away with an angry swat of her hand. "You know, he told me he loved me. That he wanted me to live with him here so he could take care of me. He said everyone who lived in Grim Road had to earn their keep and he'd find something for me to do that wasn't too strenuous. I was in a car accident when I was younger and my back sometimes spasms. He told me he'd promised my work wouldn't be that strenuous and he didn't lie. All I had to do was lay on the bed and spread my legs. The men would do everything else." She sniffed as another tear spilled down her cheek. "He actually made it sound like he'd done exactly what he promised me."

"Hammer was a first rate bastard, Gina. He wasn't worthy of you or this club. The men here aren't like Hammer."

"I know," she said softly, but I could tell she wasn't really convinced.

Then a thought occurred to me. "Gina? Did any of the guys, you know, hurt you? During sex?" I was trying to tiptoe my way through a fucking mine field and thought I wasn't doing such a bang-up job.

"There were a couple who were rough, but not overly so. They've both talked to me. Which surprised the shit outta me." She gave a small laugh, trying to play off the situation as a big misunderstanding when she was still obviously traumatized. "None of them seem like the type to explain themselves."

"They're not what I'd call exactly sensitive to a woman's feelings. But they're all very proud. Knowing that they'd same as raped a woman will never sit well with any of them. If they got rough during sex? Yeah. It would haunt them. Assuming they're all like Rocket, they like rough, aggressive sex. But forcing it on a woman? Forcing *any* kind of sex on a woman would be unforgivable to them. So yeah. If you ask them, they'll tell you taking you for rides on a pink Harley doesn't even begin to scratch the surface of what they owe you. And, by the way, the Harley sacrificed to the cause was

Falcon's."

She gasped, her eyes going wide. "He… painted *his own bike*… pink?"

"Yep." I omitted the part where *I'd* actually been the one to sacrifice his bike, but I was pretty sure Falcon would thank me for this later. The girl was interested in him, or I'd suck my own dick. "Ask him if he did. I guarantee you he'll confirm what I just told you." Falcon might be a smartass, but he wasn't a *dumb*ass. If he wanted to try to make Gina his, assuming she ever got comfortable with the idea, he'd take credit for that shit in the blink of an eye. Especially if she told him I'd said painting the bike pink was his idea.

"I think that's the sweetest thing anyone's ever done for me."

Fuck…

The tears really did start flowing then. Gina was still pretty Goddamned fragile, and I completely got it. I hadn't meant to cause her more distress, but I think maybe she needed to hear that she meant something to someone. What better way to show he cared than painting his bike pink just to make her smile? Yeah. Falcon owed me. Big fucking time.

It took everything in my power not to pat her shoulder and say, "There, there, dear," and hope she quit crying. I would not be the old granny woman taking care of everyone. I might at some point be able to pass for the motherly type, but I doubted it. There was no Goddamned way in the whole fucking universe I would *ever* be the grandmotherly type.

Thankfully, Gina finally sat up and wiped her nose with a tissue from the box on the coffee table. "I'm sorry." She sniffed and dabbed at her eyes. She wasn't a pretty crier, but she tried to keep the snot to a minimum. "I'm still a bit of a hot mess."

"Nothing to be sorry about. If you feel the need, you can make it up to me by making every single man in this compound who ever touched you take you on a ride on that bike. It will be the highlight of my day."

She gave a watery laugh. "Yeah. I think I can do that."

"You believe me when I tell you they won't hurt you?"

"Yes." She nodded and dabbed at her nose again. "I do. I had the feeling there was something not right, and none of them ever hurt me or got as rough as I'd heard some of the girls here mention."

"What do you mean?" I tilted my head, wanting to make sure I understood anything she was about to say.

She shrugged. "A couple of the guys -- Falcon being one of them -- always asked me if I was good. Like *before* they had sex with me. I knew better than to answer in any way other than yes because saying no meant someone confronting Hammer. If he got the best of them, then Hammer would've hurt me worse. So, it's not the guys' fault."

I sighed. I had to be careful here. What happened to Gina had been a tragedy. No woman should have to surrender her body to anyone if she didn't want to. I got how the guys missed that she wasn't willing, especially if they'd asked her and she'd said she was good.

"That whole situation was fucked up, Gina. I'm not saying it wasn't their fault because you don't seem to think it was. You're scared and I get why. But I'm not sure I'm willing to say it was entirely their fault either. Hammer did a number on everyone. Because of him, the guys are finding it hard to trust each other without there being some standoffishness." I omitted the part about how they'd never been a really open bunch, holding everything close instead of trusting their brothers to have their backs.

"I never thought about it that way," she said. "I guess Hammer took us all for a ride."

"I can't tell you to give them a chance to make it up to you. If you don't feel safe, you don't feel safe. This is your home. You don't have to be social with anyone you don't want to. But I can promise you that none of them would ever hurt you intentionally. I'm not asking you to take my word for it, though. You test them out any way you like. Or not at all. I'll do anything I can to make you more comfortable, Gina."

"No. I believe you. Like I said, I knew they weren't aware. I didn't trust them not to rat me out or, worse, laugh or tell me it didn't matter. I think that would have broken me."

"If you want to get out of here, I can talk to Brick at Iron Tzars for you. It's a long way from home, but the Iron Tzars are a good club."

"No. I'm really OK here. More than anything, I think I'm embarrassed. Over all of it."

She paused for a moment, looking down at her hands before finally meeting my gaze again. "I just... I don't know. It's like I've been living in this constant state of fear and it's hard to shake it off."

I nodded, understanding her struggle. "It's hard. I know. Just remember I've got your back. You need something, you call me. Anytime. Day or night." I smiled before standing. "Besides. Us girls gotta stick together. There's entirely too much testosterone in this fuckin' place."

That got a genuine laugh from Gina, and I almost sighed in relief. I wasn't a typical girl with my emotions. Being careful didn't come easy to me. If I had a problem, I faced it head on. My sisters, Apple and Danica, were kind of the same way, just more subtle about it. I was more like a steamroller. *So* not what Gina needed.

"Good." I grinned at her. "You have my number. Use it."

"Thanks, Lemon." Gina stood, leaned over and hugged me tightly before letting go and wiping her nose again. "I'm not sure I'd have made it through this without your help."

I waved her off. "It's the least I can do after everything you endured at the hands of the club. Keep your chin up. And remember, no one here is gonna hurt you. They do and they answer to me, and by extension, Rocket. And let me tell you, that man wouldn't hesitate to kill a motherfucker if he ever hurt you."

That seemed to be what she needed to hear. Gina's shoulders relaxed and she smiled. "I appreciate you taking my side. I think the guys are more than half afraid of you."

"Nah. They're afraid of Rocket if they retaliate when I attack. Puts me in a really good position overall. I know how to take advantage of that shit to get what I want."

"What *do* you want here, Lemon?" She cocked her head, genuinely curious.

"I want this place to be a fuckin' family instead of a bunch of people coexisting in this compound. Right now it's like an apartment building of introverts. I want them to support each other in everything they do. It'll make the club stronger for it."

"Good luck. I hope you succeed. Outside of Hammer, I really don't think the guys here are bad. I just have no idea what to do with any of them now. I don't know how to not… remember."

Crap. That fuckin' sucked. "Yeah. I get it." I cleared my throat. "You're a strong woman, Gina. Hold your head up."

She smiled again, but it looked a little sad. "I will."

Fuck my life. Normally I'd say she wasn't my problem, but she was most definitely my problem. As vice president of this club, and a woman, I had to look out for the women here. Me. Not Rocket or any of the other men. Me. More because I was a woman in a man's domain than because of my position in the club.

As I left Gina with a wave and climbed on my own bike, I had to wonder if I'd bitten off more than I could chew. A nurturer I was not. I knew I'd learn to become one if I had to, though. Because of Scarlet and all she'd gone through. She was my best friend and she'd suffered horribly. Same as this girl. I'd figure it out for Scarlet and Gina. And just maybe along the way, I'd truly believe I was worthy to be VP to Grim Road.

Chapter Four
Lemon

It was truly gratifying watching man after man take a turn on that fucking pink Harley. Their disgruntled but resigned expressions did my heart good. I'd caught them more than once standing around it with a can or three of spray paint, each daring the other to start on it. Then they'd see me leaning against the door to the garage and scatter. Just like naughty schoolboys caught smoking in the boys' room. (Love the song, by the way. Bit old, but... *classic*.)

Today, they just washed it down, parked it outside -- probably hoping someone would steal it -- and shuffled away. I grinned. Honestly, pink wasn't my thing, but the bike had grown on me. Who ever heard of a pink Harley? I heard the guys talk. Apparently the words "pink" and "Harley" should never have been uttered in the same sentence. Who knew? Just made me embrace the monstrosity all the more.

On impulse, I climbed on and started it up. I loved the bike Rocket had gotten for me. Wylde had taught me how to ride while I was at the Iron Tzars, but Rocket had actually sprung for a bike of my own. He said I was his woman and I would ride with him, but every MC vice president needed their own bike. Yeah. That had gotten him a blowjob and me railed from behind by a man who acted like he hadn't gotten any pussy in a fucking year. While the pink Harley was still Falcon's even if he didn't want to claim it, I was betting he'd take my bike in trade for it. If for no other reason than to not have to fuck with getting it painted again. Not that I'd ever get rid of my bike. Rocket had given it to me, and it meant the world to me.

Fuck it. I could probably just get Rocket to buy it off Falcon. I was betting that -- since it was already damaged goods because it was pink -- once I planted the idea in Falcon's mind, he would probably sell it if Rocket priced it right. It'd be the easy way out. Just like I'd wanted him to. In a way, I kind of felt sorry for the guy. This was the second time I'd basically trashed his bike. He had to be getting a complex.

I revved it a couple times before taking off toward the gate. I didn't even slow as I approached. I'd seen Rocket do this plenty of times and always thought it was cool as fuck. Head up, hair blowing in the breeze behind me, I approached the guarded exit like a boss. They'd either open the fucking gate for me or I'd bust through it. And quite possibly hurt myself, but I'd take great satisfaction watching Rocket beat those motherfuckers to a bloody pulp because I got hurt.

Unfortunately, they were ready for me and opened the gate. I halfway expected them to try to make me stop because Rocket wasn't with me, but they didn't. I sighed. Yeah, I was a little disappointed there wasn't going to be lovely chaos, but the upside was I was riding through a cleverly cut path through the reserve that blended perfectly with the landscape while still providing stable, even ground for the guys to ride off the property.

Once I was back on the main road leading toward Palm Beach, I opened the bike up and embraced the power as I rode off into the proverbial sunset. Except it was high noon. And I always thought that was a stupid saying anyway. Yeah, I was aware everyone around me thought I was crazy and maybe I was. But life was too short to live a boring life always repressing your true nature. I didn't have a death wish, nor was I sick from some debilitating, flesh-eating bubonic clap. But I'd seen death. I'd fought death.

I'd borne witness when Iron Tzars and Grim Road had literally sawed a man into tiny pieces and kept him alive so he could watch it all happening. I'd been there to witness his screams and look into Hammer's eyes as he'd been made to watch someone cut out his balls and saw off his dick. It made me ill even as it gave me great joy to watch Hammer suffer. I especially loved watching the anticipation as he saw yet another member of either Iron Tzars or Grim Road wave the knife in front of his face, taunting him with the possibility of what they were going to carve out from his body next.

I headed to Palm Springs. It was only a ten-minute drive and I loved the views. It was safe territory because of a sister club of Bones MC in Somerset, Kentucky. Salvation's Bane MC made their home in Palm Beach, so if I got in trouble, there was someone to have my back.

Then a thought occurred to me. I'd yet to meet with anyone from Salvation's Bane other than when Rocket was with me. There were a couple women I wanted to touch base with. Neither were officers or even members, but the rumor was the Bane president, Thorn, was considering giving them the distinction of being patched members. I wanted to meet with the old ladies of Bane, but that seemed too much like me coming to them as Rocket's property more than the vice president of another club. I wanted to be there as VP. If I met with one of the prospective female members of Bane who wasn't an old lady, it would assert my position in Grim as more than just Rocket's old lady.

I'd heard about one of the women. What was her name? Venus? Yeah. That sounded right. Though I'd visited the Salvation's Bane compound with Rocket and the guys a couple of times, I'd yet to meet the woman. I'd heard she was pretty awesome. Apparently she dressed in hot pink, from her leather outfit to her hair and razor-sharp nails, to pink contacts. And…

She had a pink Harley.

I hoped she was as cool as I'd heard. It'd be lame if she wasn't. While pink wasn't generally my thing, I had to admit the thought of those freaky eyes staring straight into the heart of some overly aggressive club whore made me more than a little wet. Not for Venus. To each his own, but I didn't swing that way. But giving a club whore the stink eye with pink eyes staring back at the bitch would have to be just all kinds of fucking creepy. The thought of fucking with those bitches got me all kinds of horny. Mainly because Rocket loved it when I got mean. Which got me laid. It was a vicious cycle.

Once inside Palm Beach, I thought I might head over to Tito's Diner. Tito, Elena, and Marge were awesome, and Marge made the best milkshakes I'd ever had. I could seriously gain fifty pounds if I went there on the regular.

I pulled into the diner parking lot and parked in the front. It was just after noon and the place was hopping. I smiled. Of all the fancy places to eat in Palm Springs, anyone who knew the area came here to this little diner. But no matter how busy, Elena and Tito always had fast, friendly service. One rarely had to wait longer than a couple minutes for a table. How they managed it I had no idea.

When I stepped in, the bells on the door gave a little jingle. Tito turned from the griddle where he was flipping burgers, among other yummy-smelling things.

"Lemon! You haven't been around in a few days." He gave me a bright smile like we were old friends, when I'd only met the guy a few weeks before.

Elena, Tito's wife, poked her head out from the back. "Did you say Lemon's here?" Her gaze automatically went to the door. When she spotted me, her face split into a wide grin. "*Mi niña bonita*! You should come by more often." She waved in my direction. "Marge, her meal is *en la casa*."

Marge gave me a wide grin as she smacked her gum. "That'll teach ya to not come 'round more often." The three of them laughed. The place was packed, but Marge managed to find me a place at the bar where she knew I liked to sit. I loved watching Tito sling hash. The man had seriously flipped an egg a few times.

I scowled at Elena. "I can pay my own way, Mama E."

She shook her finger at me. "None of that, young lady. Or you'll find yourself never paying for anything here."

"Elena! What the fu -- err... fudge?"

She chuckled. "That's my girl. You're learning manners."

"Well, don't tell anybody. The guys all think I'm a heathen."

"Sweet girl, those men adore you. Especially yours. Rocket believes you hung the moon. And for him, you do."

I grinned. "Yeah. He does. Ain't it awesome?"

"It most certainly is, *bebé*. Now. You tell Marge what you want. Tito will make it happen."

Tito grinned over his shoulder at me. "I got that steak and eggs you love so much. Or do you want the big burger?"

"Steak and eggs, Tito. Over light."

"I know what my girl wants." He winked at me before starting my order. Marge set what I knew would be a chocolate malt in front of me, while Elena gave me an affectionate smile before going back to her office off the main kitchen.

"Them boys treating you right, darlin'?" Marge smiled but I could tell she genuinely wanted the answer to that question. Like if I told her they were all assholes and I hated them she'd not only displeased, she'd fucking do something unpleasant about it.

"They are, Marge. Every one of them is great."

"Seen that pink motorcycle around more than once. Different guy ridin' it each time. Same girl. Couple of 'em brought her here, but I didn't get the feeling she was with any of them. More like they were making sure she was having a good time or something. Seems like a sweet girl. Bit shy."

"Yeah. That's Gina. She is sweet."

"You trade your bike for that pink one?" Marge smiled, not prying further when I had been afraid she would. They seemed to keep tabs on everyone. Not in a nosy, busybody kind of way, but in a genuine, caring way.

"You think I should?"

Marge tapped her finger against her lower lip, thinking about her answer. Then she grinned. "Yeah. If nothing else, it will make them all uncomfortable when you ride with them."

I laughed. "I like the way you think, Marge. How's the Pinto holdin' up?"

"Purrs like a kitten, thanks to Rosanna." Marge turned to get my order that Tito set on the counter. She set it and napkin-wrapped silverware on the bar next to my plate. "Red really found himself a gem in that one." Red was the road captain for Salvation's Bane.

Rosanna was a mechanic at his garage as well as his woman. I hadn't met either of them yet, but hoped to soon.

"Anyone who can keep your Pinto running the way you want it is OK in my book, Marge." I grinned before digging in. The food, as usual, was absolutely delicious. I enjoyed every single mouthful.

"Where's that man of yours, huh?" Tito frowned at me. "Figured he'd be here before now. You must have gotten a jump on him."

"This was a spur of the moment ride, Tito. There was no way I was ridin' out this way without stopping by for lunch."

Tito beamed. "That's right. I better never hear of you being in this area without coming by for a bite."

"Wouldn't think of it." I grinned as I pulled out my debit card.

Marge frowned at me as she took my plate -- which I'd barely restrained myself from licking clean, and only because Rocket wasn't here to mitigate the damage if someone said something to me for having the table manners of a pig. "What's that?" She nodded at my card like it was contaminated with something unspeakable.

"What's it look like?" I knew where this was going but I'd hoped to bully my way through it. Shoulda known better.

"What did Elena say? What part of 'on the house' did you not understand?"

"The part where I pay for my own meal? Ain't no freeloader. Danica would have my hide if she found out and I wouldn't blame her."

"You want to pay? You take it up with Elena." She smirked. "Let me know how that works out for ya."

"No need to come all the way back here," Elena called from her office somewhere beyond the front kitchen. "I can tell you how it'll work out for you, young lady, and that would be not well at all."

Marge smacked her gum with a smile. "Sorry. Boss's orders."

I scowled, but had to hide a smile. "I'll get even."

"Keep it up and you'll never pay in this place again." Elena was like a dog with a bone when she was trying to take care of those she considered hers. Apparently, she considered every motorcycle club in the area hers and Tito's. Marge too, but she tried to pretend like the other two were in charge since they owned the place. From what Rocket said, everyone knew better. Marge was as much a part of the decision-making process as Elena and Tito.

I chuckled. "I think you three are the only people in the world I've met who I can't get around."

"Sounds about right." Marge gripped my hand. "You do right by that club, honey. They might not like it getting out what they are, but they help people. Everyone knows that."

"How do you even know they're a club?" I tilted my head. I'd wondered how they managed to keep everything on the DL when there were so many of them and they were all rather distinctive-looking.

"That don't take much to figure out, honey." Marge rang up a customer's bill and took the guy's money with a smile and a thank you. "But we got inside information from Mama and Pops. Been lookin' out for those boys for years."

That surprised me. "Really?" I raised an eyebrow. "Do tell."

"Ain't my story. Might wanna check with Mama. She's Thorn's aunt. When you go to Salvation's Bane, have him put you in touch with her."

"I might just do that. How do you know Mama?"

"She and Pops helped me get this place started when I first moved here from Cuba." Tito said. His lightly accented English had him pronouncing his homeland "Cooba." "I was in trouble with the Cuban government and fled with my Elena. But when we got here, they wanted to immediately deport us. Mama worked some magic and the next thing I knew, Elena and I were US citizens. Once that happened, they had no way to deport us without divulging who they'd been in contact with. And no, I have no idea who 'they' are. But the Cuban government wanted me back at any cost to them. Mama ensured that price was too high for them to want to pay anymore."

"Wow. Cryptic much?"

Tito grinned. "Only when I have to be." It hadn't escaped me that the lunch crowd was gone, leaving only me, Elena, Tito, and Marge.

"Sounds like you're a very important man."

He shook his head. "I might have been once, but now, my greatest importance is keeping the people of this community safe. That means I feed them and keep the people who protect them happy. Grim Road should be a part of that. *Si?*"

I nodded. "I take your point. I think they already help some, but being in the limelight isn't their strong suit."

Tito tilted his head. "So… you have no say in that?" He nodded to my cut where one side had my name, the other my title. Vice President.

I scowled at him, pointing at him. "You, sir, are insufferable."

Marge cackled. I even heard Elena chuckling from the back. "She's got your number, Tito." Marge said through her laughter. "And knowing Lemon, I'm sure there were other colorful words after it. But she's a good girl and learning self-control."

"I am not!" I protest hotly. "I'm a fucking badass!"

Tito chuckled, shaking his head. "Well, you do have a say in how they proceed. I suggest you have your man and his enforcer figure out a way to balance the two. The people of West Palm Beach could use everyone's help. Along with other communities on the outskirts."

"A problem for another time. But you're right. I think I said much the same thing to the guys a month ago. Same. Only different." I wanted them to work together. To have each other's backs and no more secrets. I knew we'd accede to Tito's wishes. Who better to protect the people who couldn't protect themselves than a bunch of Black Ops bikers? It would take time to get them there, and that was OK. Rome wasn't built in a day.

"You're a good girl, Lemon." Tito lifted his chin at me. "You're good for the whole bunch."

"And you know way more than's good for you, old man."

At that, Tito outright guffawed. Marge had to sit down and Elena poked her head out from the back, trying to look stern, but I saw her lips twitch.

"Some of us have work to do, *flor pequeña*. I suggest you get back to your side of town before Tito decides to go with you and leaves me all alone."

"Geez Louise, Elena! Don't wish that on me. One man is hard enough to deal with. I'd have to kill someone if I had two of the bossy bastards telling me what to do."

Marge chuckled once again, and I waved and

smiled as I walked out the door. The afternoon was hot and humid, a far cry from the climate I was used to in Evansville, Indiana with the Iron Tzars. I'd be lying if I said I didn't miss the Tzars and, more importantly, my sisters. They belonged there. I belonged here. With Grim Road.

It wasn't that they'd made me vice president, though I wanted to be the best vice president I could. It wasn't even Rocket, though I loved that man more and more every single moment I spent with him. No. It was the whole club. I thought that every single member was a little broken inside. Dead. It was there in their eyes. I saw the way some of them looked at me and Rocket. It wasn't that any of them wanted me. In fact, I think most of them would rather go to prison than spend a lifetime shackled with me. They wanted what Rocket had with me.

I'd been trying to figure out a way to fill that gap for them, but short of mail order brides I didn't see any woman with any backbone putting up with the bullshit. And these men had to have women with backbone. Any woman claimed by any member of this club had to be in it for the long haul. To do that, they had to be able to stand up for themselves. Yeah. I was drawing a blank.

I climbed on the bike, chuckling softly as I stroked the pink gas tank. The guys hated this bike, but they drove it. All to put Gina at ease because of what they'd done to her. Sure, they hadn't known she wasn't willing, but they still saw it as a failure. I couldn't reassure them they were wrong. Every single man who'd fucked Gina. Every. Single. One. They took her for rides on this Goddamned bike every fucking day the weather was fit. This club was full of honorable men, no matter what shady shit they'd done. They kept to their code and hurting innocent women -- especially like they had Gina -- was most decidedly not in their code.

Just as I reached down to turn the key, something hit me in the head. Fucking *hard*.

I fell with a groan, the world spinning. My ears rang and I tried to shake it off, but someone grabbed me by my hair and hauled me up. Or, rather, dragged me as I stumbled, trying to get my legs under me. I knew I needed to call out, scream, something, anything, but my head was still swimming and I wasn't exactly sure I was capable. I was barely able to struggle and what I did manage was damned pitiful.

"Get her in the fuckin' van before someone sees." A gruff voice snapped the order. I grabbed at the guy's hand on my hair, trying to ease the pressure on my scalp. Someone groped me, lingering on my ass. If these guys decided they were going to rape me, there was no way I was in any shape to stop them after that blow to the head. Fortunately, as quickly as it started, those hands stopped.

The next thing I knew, someone tossed me inside the van and slid the door shut with a slam. I still saw stars in my peripheral vision and wasn't altogether certain I wasn't gonna be sick.

I tried to look around, but rough hands shoved me to my front, snagging my hands behind my back and securing them.

"You're not anything like I was expecting," the guy said, his voice whiny and grated on my nerves like fucking sandpaper. I tried to look over my shoulder and wished I hadn't. The guy had so many facial piercings he looked like he'd been in a fight with a nail gun. And lost. "Thought there'd be more *pink*." Like the bike wasn't pink enough.

I wanted to ask what was going on, but couldn't quite make my voice work. I shook my head, trying to clear it only to have the guy shove my face to the floor.

"Stay the fuck still, bitch."

I took a deep breath, the panic inside me very real and hard to overcome. But I'd do it because I had to. I was Rocket's woman. Not a pussy. Because the only pussy Rocket wanted was between my legs, not my ears. Or something. It was hard to think. But one thing was for sure, I was *not* a pussy. That thought finally helped me shake off some of the dizziness, though my head was beginning to throb.

"Of all the people I could have gotten kidnapped by, it had to be fuckin' Pinhead." In retrospect, that was probably the exact wrong thing to say, but, Goddamnit, the guy shoulda known better than to fuck with me. Even if he didn't know me, no one rode a fucking pink Harley if they didn't expect to be assaulted. The mere fact I was willing to risk it really should have told this guy how badass I was.

Except, right now, I didn't feel at all that badass. And that comment? Yeah. It cost me.

Chapter Five
Rocket

"Falcon!" I called out across the main room. Everyone was gathered tonight for a party which was usual on Friday night. It meant club whores were everywhere, fucking anything that moved. I'd already had to threaten to ban more than one if she touched me again. I needed a buffer. "You seen Lemon?" More than one club whore backed off even farther than she'd been before I mentioned Lemon's name. She'd made a grand impression on the club whores, and she hadn't had to lift a finger. Of course, it could have been due to the fact that she'd had blood splattered all over her hands, face, arms, and T-shirt.

I wanted Lemon here because I loved showing her off. That stunning, brash, tough-as-nails woman was with me. I got the added benefit of Lemon's mere presence keeping away any whores, and it reinforced to my men that Lemon was mine. There weren't many who were strong enough to deal with a woman like Lemon, but there were a couple I knew I'd have to keep an eye on. They'd never disrespect me as long as I treated my old lady right, but if they thought she was unhappy with me? Yeah. They'd jump all over that shit. Then I'd have to kill someone, and I didn't much want to have to kill any of my brothers.

"Not since early afternoon. She took the monstrosity and left."

"Monstrosity? You mean your bike?"

"Ain't my fuckin' bike no more." Falcon stuck his chin up. "Just ain't had time to give it to its new owner."

"Oh? Who the fuck'd you get to buy that thing?"

Falcon shrugged. "Just some chick. Freaky as

shit. Made sense she wanted the fuckin' bike. She was dressed from head to toe in the same shade of pink. It was like Lemon had it custom painted to match that bitch." He took a pull of his beer like the mere memory was more than he could take before continuing. "And when I say head to toe in pink? I mean that literally. The fuckin' bitch's *eyes* were fuckin' pink, Rocket! Who the fuck does that?"

"Don't know. Don't care. Where's my old lady?"

"If she left you, Rocket, I'll be happy to console you." Chyna, one of the fuckin' club whores, sauntered up to me and would have thrown her arms around my neck. Not only would it have given her leverage to pull herself up to kiss me, but it would have helped her retain her hold when I tried to shove her off me.

I took a step backward. "You fucking touch me, you die." I was sick and tired of this horse shit.

"I only want to make you feel good, Rocket. That bitch ain't nothin' compared to you. Just a kid playin' at bein' an MC queen."

I took back the steps I'd retreated plus another step toward the woman, intent on backhanding her. Had Falcon not been there to catch my arm, I have no doubt in my mind I'd have truly hit a woman in anger for the first time in my life. I might have felt bad about it afterward, but... OK. No. I wouldn't feel bad about it. Even now, I was trying to shove Falcon off me so I could go after her skank ass.

"Rocket," Falcon said as he kept a firm grip on my arm as he stepped between me and Chyna. "You can't hit the bitch."

"I'd like to know why the fuck not." My gaze never left the bitch in question.

"Because -- you hit her, she rats us out. Gonna be questionable as it is. Any woman here you reject's gonna take it as a personal affront. You knew that when you claimed Lemon."

I heaved an exasperated huff. "First of all, *she* claimed *me*. I only say that because she'd hand me my ass if I tried to take that claim away from her. Thinks she's special because she claimed her man instead of waitin' for him to claim her. I will absolutely give that to her." I turned my gaze back to Chyna with what I hoped was a death stare. "Second, any of 'em even think about doin' something to get even with me or Lemon and put this club in danger, woman be damned, I'll work out my frustrations with my fists. So, no. I'm *not* gonna worried about insultin' any of 'em." I was generally well-spoken, but when I got this angry and frustrated, my southern accent leapt to the fore.

"Fine. I still want you to step away from her. She got the message, and I'm sure she'll pass it on to anyone not here."

"She fuckin' better."

Chyna had gone white, and I knew I'd finally gotten my point across. She wouldn't tell the other women anything, though. It was not what club whores did. While they would be loyal to the club at all costs, the other whores were their rivals. No matter what Falcon thought, I knew every woman in this compound well enough to trust they wouldn't bring outsiders into club business. Even Chyna was only in it for the social status. She couldn't give two shits about me. Any jealousy on her part toward Lemon was because Lemon was the president's old lady. 'Course, the fact Lemon was VP kinda trumped the old lady status. And that was something none of them would ever have. Even if I resigned as president, none of the guys would take her for his old lady. Not because she wasn't attractive or wasn't smart enough, or even because she was a club whore. It was because it would be hard taking an old lady when every brother in the club had fucked her at one time or other. Not because she didn't deserve to have a good a time as everyone else, because it was hard not to think about men you see and talk to every day knowing what it was like to fuck your woman.

"Plush, take Chyna out," Falcon said, his voice harder than I normally heard from the other man. "She can either get her shit and leave, or she can go back to the whore's section. But she doesn't need to be here right now."

"I's jus' tryin' ta have a good time." Her words were slurring now. Apparently whatever her recreational drug of choice was was starting to kick in. I'd say it explained her behavior, but Chyna was one of the more aggressive whores. She didn't need a drug to enhance her personality.

"Not now, Chyna," Plush said, casting quick glances at both me and Falcon. Yeah. She got it. Plush would spread the word, and maybe they'd back off me. "We need to go."

With a huff and a sigh, Chyna went with Plush without any other argument. I watched until the door closed behind them. The other whores all moved in different directions away from me like I had the fucking plague.

When Chyna was gone, I turned my attention back to Falcon. "Now. My woman."

"Told you, prez. Ain't seen her in a couple hours."

"It's not like her to ignore texts from me." I mused as I pulled out my phone and scrolled down, trying to see when the last time she called or texted was.

"She ignores me all the time," Falcon grumbled.

"Are you… sulking?" I gave Falcon a disbelieving look before going back to intently study my phone.

"I'm not sulking, Rocket. What the fuck? I'm just saying she never answers my texts or calls about club business."

"And are all your calls and texts about club business important enough that I'd have answered them if you'd sent them to me?" Falcon just blinked at me. He opened his mouth, then shut it. "That's what I thought." I raised an eyebrow at him. "She's vice president, asshole. Not your mother."

"Thank God." Falcon muttered his response, but I also knew he was just messing with Lemon. All the guys did. The sooner they accepted that she was exactly like me when it came to bullshit, the better off they would be. Lemon would absolutely deal with anything important. She would not take on all their bullshit just to keep them from having to deal with it.

"What was that?" I snapped, wanting Falcon to know I wouldn't tolerate disrespect. Though, I'd have thought he'd have learned his lesson when I beat the fuck outta Ringo.

He raised his hands. "Nothin', prez. Just that if Lemon were my mom, she'd have busted my balls a long time ago. That woman's got a vicious streak." He grinned. "I like it. But I'm glad she set her sights on you and not me."

I snorted. "Like you could take Lemon on."

"That's exactly my point." Falcon pointed a finger at me. "Ain't too proud to admit it either. She's way the fuck more woman than I could handle."

"Good. Glad we got that straight. But you still

don't get to disrespect her."

"Wouldn't dream of it, Prez."

"Now that that's outta the way, where's my woman?"

"It's not like her to not be at a party when she knows you're gonna be here."

"Yeah." I took out my phone and checked it. Didn't look like she'd read my messages. Which was damned odd. "Crush in his office?"

Falcon nodded. "Last I saw."

Without another word, I stalked in that direction. A couple of the girls tried to approach me, but one look at my face and they backed off. I didn't like Lemon not being here. She was capable of taking care of herself, but I still didn't like it. I'm sure my expression told how much I didn't like it. And how much I wasn't in the mood for bullshit. Neither woman came closer.

I'd rounded the corner as Crush opened the door and hurried out, his expression tight. When he saw me, he stopped.

"You need to be looped in on this, Prez."

I followed him inside. Crush shut and locked the door behind us. Byte was busy at his computer, talking to someone as he pulled up several camera feeds.

"Is that Tito's restaurant?" I leaned over Byte's shoulder to get a better look at the screen."

"Yeah."

"What's Falcon's bike doing there? Did Gina go out with one of the guys?"

"No. Lemon's on it."

That surprised me. "Lemon? At Tito's?"

"Yeah. But that doesn't matter. Watch." He started the camera feed.

"What am I looking at?"

Instead of Byte answering me, a voice from the

speakerphone spoke up. "Lemon's been kidnapped."

That was Thorn's voice. President of Salvation's Bane. We had a loose alliance with their club, but we weren't exactly friends. More like we agreed to stay out of each other's way and to help each other out if things got too out of hand. Looks like they were. Had Thorn punched me in the balls, he couldn't have dealt a more debilitating blow.

"What?" I barked the question. "You better be fuckin' with me, Thorn. Then you better take your ass beatin' like a fuckin' man."

"I wish like fuck I was, Rocket. Venus was on her way to Tito's when it went down. She thinks they were looking for her."

"Lemon looks nothing like Venus. Not to mention all the pink." Then a thought occurred to me. "The bike," I whispered, glancing over at Crush. His expression was hard but resigned. "That Goddamned bike."

"Yeah. She was riding Falcon's bike." Ringo stuck his head inside the room. "You think they thought Lemon was Venus?"

"That's exactly what Ripper thought." Thorn continued. "When Venus contacted us, Ripper started pulling camera feeds all over the city. Those guys are good. They know what they're doing and how to stay off the cameras. Venus is on 'em, though. She'll keep on your girl, Rocket. Venus is deadly as any of us."

Ringo snorted. "That's not what I heard."

I gave him an exasperated look. "Run along, little boy. The grown-ups are having a conversation."

Ringo barked out a laugh. "The little hellion's rubbin' off on you, Prez. You sound just like her."

"I must not have beat you hard enough before." Even though the man sported a still swollen-shut black eye, he couldn't keep his mouth shut.

"You beat me plenty, Rocket, but I'm bettin' you no one's considered Lemon's sharp tongue and how it's gonna affect her kidnappers. Because that woman could try the patience of a saint. I say that with the utmost affection, Rocket. But you know it's true."

Yeah. My little sourpuss could rip a man to shreds without batting an eyelash. "I hear you, Ringo." I turned my attention back to the phone and Thorn. "Where's Lemon?"

"Venus is following them. Ripper has a GPS on everyone's bike, so he's following her. She's also got an open phone connection with Ripper, giving him real-time information. They're headed to the reserve. Your direction. They know you guys are there?"

"No," I said without hesitation. "We all take great pains to protect our area out here. I'm not saying no one knows where we are, but in this case, I'd be willing to bet my life they're looking for a place to hole up and think the nature reserve is the perfect place because no one is allowed in here."

There was a slight pause, then Thorn spoke again. "I agree. I'm assumin' you have places to get rid of the motherfuckers."

"Plenty of gators out there. We cut 'em up in small enough pieces, even if someone did find 'em they wouldn't know what they'd found." I moved across the room. The main weapons locker for the club was in Crush and Byte's office. I entered the code for the locker and chose a SIG-Sauer and a couple of clips. "Get a team together, Crush. You get all the information Ripper has. I want to know exactly where those motherfuckers are."

"Roger that," Crush's fingers flew over the keyboard as I snagged another gun. Ringo was right beside me, packing up his own weapons.

"What'er you doin'?" I raised an eyebrow at him. Ringo wasn't exactly who I thought would want to help me rescue Lemon. Not considering how the two of them clashed.

"Goin' after my VP." He leveled his one-eye-gaze on me. "Got a problem with that, Prez?"

"Nope. Just don't accidentally shoot her."

"Hey. She gets on my ever-lovin' last nerve, Rocket. She's a pain in the ass on the best of days. She seems to get a kick outta bustin' everyone's balls. But she's the VP of Grim Road. We all voted her in. Unanimously. I might want to throttle her sometimes, but no one else better touch one hair on her head."

I snorted. "You better not either."

"I have no desire to get my ass handed to me again, Prez."

"Good. Crush, tell the team they've got five minutes to gear up, then I'm leavin'. I'm gonna find these bastards. We're gonna make what happened to Hammer look like a fuckin' picnic."

Chapter Six
Lemon

"Get up, bitch." The guy was dancing all over my last fucking nerve, but there wasn't a Goddamned thing I could do about it.

"Go fuck yourself." My mouth hadn't caught up with the pain in my body yet. Too bad, too, because I really wasn't sure how many more beatings I could take. Just like all the other times since I'd been taken a few hours ago, I got backhanded. Pain exploded across my cheek, and I sucked in a breath. When this had started, and I realized I was on my own until Rocket and Grim Road found me, I'd made a promise to myself that, no matter what they did, I would not give them the satisfaction of hearing me scream or seeing me cry. So far, all they'd done was hit me or kick me. I was pretty sure things wouldn't stay that way long. If Rocket didn't find me soon, I was going to be in some serious fucking trouble. Hell, I was already in serious fucking trouble.

"When I tell you to do something, you do it, bitch." The guy grabbed me by my hair and dragged me across the short length of the tiny hunting shack. I had no idea who owned the property, but I was fairly certain we were close to Grim Road's territory. The place was pretty well hidden. Unless there were cameras or sensors in the immediate vicinity, I doubted anyone could find the place.

Once he had me where he wanted me, he snapped handcuffs on my wrists and hung the chain on a hook from the ceiling. My feet were touching the floor but only with my toes. The cuffs were cutting into my wrists. My face and head throbbed, and I thought I might have a broken rib. It felt like a repeat of that beach house in Riviera Beach. Only these guys meant business. The big one was bad, but I was pretty sure Pinhead wanted to torture me more than they already had. The really shitty part was, I wasn't certain how long I could hold out.

I kept my one good eye open. The other was starting to swell shut. The last thing I wanted to do was lose track of them. There were only three, but that was way more than I could take on by myself with any degree of positive outcome. Yeah. I was well and truly fucked.

"What'er we gonna do with the bitch?" The one who'd been beating on me the most, Pinhead, looked like he wanted to start on me again. Relished the idea, even.

"We're gonna wait until we get instructions from that freak, Victor." That one was the biggest and seemed to be the leader. Neither of them seemed too bright, but this guy kept staring at me like he was looking for something specific. "He said she'd be ridin' a pink bike, but also that she'd be dressed in pink. I was also expectin' another woman with her. And some bigass black guy. Only thing this one matches is the bike."

"What? You think we got the wrong bitch?" The last one had a full head of bushy hair he was continually brushing out of his eyes. Looked like he hadn't washed it in a couple months. Smelled like the rest of him hadn't been washed in that long either.

"Not sure." The guy kept eyeing me. I didn't let him stare me down but met his gaze with a steely one of my own. Well, with one eye anyway. "But I need to find out before Victor gets here. If we didn't get the bitch he was after, we'll be in a world of hurt."

"True," the smelly one agreed. "How we gonna

be sure?"

"I'm gonna go scout out that motorcycle club. See if I see someone who looks a little more like the description we got." He pointed a finger at Pinhead. "You touch her again, when I get back, you die. Get me?"

"Ah, come on, Butch! It's boring and I wanna have a little fun." Pinhead looked almost gleeful as he stared at me, licking his lips and playing with the stud in one corner of his lip with his tongue. Gross. Oh, I was gonna have so much fun with that piercing when Rocket got me loose...

"No more! If she's the right woman, Victor ain't gonna be pleased. He gave explicit instructions we ain't supposed to hurt her. Not 'til he said."

"Oh, I ain't hurt her." He stared at me and flashed me an evil grin. If I'd been a weaker person, I might have shivered. This man would kill me if he got the chance. Just not right away. "Those were just little love taps."

"Just shut the fuck up and leave her alone. I'll be back in a couple of hours."

Yeah. I could tell that wasn't happening. I'd be lucky to be conscious when Butch came back. And who the hell was Victor? More importantly, how did I get word to Venus she had someone after her? Because there was no doubt in my mind it was Venus they wanted.

The door slamming shut sounded like a death knell. Mine.

Pinhead waited until I heard the van start up and drive off before he gave me an evil grin. "You gonna scream, bitch?"

I knew better than to say anything. Knew it like I knew my own name. Still, my mouth just couldn't get the message. "Too soon to tell. The better question would be how loud are *you* gonna scream when my man gets here?"

He laughed. It wasn't a pleasant sound. "You really think someone's gonna find you out here? We're on a nature reserve, you fuckin' cunt. No one's even allowed in here. Yet here we are." That kind of surprised me. There hadn't been any windows in the van so I hadn't been able to look out, but the length of the trip and the general vibe of the place told me it was entirely possible I was in my home territory. Which meant these guys were even more fucked than I was.

"Hmm… nature reserve? And there just happens to be a hunting cabin? You guys build it?"

Pinhead snorted. "Didn't have to. This place has been here for years. Probably here from before the government took over. Nah, bitch. We didn't build it. But we're damned sure gonna use it."

This couldn't really be happening. There was no way I could get this lucky. "So, let me get this straight. You happened upon a random cabin in the woods and just… decided to use it?"

"Wuddent no one usin' it. Hell, no one comes out here." That from the smelly one.

I sighed, shaking my head. "No fuckin' way this is happenin'." I muttered the comment more to myself but Pinhead thought I was talking to him.

"Oh, it's happenin', bitch." His sneer made me want to cunt punch him. "It's really fuckin' happenin'. And when I get through with you, you're gonna wish you'd kept that fuckin' mouth of yours shut. 'Cause I'm gonna fuck the bitchiness right outta that blow hole of yours."

"Did you think this was a conversation?" I tilted my head, trying my best to look confused no matter how much my face was hurting. No matter how scared and in pain I was, I absolutely would not let him see it. I was the vice president of Grim Road MC. I couldn't tell this bastard that in case he got away before I could kill him, but I could act like it. I *would* act like it, Goddamnit! "I'm talking to myself. Because there is no possible way in the history of mother *fuck* you could be this Goddamned stupid on purpose."

As expected, he backhanded me again. The force snapped my head to the side and I tasted blood. It took every bit of mental strength I had to keep my toes on the ground and not let my knees buckle. Strong. I had to be strong.

"Now who's stupid, you fuckin' cunt!" He was up in my face, just looking for a reason to hit me again. I knew it. But I wasn't about to back down now.

I laughed and I knew it sounded more than a little bit crazy. "You are." I laughed in a sing-song voice. "You have no idea where you are or who you're getting ready to have to deal with." I grinned at him. At least I hope I was looking at him. That one eye was now completely swollen shut and there were dots dancing at the edges of my vision in my good eye. I tilted my head and tried to project the same effect on him I had to the club girls when I'd first come back to Grim Road as Rocket's old lady. I leaned in and whispered, "You've stepped onto a very… grim… road…" God, could I get any cheesier? But Lord, it was too funny. Well. It *would* be funny. Weeks from now after I'd healed. And had a proper meltdown.

Pinhead laughed, then snarled and backhanded me again. This time, my feet slipped and the cuffs on my wrist took my entire weight. How I managed to stay conscious I had no idea. Probably because I was just that Goddamned stubborn. I wasn't going to pass out and give this fuck a chance to touch me without me fighting back. He might hurt me. Might even kill me. But I would not go without a fight or giving back as much as I could. I was the vice president of Grim Road, Goddamnit! And if I kept telling myself that, it would help me be strong. I would prove myself worthy of their trust in putting me in this position.

"I'm gonna enjoy playin' with you, little girl." Pinhead leaned in and licked up the side of my face. "When I'm finished -- if there's anything left -- I'll give you to some friends of mine. After *they're* through? Maybe I'll ship you back to this man of yours. In multiple boxes."

I grinned. "You're so fuckin' fucked, and the sad part is, you don't even know it. When they get here, I'm gonna remove every piece of metal from your face. With needle-nose pliers."

He raised his hand to hit me again, but before he could, the door to the tiny cabin burst inward. I used the opportunity, kicking out. My foot connected with Pinhead's crotch. He cried out, stumbling backward before falling to his knees.

I struggled to free myself, but I was just that little bit too short to slip the hook where my cuffs hung from the ceiling. That's when my attention focused on the woman who'd come barging in like a bull.

Venus. I'd never met her, but there was no mistaking who this woman was. Long pink hair. Pink leather. Pink boots. Pink nails that looked sharp enough to disembowel a man. And when she turned her head? Yep. Pink eyes.

Cool!

I had just enough left in me to appreciate the efficiency with which she dispatched both men. One kick to the head for each and they were lying on the floor either completely dazed or unconscious. Then she moved to me.

"Which one hit you?" It was a demand, her expression as hard and cold as any of the guys in Grim Road. She was taller than me by several inches and looked to have several pounds of muscle on me. Her pink top was a leather vest displaying toned arms and a small strip of muscled midriff. She helped me get the links of my cuffs off the hook and steadied me so I could keep my knees from buckling. When she tried to ease me to the ground I shook my head, bracing myself with a hand on her shoulder for a few more seconds before I nodded and stood on my own power.

"Pinhead there." I nodded at the man in question. He was out but starting to stir. "I'd appreciate it if you helped me tie him up. Me and him got unfinished business."

The corner of her lips up with a satisfied smirk. "Woman after my own heart." Her accent was Russian, though not really heavy.

We secured both men before I sat back on my ass next to the wall. "Give me a minute. I want to enjoy the fuck outta this."

"No problem. We can take as long as you like. Your club will be here soon. They can take these fucks to secure location for you to play to your heart's content."

I chuckled. "Yeah. That's a real thing." Then I groaned. "I may have to take a few days before we start good and proper. Though I promised Pinhead there I'd be removing a couple of those piercings with needle-nose pliers. I should probably do that now so he knows I always follow through."

"As you should." Venus sounded approving. "While I always like to do torture when at full strength, follow-through is very important. And if you're not physically ready for the torture, it hurts you more than one you're hurting."

"Sound advice."

"I'm Venus," she said, offering her hand which I took. "I got word to Thorn they took you. He reached out to Rocket."

"Lemon. I'm VP of Grim Road." I put my shoulders back, proud of my designation in the club. "You have no idea how much I appreciate your help, Venus. You need to know, these guys were looking for you."

Her gaze hardened. "You know this how?"

"There's another man. He was going to scout out Bane. See if he could find a woman riding a pink Harley in case they were mistaken about me. Which, hello, Captain Obvious. The pink Harley was the only criteria I met on his list. When they got me, they made the comment that they thought I'd be more… pink. Unless you know of anyone else in this area fitting the description…"

She turned her attention to the men tied up on the floor. "Well, little boys…" She grinned, standing to her full height to look down at both men. "You have one chance to tell me who wants me. Then we take you apart." She tapped one pointed nail against her lip. "How *long* that takes? Depends on how quick you tell me what I want to know."

Chapter Seven
Rocket

My heart was pounding in my chest. I was actually shaking as we followed Ripper's directions. The first time she'd been taken I could hardly believe they'd brought her back into my territory. Dumb luck on my part but I'd take it.

I didn't check to see where my brothers were or even try to hide the noise of my bike as I pulled up outside the tiny watch cabin. No one had used the place in years, but it was meant to be a place to keep watch over this section of our home. The fucking clubhouse was only a mile or so to the east, but Crush had set up cameras so no one had to use the shack unless they just wanted a place on the property to hide out by themselves a while.

When I shut down my bike, I heard a man's shrill scream, followed by an angry, harsh female voice. It wasn't Lemon's voice. Rather it was more alto with a Russian accent.

"What the Goddamned fuck?" I hurried to the door, which had been kicked in. The cabin was more of a shack. One room with only a table, chairs, and a wood stove. The place was dusty and musty smelling, but not cluttered, so taking in the whole thing at a glance wasn't difficult.

In the corner a man with black, greasy hair had gashes down his face that looked like claw marks. Blood oozed steadily, and that guy would definitely be scarred for life. Or rather, he would if he lived long enough for them to heal. Which I had it on good authority he wouldn't. The other guy was a bloody fucking mess. Lemon knelt in front of the second guy, speaking so softly, I had no idea what she said.

Whatever it was, though, had the guy whimpering and shaking his head so violently that blood was flung out from the mess of his face.

Venus stood well back, as if keeping watch. Her bike hadn't been out front, but the woman was too smart for that. She'd have parked away from this place or camouflaged it carefully. She turned her head in my direction, not the least bit concerned, and acknowledged me with a lift of her chin.

"Please," the guy Lemon was kneeling beside begged. "I'm sorry! I'm really sorry!"

"Oh, I'm sure you are," Lemon replied mildly. "*Now*. But you see, the way you smacked me around, the threats you made to give me to your friends before you shipped me back to Rocket in multiple boxes, aaaallll that speaks way the fuck louder than your pitiful beggin' now."

Lemon had a pair of pliers in her hand. Likely from the tool kit we kept alongside the first aid kit and case of bottled water on the other side of the cabin. Her voice was calm. Almost conciliatory. But I knew my woman. Whatever she was planning on doing, she wouldn't stop just because the fucker said he was sorry. She hadn't turned her attention to me. I wasn't even sure if she knew I was here or not. I hadn't had the chance to examine her yet, but I did see bruising around one wrist. It was enough for me to know these guys were dead men. The only question was how long it was going to take for them to die.

"Come on! I said I was sorry! What do you want from me?" The guy was stressed to the max. Given the state of his face, I could understand. When Lemon raised those pliers to his face again, then gripped a studded piercing at the corner of his lip, the guy thrashed and tried to turn his head away from the instrument she held.

"Hold still, Pinhead, or it won't come out clean." Lemon's voice sounded like she was trying to reason with him. Like a parent telling a child this was for his own good. I knew better. She wanted him to fight. To fear. The woman was vicious in a way a man could only dream of. Admittedly, there weren't many men willing to take on a woman this brutal, but I wasn't most men. And the sight only turned me on. My woman might take a beating, but she was anything but a victim. She'd bide her time. When the opportunity presented itself, she struck.

"No! *NO!*" The guy's voice broke, and he sobbed as Lemon pulled at the stud. She took her time, stretching the skin taut.

"You ready?"

"NO! Stop! NOOOO!"

"I have to wonder." Lemon tilted her head. I could see one side of her face and her lips were pursed. "Would you have stopped hurting me if I'd begged you?"

Everything inside me stilled. When I'd first brought Lemon back to the compound with me as my woman, she'd been taken by a couple of guys who had kidnapped a young girl off the beach. Lemon had gone after the girl, Effie, who was now with us at Grim Road. Lemon had taken several blows before I'd gotten there, during the ensuing fight. I'd lost my shit then, but I had a feeling this was going to be worse.

The guy half laughed, half cried, trying to play it off. "I was only jokin', lady. I wouldn't really've done all that shit."

"Really. Because it felt like you meant it."

Then, with a vicious jerk of her hand, Lemon pulled the stud from his lip. She held it up to the light coming through the grimy window as if to get a better look at it. The guy she'd called Pinhead screamed and thrashed about. Obviously not one of his better days. Seeing Lemon acting in character with her typical self eased my rage and fear somewhat, lessening the band around my chest. She was here. She was safe. I had no idea what injuries she had, if any, but she wasn't so hurt she wasn't up for a few shenanigans.

This Pinhead screamed over and over, sucking in one breath after another only to let out more screams. Judging by his face, she'd done this several times. Which made sense. He'd reached the point where he'd given up trying to be stoic about the whole mess, but she hadn't gone so far he didn't have the strength to fight.

"Oh, look, Venus," Lemon said as she held out the bloody bit of steel. "Another souvenir. I think I want to melt them all down and make a cock piercing for his dick." She straightened then, as if a thought had just occurred to her. Knowing Lemon, this was the exact moment she'd been leading up to. "Wait. He's got a metric crapton of piercings in his face. I bet he has them other places too."

Pinhead screamed in what I could only describe as abject terror. Because he obviously knew what I did. Lemon absolutely would rip out every piece of body jewelry the man had.

"No doubt, Lemon." Venus gave a supremely satisfied smirk. My guess was she'd been waiting for Lemon to come to this conclusion, and now realized there had been a method to the madness for Lemon. This was where she'd been going all along and had played it to perfection. "You and I need to hang out more."

"You sure Thorn would approve of that?" I

couldn't keep to the shadows any longer. I mean, I hadn't been exactly subtle in my approach, but the men hadn't noticed and it was time to make my presence known. I frowned at them. Venus didn't turn her head to acknowledge me. Lemon did...

And all that rage inside me I'd just tamped down rose to the surface in a white-hot explosion.

"What the Goddamned fuck?" I shouted as I took the two steps necessary to get to my woman. "Who the fuck hit you? He's a fuckin' dead man!"

"Relax, sugar," she said, standing to wrap her arms around my neck. She was splattered with blood and one whole side of her face was swollen. Dried blood trickled down one corner of her mouth, but she was acting like she felt none of it. This was becoming a theme I didn't like. "I'm fine. Just a couple bumps and bruises." She hiked a thumb over her shoulder. "You should see the other guy. Besides, once Venus got here, it was all good."

"Don't care. I'm done with you getting beat up, Lemon. This has to fuckin' stop." I pulled her solidly against me, wrapping my arms around her tightly. She clung to me as well and, though I knew she'd never admit it, she was trembling. Every instinct in me screamed at me to remove her from the situation. Whether she wanted me to or not.

After a couple of moments, she gave a half-hearted attempt to push me away. I recognized it for what it was. She needed comfort but didn't want to look weak in front of the man she was torturing.

I wanted to take her and leave. I wanted to strip her of her rank as VP in my club and demand she keep her ass in the compound at all times unless I was with her. I wanted to forbid her from ever torturing someone like she was doing now ever again because I knew that, though she was more than capable -- I mean, she was playing this session like a fucking pro -- it took something out of her. It would also give her nightmares. Just like Hammer's torture had. She'd never admit any of it though. She'd put on that cocky grin and parade back to the clubhouse covered in blood, sporting her injuries like a fucking badge of honor for all to see. But inside, she would be emotionally scarred and broken.

"Maybe this should be finished in more… secure place. *Da*?" Venus looked amused. "I am very sure no one will hear their screams -- they weren't complete dumbasses in choosing their location -- but now we have options…" She trailed off before giving a crisp nod like she'd only just come to this conclusion. "I think would be best. More comfortable for us so we have break between sessions. More secure so they know there is no way out for them, no matter who they manage to get past." I knew she was passively taking charge when she didn't think I was capable of being objective.

Venus wasn't a young newcomer to MC life. Or even military life. She was a hardened, seasoned warrior who'd been involved with an active club and military organization for the better part of twenty years. She might not look like it, but she was in her late thirties or early forties. I knew she planned every move she made or word she said before she showed her hand. This idea got Lemon away from these bastards long enough for her to regroup, and time for me to get myself under control. I wasn't too proud to admit I needed that at the moment.

I gave Venus a nod of acknowledgment. "The rest of the men are right behind me. We'll get them tied more securely, shove a gag in Pinhead there, then get them to the dungeon."

Venus cocked her head. "You have dungeon?"

"We have lots of things." I felt my face split into a grin when I didn't really feel like smiling as I tightened my arms around Lemon. She continued to struggle but it was still half-hearted, so I chose to ignore her protests.

"Dungeon would be perfect for these two." She narrowed her eyes at me and I knew what was about to happen. I also knew I'd give her whatever she wanted simply because she'd come to my woman's aid. "Your vice president says they were after me. She also says there is man headed to Salvation's Bane to scout out place. See if anyone in compound matches description they were given. They grabbed Lemon because of pink bike. Not because she fit profile."

"And you want a chance to find out why." It wasn't a question.

"*Da*. I am very interested in knowing who and, more importantly, why."

I stared at her for several moments, trying to gauge her mood and her intent. She held my gaze without flinching and, I had to admit, those pink eyes were freaky... as... *fuck*. Besides that, I could see she wasn't asking permission.

"I owe you for helping my vice president out of a tight spot, Venus. But you're not a member of my club, nor do you give orders. As long as you understand that, I'll allow you to participate in this. Understood?"

"*Da*. What else?" She didn't even flinch. If she saw it as a reprimand, she didn't let on.

"No one knows where our compound is." I gave her a pointed look, letting her draw the necessary conclusions.

She waved me off. "Easily resolved. I got here on

my own. Let me take bike back to Bane, and you can send cage after me. I can fill Thorn in, we can look for third guy, you can blindfold me when you take me back. Might even come back heavy one captive."

"You can call Thorn from here. You leave your phone here and my tech people scan you for bugs. And you're blindfolded from here to the compound."

Normally, her coming back with us would be a nonstarter, but two things swayed me. First, she'd saved Lemon from more of a beating than she'd taken as it was. Second… well. I'd address the second later. Venus wasn't ready, I hadn't discussed it with Lemon yet, and I wasn't entirely sure I wanted to address the second reason I was allowing her a way into our compound.

Venus didn't even flinch. "Deal." She stuck out her hand, expecting me to shake it. I did, but didn't let go of Lemon.

That was when three members of Grim Road entered the cabin. Bear was first, followed by Knox and Piston. To say the tiny shack was overcrowded was an understatement.

Bear's gaze went to the two men on the floor before moving to Lemon. "Looks like you took care of things with your usual finesse, Lemon."

Lemon shrugged. "See me, love me, motherfucker."

Venus snorted out a laugh before putting a hand on Lemon's shoulder. "You will be fine. Little sister for me and Millie."

"What'er we doin' with that lot?" Piston asked. "Not much left of 'em. We gettin' rid of 'em here?"

"No." I shook my head, finally able to let Lemon push away from me, but only because I knew she'd never forgive me if I let the other men see her as anything less than an officer in Grim Road.

"We're takin' 'em back to the compound," Lemon answered. "Venus is coming with us, so I need you to have Byte come here with whatever he needs to scan her for tracking devices."

"You got it." Bear nodded, taking out his phone and making the call as he stepped outside.

"You want a cage to take them back to the compound?" Knox indicated the two men on the floor.

"Yep." I nodded to Venus. "She can ride with you, though she'll need to be blindfolded."

"No." Piston moved and indicated Knox should go. "Get the cage, but that one rides with me."

"Not sure it's safe for her to ride blindfolded, even if she ain't drivin'." I frowned. What was he playing at?

"She won't be. Claimin' that one. I'll discuss her patchin' in once we get all this other shit figured out."

Venus laughed. "Taking much for granted, are you not?"

Piston leveled a look on her that brooked no argument. "No."

"Have you said more than two words to her?" Lemon stepped closer to Piston.

"Nope. Don't change nothin'. She's still mine."

"Well, all right then." Lemon gave Venus a cheeky grin. Even with her face all swollen I could tell she was enjoying this.

Venus looked less than thrilled but wasn't balking. Likely, she thought she'd get a free look inside our compound before she blazed. Piston was the one who surprised me. The man wasn't playing. This was happening whether Venus realized it or not.

Chapter Eight
Lemon

The ride back to the clubhouse was painful. Rocket was right. I needed to stop doing this. Which meant I needed to learn self-control. Yeah. I'd have better luck winning the fucking lottery.

We pulled into the compound and up to the clubhouse front door. "Feels like *deja vu*," I muttered.

"What?" Rocket looked over his shoulder at me while the others pulled up and parked. "You walking into the clubhouse with blood all over you? Or sporting a swollen face?"

"Ouch. Way to hit a girl's ego."

"Come on, sourpuss. Go scare the shit outta the club girls, then you and me gotta have a talk."

"About me keepin' my fuckin' mouth shut?" I looked away and took a deep breath. "You gonna make me resign? I know you can't have a VP who continually gets herself into trouble."

He sighed but took my hand. "Come with me, baby. We'll talk about this upstairs."

Yeah. He was totally gonna let me down easy. For some strange reason, it made my eyes sting. As a rule, I never cried. Sure, there were times I needed to let off some steam that didn't seem to want to go any other way, but never in front of others. And not in front of Rocket if he was making me not be vice president. I knew I was shit at this. But I was trying, Goddamnit!

Frustration roiling inside me, my emotions as high as they'd been at any other time in my life, I stepped into the clubhouse with Rocket…

And he was immediately swamped by fucking club whores who managed to dislodge my hand from his and shove me away from Rocket.

I thought I had that shit under control. I thought that, with me not only being VP but sporting Rocket's property patch, they'd leave us all alone. I'd done my best to avoid them since the incident with Plush when Rocket had brought me home covered in blood the first time. I hadn't even had to lift a finger. Looked like that was changing.

"So Goddamned sick of this." My muttered curse caught a few of the girls' attention. It didn't escape my notice that Plush wasn't in the middle of this bunch. Unfortunately there were at least three others. I couldn't really tell because my stupid eyes chose that moment to tear up. Now I couldn't see out of either eye.

The way I saw it was this. No matter what happened in the next few minutes, I was fucked. If I left to go have my breakdown, I left Rocket with greedy club whores and I was fucked. If I stayed and started crying, I was doubly fucked. The men wouldn't want a hormonal, emotional mess being their VP and I wouldn't blame them. The only option I had was to beat the shit outta someone and quite possibly break some code of conduct I wasn't aware of by killing someone I shouldn't and... I was fucked.

Well. If I was fucked either way, I'd take the most satisfying way out.

Without a word, I snagged a bottle Rattler had set on the bar. Probably for Rocket.

"Ah, hell. Rocket! Look out!" I wasn't sure who shouted the warning but it was too late. I used the neck as a handle as I took the few steps separating me and the group of women and Rocket.

Rocket's gaze found mine and his eyes widened. It wasn't until I brought the bottle down on the head of the first woman that I realized Rocket thought I might hit him. He hadn't lifted his hands in defense, nor did he try to stop the carnage I was currently unleashing. In fact, he took a couple steps backward.

"Imma kill every fuckin' woman who laid a hand on my man," I said in a low voice. "I'm done fuckin' with you lot."

The broken end of the bottle was still in my hand and I jabbed one woman in the thigh. She shrieked, backing off. The rest didn't move fast enough to suit me.

"So done with this fuckin' shit!" I stabbed another one in the shoulder, leaving the glass shank when she backed off. From there, I used my fists and feet. One of them landed a blow to the already injured side of my face. The pain was more than I was prepared for, and I staggered back though I managed to hold back a cry that wanted to escape.

Tears streamed down my cheeks as I fought to get my footing. That one misstep seemed to be a silent signal to the other women because the next thing I knew there were four of them pounding on me.

My ears rang under the onslaught, but I thought I heard Rocket's ferocious roar of anger in the background. Not that it mattered.

"Let her go, man. She needs this and I think the whores do too. They've been pushing at her boundaries. Time they find out where they are." I wasn't certain who spoke, but I thought it might have been Bear.

"If they hurt her, I'll kill every fuckin' one of 'em." That was definitely Rocket. Taking my attention away from the fight got me smacked on the sore side of my face again but I didn't cry out or do more than turn my head before punching the woman's crotch. She screamed in pain and backed off, clutching her crotch.

"Ha! Cunt punch, bitch!" I yelled as I continued to fight, getting to my feet. Grabbing the closest woman by the hair, I slammed her against a nearby table where I found another bottle. I broke it over the same woman's head, then threw myself back into the fray. That was when I noticed Venus taking out women close to me. There was more than a little bit of blood around the room, most of it from the women we fought.

"That bitch is rabid, Rocket! Put her down! We aren't safe around her!" That fucking cunt! She had the audacity to complain to my man about *me*? When she had her hands on him? I bared my teeth and stalked to her. "You ain't seen rabid. But you're fixin' to." I swiped out with the broken bottle neck, catching her across the cheek in a deep gash. "Bet that'll leave a mark."

Venus was beside me. I turned, afraid I'd have to fight her, and I knew there was no way I could win against the other woman. Not only was she taller, stronger, and generally more experienced than me in every aspect of fighting, life, and pretty much everything else, I also wasn't sure how much gas I had left in the tank. I was hurting. Inside and out. I'd thought I had at least this much under control. Obviously, I was wrong. Was I wrong about Rocket as well? He said wanted to talk to me. Was this when he'd tell me he'd underestimate the amount of trouble I was and that he'd had enough?

The thought of losing Rocket through my own stupidity unleashed a torrent of grief I hadn't known was inside me. I turned that grief to rage. I wasn't certain exactly what I'd done, but the next thing I knew, Venus was pulling me off a club girl and handing me over to Rocket.

"Get off me, Rocket! You want your skanky club whores? You can fucking have them!" I screamed and kicked. Rocket took my blows but didn't let me go.

"*Malishka*, stop." Venus moved into my line of sight. "They got message, little sister." She stroked my hair off my face and cupped my cheek. "You make fine vice president. You make even better old lady." She grinned and raised her voice so everyone heard her. "I hear men you were torturing are waiting for more in club dungeon. Do you wish for me to continue or wait for you?"

I looked up at her. Her gaze was steady on me, and I knew I was going to have to say something. Taking a deep breath, I pushed back from Rocket. I was afraid he wouldn't let me go but, surprisingly, he did. Which made me want to cry all the harder. I wanted him to force the issue. Like he had back at that fucking shack. I wanted him to want to hold me and never let me go. To protect me even though I didn't need it.

Only… maybe I did need his protection.

"No." I straightened, not bothering to swipe at my tears. Leaving them was bad, but acknowledging them was worse. "Build their suspense. I need a bit of time to ice my face and take a Tylenol, then I'll be down."

Venus nodded her head and gave me a small half grin. "Is there anything you need from me while you take care of personal business?"

I started to say no, then thought better of it. "Yeah. Have Falcon take you to Gina. She's had a hard go of it. Though she's doing better, I like to check on her in the afternoon. Just to make sure she's good, but I don't think she needs to see me with my face all bruised and swollen. Might scare her worse than she already is. Would you be wiling to do that for me?"

"Absolutely."

"She's still a little nervous around the guys, though she's getting better. I think she likes Falcon. It's why he needs to be the one to take you to her." Talking about mundane, routine things helped settle me, though I knew my voice still shook with emotion. I tried to project the calm Rocket often did in the face of chaos. But, like had been said about me, I was chaos embodied. How did one project calm when one was anything but by nature?

"Good. Also, thank you for letting me know about threat to Bane. Thorn found guy lurking around fence to compound. They have him locked away until you or Rocket are ready to send someone after him." I didn't miss how she put me in a position of authority the same as Rocket. It helped me keep what little control I'd managed to grasp. When this was all over, I owed Venus more than I could ever repay.

"Knox. Take Bear and Leather with you. Go get that bastard and bring him back." I gave the order with confidence, not once looking at Rocket. He had his hand resting on my shoulder and, though I thought maybe I should shrug him off, the connection felt too good.

"All over that shit," Knox growled. Then he asked the strangest question. "He the one who bruised up your face, Lemon?"

I just looked at the man. Knox was pissed. Nearly as pissed as Rocket looked. "No. I think he hit me outside Tito's, but it was Pinhead who hit me the most." I waved it off, trying to get my bravado back when all I wanted to do was break down and have a good cry. "I got him back, though."

"Pinhead?" Knox looked from me to Venus in confusion.

"Yeah. Like in the movie," I supplied.

Venus shrugged. "His face was covered in piercings." She grinned, lifting her chin and looking for all the world like she was a proud mother. "Emphasis on *was*."

"Was." Knox gave her a blank look.

"Where do you think all that blood came from?" She gestured to me. "There might be a few left in his face but not many. She'll be starting on other body parts when she's had chance to rest." Venus's gaze roamed around the room until she landed on the few remaining club whores. "Torture is nasty business. Hard work. Makes woman… thirsty." She shrugged. "Usually for more blood. My suggestion would be to keep hands off what does not belong to you. Lemon appears to have… vicious streak." Then her gaze landed on Piston. "As do I. And it appears this one has decided to claim me." She raised an eyebrow at Piston. "Unless he changed his mind?"

"Nope." Piston's expression didn't change. The two didn't go to each other or do anything else. It seemed like a quiet understanding passed between them. I knew this meant the next few days to come would be interesting and normally I'd be gleeful. But just now, I was desperate to get back to mine and Rocket's room, because I had reached the end of my endurance.

"Good," I said, clearing my throat and turning toward the back of the room. "Carry on. I'll be down in an hour or so."

"Tomorrow." Rocket's voice was close behind me. Before I'd made three steps, he scooped me up and hurried down the hall and up the stairs with me in his arms. "She'll be down tomorrow. No more torture until she gives the word. Let the fuckers stew."

"Rocket, put me down." I didn't really want that, but felt like I had to put up at least a bit of a protest.

"No. And if you start squirming, I'll spank you when we get to our room."

"Fuck you." There was no real heat behind my words, and I knew there never would be. Not in the sense I was angry with him. It wasn't his fault I was a handful and kept getting myself into trouble.

"Yep. In just a few minutes."

Chapter Nine
Rocket

Lemon had reached the end of her endurance. I wasn't sure what was going on with her, but I had the feeling it was more than just the recent trauma of being kidnapped. Sure, I could be wrong. She was strong, but she'd been through a lot in the last couple of months. I mean, how could one small woman get into so much trouble?

Scratch that. Lemon wasn't just a small woman. She was a force of nature. It was one of many reasons why I loved her so much. Which is why I was surprised she lay passively in my arms on the way to our room. Actually wrapped her fucking arms around my neck and buried her face in my chest. Yeah. This was serious.

When I reached our room, I found Bullet waiting at the door. "Heard our VP might need a little patchin' up."

"I'm fuckin' fine!" Lemon surprised me by really making a concerted effort to get out of my arms this time, which is how she escaped. "I just need a shower, which you absolutely will not help me with." She gave Bullet a fierce scowl before turning and marching toward the bathroom.

Bullet raised an eyebrow at me and handed me a chemical ice pack as well as a bottle of pills. "Painkillers. Two to start, then one every six hours. If she still ain't relaxed enough to let you take care of her, have her drink this." He handed me a bottle of…

"Fruit punch? Really, Bullet?"

The big man shrugged. "It's got cannabis in it. It'll mellow her out and let her sleep. And quite possibly let you keep your balls intact."

I scowled, then looked over my shoulder in the direction Lemon had gone. "You know, you're probably right."

"Everything's finally caught up with her." Bullet wasn't above joking around, but not about this. "Not sure what's goin' on in the dungeon, but you keep her out of it."

"She's vice president of this club, Bullet. I wouldn't hold back any of the others."

"She's still a teenager, Rocket. And your woman. It's time for her to be your woman for a while. You wouldn't hesitate to pull any of us back if you thought we were in over our heads." He stabbed a finger in Lemon's direction. "She is. Whether she wants to admit it or not."

He was right. In truth, I'd been waiting for this moment. The trick would be to figure out what exactly she was most upset about. I knew it was a combination of things but one stood out. During the fight downstairs, she'd told me I could have my skanky whores. If the main problem was her doubting me, we'd have to have a come-to-Jesus meeting.

I found her in the shower, scrubbing the blood off her skin so hard I winced. The bloody clothes she'd worn were in the middle of the bathroom floor, so I added my own to the pile. When I stepped in with her, she pushed away from me.

"Don't touch me! You smell like whores!"

"Then wash me, baby. Get their stink off me."

She turned away, muttering, "Wash your own fuckin' self." It wasn't like Lemon to sulk, which meant she was saying what she thought she should say. Not what she wanted to actually do.

I stepped forward, reaching around her for the shower gel. I put my other arm around her middle, pulling her back against me. She tried to bat my hand away, but it wasn't even a half-hearted attempt.

Squirting a generous amount over my torso, I turned Lemon around to face me and took her wrists in my hands, placing her palms against my chest. "I said wash me, Lemon."

"That an order, Prez?" The snarky comment was said without any real heat. In fact, she looked more like a sullen teenager. Which she kind of was. Though she was of legal age for me to have her as my woman, she still wasn't twenty. It was easy to forget sometimes, because she saw so much of the way things really were when none of the rest of us in Grim ever had. We'd kept our heads down except when we were forced to pay attention. That had started to change, and it was all because of the woman in my arms.

"Yeah, baby. It's an order." When she actually pouted, her delicate brows knitting together in disapproval, I had to clear my throat to cover my chuckle. I wasn't stupid.

"Fine." She settled her hands over my chest and rubbed the soap over my skin until she finally started to relax a little. And yeah, I noticed the tears slowly leaking from her beautiful eyes, even though one was still swollen most of the way shut. Wasn't stupid enough to mention it. I would question her about them later. Now wasn't the time, though.

"Been thinkin'." I thought she might need a distraction for a bit. Take her mind off things.

"Here it comes," she muttered. Before I could question her, she plowed on. "What exactly have you been thinking, oh great leader?"

I raised an eyebrow. "You mean besides that I need to take you over my knee?

She snorted. "Yeah. Besides that."

"Uh-huh." I waited to see if she'd look up at me. She didn't. "Been thinkin' me and you need some alone time. Away from the clubhouse. Just the two of us. Anywhere in the world you want to go."

To my complete and utter horror and mortification and all kinds of other terrifying shit, Lemon -- my brave, beautiful Lemon -- burst into tears.

"Christ." I pulled her against me, wrapping my arms around her as tightly as I could. I knew she was close to shattering, but I never thought she was this far gone. "I've got you Lemon. I won't let go. Not ever."

"Why?" she cried. "Why would you even want to be around me?"

That... didn't compute. I thought about her question for long moments, trying my best to figure out what she meant and simply came up blank. "You're gonna have to explain, baby. I don't understand the question."

"I'm too much. I've always been too much." She clung to me like a child not wanting a parent to drop her off at daycare. Which was as funny as it was sad. This beautiful, wonderful, caring woman should never feel like that. "Why would you throw over all those beautiful, normal women down there for someone who can't keep her fucking mouth shut!" She practically yelled that last part.

"Who said you *should* keep your mouth shut? Keeping our mouths shut is what got Grim into the shape it was in before you got here. That's on me. You keep on speakin' your mind, honey."

"It got me beat up again." Her voice was so soft I almost didn't hear her over the water. "I'm sorry."

"Honey..." I tried to push her back a little so I could look at her face, but she refused to lift her head, even when I tried to force her. "Lemon, honey. Look at me. Right now. Look at me."

She took a deep breath and slowly, reluctantly, raised her head. Even through the shower spray, I could tell she was still crying. She sniffed once, and wiped her nose on the back of her wrist before meeting my gaze.

"Yeah. You got beat up, and it makes me fuckin' *furious*." Her face crumbled before I could plow on. "But not at you, honey. *Never* at you. Never for that. I'm angry that I wasn't with you when it happened, so I could kill those motherfuckers." I brushed my thumbs under her eyes as I continued. "I'm angry that any man would hit a woman because she got the best of him in a verbal confrontation. Because I know that's what happened. You're wicked smart with a sharp tongue. I wouldn't have you any other way."

"You're gonna tell me the vice president thing isn't working. Aren't you? Because, I mean, you're right. Who wants a vice president who keeps getting beat up and in trouble?"

I sighed, shaking my head. "Lemon…"

"Because I'll resign. In fact, I really think Bear or Piston would be better in that position. Piston has some season on him. He's smart, quiet, and very thoughtful in his decision-making. He's not going to say or do anything that would embarrass you or set someone off and cause some kind of turf war."

"Lemon."

"And if he's serious about claiming Venus, you'll have her too. If it hadn't been for Venus, they'd probably have killed me before the third guy got back from scouting out Bane. She's the real deal, Rocket. She's a member of Salvation's Bane, but maybe you could convince her to move here?"

"Lemon. Stop."

"But --"

I cut her off the only way I knew how. I kissed her. Hard. Our mouths crashed together with a fervor that matched the intensity of our conversation, and for a moment, the world outside the shower dissolved away. I could feel her fighting back her tears as she responded to my kiss, her body trembling with emotion.

Finally, we broke apart, gasping. My cock was hard as fucking diamond, needing to be inside her, but I had to ease her fears first. I needed her to realize she was my woman and always would be.

She sniffled a couple times as I pulled back but said nothing.

"Now," I said, snagging the shower gel once more. "Listen to me, Lemon. Listen good." I waited until she nodded her head. "First of all, you're my woman. I'm your man. Ain't no fuckin' club whore in this place or any other, ain't no woman anywhere I want more than I want you. It's you and me, honey. Understand?"

"Not really," she muttered. "Most guys would want a woman who was easier than me. No matter how much I know I need to tone it down, I can't seem to. Even when my life is on the line."

"No one said you should. Especially not me." I grabbed her wrist and brought her palm to my cock. "You think this is just because I'm in the shower with a naked woman? I was hard long before I got in here with you." I made sure to hold her gaze. When she tried to turn her head, I brought my fingers to her chin and forced her head up. I used her hand to stroke my cock several times while she looked up at me. "Watchin' you defend your claim on me was fuckin' hot. Now, I have no desire for you to fight because any time you're hurt I want to kill someone. This?" I brushed my fingertips along her bruised cheek and swollen eye. "This makes me want to kill those sons of bitches in the dungeon. But I'd do it too quickly."

She ducked her head again, but this time, she wrapped her arms around my middle and buried her face in my chest. The feeling of her clinging to me so sweetly made my heart swell.

"Lemon," I whispered against her hair, brushing my lips gently over her temple. "I'm your man. I'll never let anything or anyone hurt you if I can help it, and if it does happen, I will annihilate whoever is responsible. And I'll always want you. You can be as fierce as you need to be, but remember that I'm here to catch you when things go to shit. So the very last thing in this world you have to worry about are the club whores or any other woman in this world catching my attention. You've got my attention focused squarely on you."

I leaned in to kiss her again before continuing on. Because I had to. And I was pretty sure she needed some TLC. I was more than happy to give that to her. I wasn't kidding earlier when I said she'd fuck me. She was getting ready to.

When I ended the kiss, I pressed my forehead against hers. "As for being vice president? Honey, the men of Grim Road elected you. Unanimously. I didn't prompt them. I didn't tell them they had to once it was suggested. They did it because they saw in you what they needed their vice president to be. That includes your lack of a filter."

"I don't believe you. I wish I did, but I don't. Any of these guys would be better than me."

I scowled at her, squeezing her shoulders and forcing her to back up a step. I leaned down so that I was staring straight at her, hovering over her in a dominant position. "What do you think would have happened to Gina if Bear had been vice president?"

She shrugged. "Ain't his problem. Hell. It ain't even my problem, I just couldn't stand to see everyone hurting because of one bastard's actions."

"Exactly!" I gripped her shoulders hard enough to bruise because I really wanted her attention. "You listen to me, Lemon. Listen good. You need to really think about what I'm about to say." When she gave a small nod, I continued.

"This club has grown together this last month. I've seen men... maybe not really breaking out of their shells, but at least coming together once a week for an hour or two to eat and drink together. This compound and clubhouse is becoming more than simply a place for them to crash. It's becoming a home. Because of you, girl. You forced the issue on them by making them all get to know each other.

"Those weekly dinners might have started out a little forced, but most of them look forward to it. Hell, I've noticed more than one of them getting together to ride or whatever on their own. And Gina? Yeah. She's still not completely comfortable with everyone, but she loves the daily rides on that stupid pink bike. And she and Falcon are more at ease than I ever thought would happen. That girl would be a broken, terrified mess if not for you." I paused, letting my words sink in. "Now, you tell me that's not something a vice president should do. You're bringing this club together like family. *You*."

"You promise I'm not more trouble than I'm worth? Don't you need to get away from me for a while? Because you don't have to take me with you if you need to go on a trip to relax a bit."

I wasn't used to this Lemon. Since the first day I'd met her, she was larger than life. A force of nature. It never occurred to me she'd been under this much stress because she handled it so well. This was stress she put on herself. I was absolutely convinced she had higher expectations of herself than anyone else ever could.

"Honey, every single day in your presence makes me realize how miserable and empty my life would be without you. I'm not going anywhere without you. We're a team."

"Oh, Rocket!" She jumped into my arms, wrapping her limbs around me as tightly as she could. I held her just as hard. "I love you. I love you so damned much!"

"Ah, baby. I love you too. I have for a while. I will never, *never*, let you go. Do you understand me?"

She didn't answer. Instead, she found my lips and kissed me like she was starving for my touch. I wanted nothing more than to devour her, to let her lose herself in my body the way I wanted to lose myself in hers. But the bruises covering her body made me restrain myself. Making love to her would be easy enough. I could make her come until she passed out. But I was going to do it my way. That meant not taking her like I normally do. Like an animal during mating season. No. This time was going to be slow and careful and long. So very, very long.

Chapter Ten
Lemon

This man. This wonderful, wonderful man...

Rocket was everything I'd never known I needed in my life. Sure, I'd committed myself to him over a month ago, but it took believing I might be losing him because of my own stupidity to really appreciate how much he meant to me. I'd said it on more than one occasion. My way of thinking had always been "see me, love me, motherfucker." I'd never cared what people thought of me. Not until Rocket. And by extension, Grim Road.

"I just want to do right by the club," I whispered. "To be the best vice president and old lady I can be."

"Honey, you are. I couldn't have asked for a more perfect partner. You... you're everything, Lemon. We need you in the club. I need you in my life. By my side. In my bed." He kissed down my neck to the place where my shoulder began. The water cascaded over us in a warm fall adding to the sensations Rocket was expertly building.

Every single time he fucked me, he taught me something else. He'd taken me at least once a day since he took my virginity. Sometimes twice or more. I craved his touch and did my best to give him as much pleasure as he gave me.

He dipped to my breast and sucked the nipple into his mouth with a strong pull. I cried out and threaded my hands through his hair as my clit throbbed in time with his sucks. I arched my back, thrusting my breasts at him and he pinched the other one and twisted lightly.

"That's my girl. Talk to me. Let me know you like what I'm doing to you."

"Nope!" I gasped out. "Hate it. Gonna have to try harder." I had no idea where that came from, but I was glad it popped out when he chuckled and the vibration went from my breast straight to my sex again.

"There she is. You're back with me, aren't you. My sassy, sexy little sourpuss."

"Rocket…" I breathed a happy sigh of relief. Maybe I'd been feeling the stress the whole time I'd been here. All I knew was something inside me unfurled and I felt lighter than I had in a long time. I guess the pressure had been building subconsciously since the beginning.

"I've got you, baby. You have doubts? You bring them to me. No matter what they are. That's one of many things I'm here for."

"I…" I swallowed and shook my head slightly, closing my eyes before taking a deep breath and trying again. "I've always been the one looking out for everyone." I have no idea where my outburst came from. I wanted to lose myself in Rocket so I could just forget everything for a while.

"Yeah. Figured." He didn't stop, but kissed his way down my belly until he knelt on the shower floor in front of me.

"What are you doing?" My hand bunched in his hair and flexed, gripping and tangling in his shaggy hair.

"We've done this enough you know what I'm doing, Lemon." He leaned in and swiped his tongue through my folds and I cried out. I abruptly sat down on the bench. "We're gonna take our time." Lick. "And do this proper." Lick. "Once I'm done, you'll never doubt me again. You get me?"

"Rocket!"

The man had a magical tongue. I'd known it since the first time he ate me out. Never had I thought in this whole entire world that anything could feel as good as Rocket tonguing my pussy.

I didn't even try to hold back my moans. The sensation was too much. His talented tongue was sending shockwaves of pleasure throughout my entire body, and I was melting into a puddle of goo in the heat of shower and his steady ministrations. He expertly teased my clit, then dipped inside me, tasting every drop like he was dying of thirst and my pussy held the elixir of life.

He held me close, his arms around my middle, his big body wedged between my legs. His breath was hot against my inner thigh. His tongue never faltered, his rhythm never broke and the passion in his eyes as he looked up at me from between my legs was unmistakable.

"I've got you, Lemon. I'll always have you. You're not alone. Never again." His words washed over me like a soothing balm as the pleasure continued to build, his voice blending with the shower's steady hum. There was an insatiable hunger in his touches that swept me up with him. All that mattered was the next stroke of his tongue. The next caress of his hands.

As he continued to pleasure me, my body responded to his touch. My hips moved, matching the rhythm of his tongue. Each step of the way, there was a growing intensity that threatened to consume me. With every touch and every whisper, I knew I was safe. I was loved. And this man was rapidly becoming the most important person in my life.

I whimpered in protest when he pulled away from me and stood. Instead of leaving me, though, Rocket pulled me to my feet before lifting me and pressing me against the shower wall. Once again, his mouth fused to mine and he kissed me with wicked thrusts of his tongue. He tasted of me. Of sex and sin and everything wonderful all rolled into one.

When he reached between us to guide his cock inside me, I sobbed in relief. As always, Rocket stretched me, making my pussy burn as it accepted his delicious invasion. My body had never felt so alive, so electric. The heat of the shower, the cool tiles against my skin, everything faded into the background as Rocket's masterful lovemaking became the center of my world.

It didn't take long for him to find a steady rhythm. He didn't move fast or hard, just a smooth cadence that seemed designed to drive me mad. His hips thrust between my legs, driving deeper and deeper into me. My body slipped up and down the cool porcelain of the shower wall. Sweat dripped from my hairline to my face, mingling with the steam and water cascading around us. Each thrust sent shockwaves of pleasure rushing through me and I gripped him tightly, pulling him closer to me.

When I tried to ride him, to force him to move faster, Rocket smacked my ass…

And I lost my Goddamned mind.

* * *

Rocket

I was only trying to get Lemon's attention, to get her to focus on me and let me have control. The second I smacked her ass I knew it had been the exact wrong thing to do. Or maybe it was the best thing I could have done.

The woman went wild.

Her eyes widened in surprise, her breathing

already ragged from our encounter, but as soon as my hand connected with her soft flesh, she erupted. Lemon's moans turned into a feral wail that echoed through the bathroom, her pussy quivering around my cock.

She rode me like she might a wild stallion she was trying to bend to her will, which was something I absolutely could not allow. Not now. Now during the emotional break she was having. She had to know I could handle anything she chose to throw at me and come back for more.

I gritted my teeth, trying to regain control. My heart was racing, my hands gripping her hips tight. I had to slow down, take this moment to calm her passions. But the more I tried, the more she bucked, whimpering like a wounded animal. Each slap of skin against skin was harsh against her keening cries.

So I smacked her ass again. Harder this time. Her hips gyrated with a fierce intensity. Our bodies slammed together as the rhythm intensified. I bit the inside of my cheek to keep from coming. I had to wrap my arm around her back and clamp her solidly against my body to keep her from falling.

We'd had wild sex before. Angry sex. Hard sex. Always it had ended with mutual satisfaction. She'd calmed my beast with her body more than once. The time in the barn when we'd dropped the bombshell on the club about what had happened to Gina came to mind. She'd known I needed the release before facing the men and she'd given it to me. The sex had been primal and hard. Rough. She'd taken all I had to give and enjoyed herself in the extreme. I guess it was my turn. I'd give her what she needed and push her a little further.

"Little witch." I snarled against her neck as I

continued to pump into her. I didn't speed up like she wanted, but I didn't slow down or prevent her from moving. I just refused to put any more force behind my movements. "Drive me insane with how fuckin' sexy you are."

"Fuck me harder, Rocket! Fuck me!"

"I'll fuck you harder when I'm Goddamned good and ready." I pushed us away from the tiled wall before pulling out of her and spinning her around. Her frustrated cry was cut off with my hand around her throat, pulling her back to me. I guided my cock back inside her pussy with the other hand before gripping her hips and starting a hard, driving rhythm.

She moaned loudly, her body trembling in response to my increased pace. I could feel her wetness coating my shaft as I thrust into her with increasing desperation, my need for her growing with each passing second and trying to surpass my need to give her what she needed. And that wasn't necessarily what she wanted either. Lemon needed my dominance, needed to know I would take charge when she needed me to. That I was capable of holding her back when I thought it was necessary. She worried that she was too much of handful for me to handle. I got it, too. For most men, she probably would be too much.

Lemon pressed her hands flat against the shower wall, pushing back against me as I fucked her. She was always aggressive during sex. It was part of the reason we fit so well. She was dominant, but I was more so. It was time to prove to her I could handle anything she chose to dish out.

"Hold still." I gave the command at her ear. When she refused, I bit down on her earlobe. She cried out but did what I demanded of her. I pulled out of her pussy, and she sobbed her protest.

"NOOOO!"

"I said hush, woman. You'll take what I give you, when I give it to you."

"Rocket! I need --"

"Hush! I know what you need. Submit to me!"

"Never!" She bit out her answer, but she didn't move.

Once she was still, I guided my cock back, sliding my wet dick along her flesh until I felt her back entrance with the head. I pressed slightly, testing her reaction.

Lemon sucked in a breath and turned her head to look back over her shoulder. "Rocket?"

"Relax your muscles. Let me in."

"I've never..."

"Didn't think so. But this is happenin'. You concentrate on me. I'll take care of you. I'll make sure you enjoy it."

She held my gaze with equal amounts of trepidation and arousal. I held my cock and circled her asshole, teasing and tempting until she rocked her hips back, seeking more.

I gripped her hip. "Stay still." She whimpered but obeyed. I rewarded her by slipping past her rim.

"Oh, God..." She whimpered but held still. Her body quivered in my arms. "What is this..."

"Just stay still. Don't fight me. Push out and I can slip right in."

She was still for a few seconds before doing as I told her. The second she did, I pushed inside her slowly until she stopped. I wasn't all the way inside, but I could take my time. Especially when she was enjoying herself, focusing on me instead of her fears and insecurities.

"That's my girl. Want more?"

"Yes." Her small gasp was sweet music. She was surrendering right before my eyes. In my arms. I knew this wouldn't always be the case, but I'd have to use my experience to shock her occasionally until she realized her worth to me beyond doubt.

"Good. Now listen to me. You, Lemon. *You*… are my world. I don't want another woman -- club whore or a woman from another club, or any woman from outside the club. I want… *you*." When she took a breath to say something, I eased my way out of her ass until only the head remained. Which made her gasp again. This time, a little whimper escaped as well. "Push out against me again." She did. I slid back inside her, this time, a little further.

"Oh, my God!" She cried out in a long wail this time. Her hands were still flat on the wall of the shower and she stood perfectly still until I pulled out once more. "Noooo!"

"Hush," I snapped. "I'm in control." She shook her head and I removed my hand from her throat to fist in her hair. "I'm. In. Control." Her breath shuddered out of her lungs but she said nothing. "Say it, Lemon. I'm in control."

"You're in control."

"That's my girl." I sank back into her, this time, my abdomen met her ass and I held myself deep. "That's my girl…"

When her body relaxed on a breathy sigh, I started moving. Slowly at first, letting her adjust. I'd planned on introducing anal sex to her slowly over several days so I could stretch her, but sometimes things change. And I knew Lemon needed this. Not the act itself so much as my dominance. To get that, I had to do something completely foreign to her. Since I wasn't sure how badly she was hurt, I couldn't just tie her up and torture her sexually for hours until she was drenched in sweat and mindless with pleasure. This was the best alternative I could think of and it was working exactly like I'd hoped.

"I've never..." She cried out when I sank back inside her ass. "Oh, God! I've never felt anything like this!"

"Good. Now. Who's in control." It wasn't a question so much as a demand.

"You are."

"That's right. And when I'm in control, you listen to me. Say it!"

"I listen to you when you're in control."

"Good. Now, I'm going to tell you this and you're going to listen. Why?"

"I --" I smacked her ass once, my cock throbbing as her ass pinkened where I'd spanked it. "Because you're in control!" She sounded almost desperate and I couldn't stop the grin tugging at my lips.

"That's right. I'm also president of Grim Road. Right?"

"Uh -- I mean. Yeah. Yes. You're president." The tension was back in her body so I reached around and found her clit with my fingers. When I strummed the little nub once, her knees buckled and she gave a sharp yell.

"No thinking, Lemon. Not now. Not when I'm in control."

Her cry turned into a whimper, but she nodded her head. "OK. OK."

"I'm president. You're vice president. Nominated and voted in to this club unanimously. The only way you're voted out is unanimously. No one is going to force you to step down. In fact, I'd probably have a mutiny on my hands if you tried. You're not in this as a joke or to appease anyone, or for any other reason other than the men in Grim Road believe you're the person they need for their vice president. You're the person who will take over in the event something happens to me. You're the person they go to when they don't think they can go to me." I slid out of her again, then back in. Starting a slow, steady pace designed to ease her into the new sensations and get her used to the burn so it could morph into the pleasure I knew was starting in her.

"I don't want to be a burden, Rocket," she whispered. "They think I'm weak because I've let myself get kidnapped not once but twice in the space of a month and I don't blame them."

I laid down three smacks to her ass. This time I put down a little more heat than the previous smacks. I wanted her to know I meant business. As I hoped, she screamed, her back arching and her ass clenching down around my cock. When it did, she gasped out again, her body shaking once again.

"Talk to me, Lemon. Does it hurt?"

"It burns."

"Not the question. Am I hurting you?"

"I don't know, Rocket! I don't fuckin' know if it hurts!"

I tried not to chuckle. I had her completely off balance, and I knew this was an experience I wanted to repeat. Maybe not too often -- the last thing I wanted to do was break her so she was completely docile in bed -- but I definitely wanted her like this again.

"Then it's not hurting." I slid back inside her again. Then out. Then I circled her clit once more. Again, she jumped and clamped down on me. Her legs refused to hold her even though she seemed to be scrambling for purchase. It didn't matter, though. My arm around her middle held her up even as she was impaled on my cock.

"I can't think!"

"Good. That's where I want you."

Her breath came in pants and I knew she was hyperventilating. It would make her dizzy but I chose to let her keep going. If she got in distress, I'd bring her back down, but the loss of control and her head spinning a little would enhance this experience for her.

When she went limp, I reassessed the situation. Her hands were still on the wall. She wasn't fighting me. Her ass was squeezing my cock rhythmically. Her breathing had calmed somewhat, but she was still panting occasionally. Her skin was damp, but I couldn't tell if it was from the shower spray or sweat. I thought it was probably a combination.

Once satisfied she wasn't hurting, I started to move again. This time, I kept my fingers over her clit, resting lightly against her wet flesh. I kept my arm firmly around her in case her legs gave out again, but kept moving in a slow steady rhythm.

"You're not a burden. No one thinks you are. You didn't let yourself get kidnapped either. Maybe the first time you did, but the alternative was leaving a child to be brutalized and that's not who you are, Lemon. If it were, you wouldn't be my woman.

"When you got taken this time, they got the jump on you. Three against one. And you're a tiny woman, honey. Still, you fought. I'm willing to bet that smart mouth of yours kept them off-balance because you didn't show any fear, no matter what they did to you. No, honey. You're not a liability. You're the strongest of us all because you run into the fray with minimal fighting skills, knowing the odds are stacked against you, simply to do the right thing."

She stilled, trying to look over her shoulder. I released her hair so she could. "You really see me that way?"

"Honey, out of a club full of badasses, you are the most badass of the bunch. And I mean that with all sincerity. Just because you're not ten feet tall and bulletproof doesn't mean you're the weak link. You're the one pushing us all in the right direction. Sure, we'd all jump in with both feet to save a child, but you forced them to come after me when they normally wouldn't have. You, Lemon. You stole the bike of a man easily twice your size, crashed it through a door to get to me. Then after we'd had it fixed, you painted the fuckin' thing *pink* just to make a terrorized woman feel better." I held her gaze for long moments as I let that sink in. "Liability? No, baby. You're anything but a liability."

I fisted my hand back in her hair and pulled her back for a kiss before I started fucking her. This time, I let nature take its course. When we both wanted more, I gave it to us. Lemon took my dominance and embraced it.

She reached down to the hand gripping her hip and wrapped her small hand round my thick wrist. I thought she wanted me to let up, but when I did, she brought it to her throat. My cock pulsed like fucking mad!

"Fuck!" I gripped her neck tight. Not so hard I cut off her air, but hard enough to give her a thrill and me the dominance I needed.

Didn't last long.

An embarrassingly few pumps later, I knew I was coming. There was no stopping it or slowing down, I was gonna explode.

"Find your clit, Lemon. Use your fingers and

play with your clit." My voice was strangled as I tried to hold on just that little bit longer. I absolutely was not going to come before she did.

"Oh, God! Yes!"

The second she touched her clit, her ass clamped down on my dick. Hard. Then it pulsed and milked me, wanting my cum inside it as much as I wanted to put it there.

"That's it, baby," I panted. "Gonna put my cum in your ass. You ready?"

"Do it! Oh, fuck! Fuckin' *do it*!"

I did. With a brutal yell, I shoved myself as deep inside her as I could and let my load go. My whole body jerked with each jet of sperm I released into her ass. The orgasm was the most powerful I'd ever had. I wasn't sure I wasn't going to fall on my ass before I could get us to the bench and sit down. Hell, I couldn't even move from where I was standing! All I could do was grip her tightly to me and stand there while my cock filled her full of hot, sticky cum.

Several seconds later, once the storm had passed, I managed to get us to the bench and sat as carefully as I could with Lemon still impaled on my dick. She shivered, but I didn't think it was from the chill. Every time my dick pulsed, she shuddered. She'd be sore tomorrow, but I think I accomplished what I intended.

"You good, baby?"

She was silent for so long I wasn't sure if she heard me, but finally she gave several little nods. "Yeah. I think so."

I grinned and kissed her shoulder. "Good. Feel better?"

She turned her head and the smile she gave me was full of wonder and... love? "I do, Rocket. I really do." The double meaning wasn't lost. Yeah. She'd needed everything I'd given her. "Thank you." She reached back to pull me closer for a sweet, lingering kiss. "For all of it. How did you know?"

"That you needed me to take control?" When she nodded, I stroked her bruised cheek carefully. "You've been through more than your share of shit that last month. You've barely dealt with all you witnessed when we took Hammer apart. Then this? You needed a break so you could get back your perspective. No one here thinks less of you, Lemon. You're a very young, inexperienced woman doing the job of a seasoned, battle-hardened warrior. You did it so well, those same seasoned, battle-hardened warriors made you one of their leaders. Their second-in-command. Don't you think that says something about, not only your character and ability to think through a situation and find an answer, but how they view you?"

"I hadn't thought about it that way."

"No. You didn't. Because you're a responsible woman, always looking out for others. You remind me a lot of Mama at Bones MC."

"You know her?"

"Eh, a little. Mostly by reputation. And only because of the work I did for the CIA years ago. She's a nurturer, but a firm believer in tough love. That's you, Lemon. There's nothing you wouldn't do for anyone who needed it. Including kicking their ass."

She grinned. "Well, if Mama is like that, then yeah. I guess I am like her."

I kissed her again, relishing the ability to do so. "Come on. Let's get cleaned up. You need something for pain and some rest."

She touched the bruised side of her face and winced. "Yeah. I hadn't realized how much it was starting to throb."

"Yeah. I didn't intend to fuck you tonight. But I won't lie and say I'm sorry I did."

"You better not," she groused. "'Cause it was fuckin' fabulous."

Chapter Eleven
Rocket

After a conversation with Bullet and assessing her pain level, Lemon opted for the spiked fruit punch. I believe her exact words were something along the lines of, "If I'm gonna be buzzed, it might as well be from something that would make Dani cringe. Pot-laced fruit punch it is." I think even Bullet's lips twitched at that one.

He gave her some ibuprofen as well, telling her the fruit punch would take a while to kick in and she needed some relief sooner rather than later. So we sat on the couch and watched a movie while she held an ice pack to her face. Until she started giggling.

"Feelin' it?"

"If by 'it' you mean, everything is soft, fuzzy, and more than a little funny, then yeah. I'm feelin' it."

She turned where she'd cuddled up against me and tilted her head up for a kiss. Who was I to deny her? And yeah. The pot made her horny.

I did what I'd intended to do when I ended up railing her ass from behind. I took her to bed and worshiped her body for the rest of the night. At first, she was stoned as fuck, but more than receptive to me eating her out. Since we hadn't talked about me taking her when she was under the influence, I didn't fuck her until nearly sunrise when the effects of her drink started to wane. And after she'd begged me, more than a few times. It made the grand finale that much sweeter.

I let her sleep until midday, sometimes cuddling her close, sometimes just watching over her. When Bullet came to check on her, it finally dawned on me how much she'd needed the sleep.

"Glad to see she's resting," Bullet said as he set two more bottles of the fruit punch in the mini fridge I kept in my room. "She should drink some of that each night until it's all gone. Let her sleep as long as she can. You talk to her about lettin' someone else deal with the assholes in the dungeon?"

"Not yet. I will when she wakes up." I had intended on doing it the night before, but of all the things going on in her head, those pukes were the last thing I wanted to bring up.

"Good. That was only my suggestion, Rocket. She's a kid compared to us, but she's stronger than most kids her age. She might be able to take it no problem, but I still think she needs a break."

"She does, and I'll make sure she gets it."

Bullet nodded once, then left the room. I shut the door behind him before turning back to see Lemon stretching languidly in bed.

I crossed back to her and sat on the edge, reaching out to sift my fingers through her hair. "How you feelin'?"

"I have to pee."

I barked out a laugh. "Yeah. I hear ya. Come on." I held out my hand for her and she took it. I helped her to her feet and let her hold on to me until she got her balance.

"Whoa," she said with a little shake of her head.

"Hungover?"

"Not sure. I don't hurt anywhere or feel sick or anything."

I grinned. "Little woozy."

"Yep. High as a giraffe's pussy. My legs don't wanna work."

She pouted prettily. Probably didn't mean to, but I thought it was adorable. My woman was a warrior through and through, but she was still my little sourpuss. She was also funny as shit. *High as a giraffe's pussy.* Who the fuck comes up with this shit? "Yeah. I can see that." When I chuckled, I expected her to frown up at me, accusing me of laughing at her, but she just giggled. Actually fucking giggled.

"Pot is *fun*."

"I'll make a note."

I helped her to the bathroom, but she didn't want to go back to bed. "I need to go to the dungeon to see about my boys." She had an almost gleeful look on her face.

"Yeah. Not happening, baby."

She glanced at me sharply. "Why the fuck not?"

"You've had enough of that for a while." I stuck a finger in her face like she was a naughty child. "No more torture. Bad Lemon."

She snorted. "You sound like Wylde. He never means it, and you don't either."

"I do in this instance. Next time there's someone to take apart, we'll talk about it."

"Rocket, this is part of my job as VP."

"Sometimes. Sure. But you did your part this time. Let the guys and Venus finish this."

Her eyes widened. "Venus. Where is she? She's got someone after her and I need to help her find the son of a bitch." She pushed off the couch and tried to hurry to the door, but I snagged her arm and brought her back to me. I pulled her onto my lap so she straddled my thigh, my hand gripping her ass through the boxers she wore. "What are you doing? Let me up."

"Nope. Not this time. Besides, Venus is already gone."

"What? But Piston claimed her! She can't leave!"

"Piston went with her. They're headed to find

the man after her. Victor Zaitsev. He's a Russian mob boss and the father of Venus's half sister. She suspects he wants his daughter back."

Her eyes got wide. "Russian Mafia? Holy shit!"

I chuckled and pulled her in for a hug. "Yeah, sourpuss. Venus has ties, however loose, to Bratva."

"When you say ties, it seems like you're implying she was part of it. Not just that her half sister's father is part of it."

"That's because I am. She'll have to tell you the details when she gets back, but I got the sense she used to be some kind of enforcer before she broke free."

"Wow. The more you know, eh?"

I chuckled. "Yeah, I guess so."

"What about the guys in the dungeon?"

"Taken care of. I don't want you thinking about them anymore. It's done."

She sighed and draped herself over my chest, tucking her head under my chin. "You take away all my fun."

"I'd say I'm sorry but I'm really not."

"Has someone checked on Gina today? And where's Effie?"

"Falcon's been with them most of the day. Effie and Gina are settling in well. Effie wants to see you tomorrow. I thought you and I would go with Falcon, Gina, and Effie to Tito's. Tito called Byte several times, checking on you. You made an impression on the whole group. You think you'll be up for a small trip?"

"Absolutely." She grinned just as her phone trilled.

I leaned over to pick it up from the end table and looked at the screen. "Your sister. Wanna take it here?"

"Sure. Though, my face..." She brushed a hand over the bruised side."

"Let them fuss over you. Want me to leave?"

"Nope. You stay here so you can protect me when Danica goes ballistic."

I couldn't help chuckle.

"Oh, my God! Lemon, what happened?" Apple's hands flew to her own face the second she got a good look at Lemon. "Dani! Lemon's been hurt!"

"Christ, Apple! Don't do that!"

That's when I saw Apple smirk. "Docile one, my ass," I muttered.

"Lemon! God! That's it," Dani said, her face a whole ass novel of distress. "You're coming home. That man obviously can't take care of you. Wylde! We're going to Riviera Beach. Right fucking now!"

"Dani, calm down." It was kind of amusing as shit to watch Lemon trying to deal with her sister. I also made a mental note not to let any of the brothers decide they were taking a liking to Apple. I knew she had a man who'd said he was claiming her, but they'd yet to make it official. Lemon was starting to wonder what the fuck was going on. "Rocket takes care of me fine. Besides. I don't need anyone taking care of me. And you should see the other guy."

Dani gave me a hard stare. "What happened, Rocket?"

"Mistaken identity. Trust me when I tell you that, by the end of the whole affair, they wished they'd never laid eyes on Lemon, let alone taken her."

I heard Wylde in the background before his face appeared in the screen. "Makin' new friends, Lemon?"

"All kinds. It's a blast here." She grinned. "Danica just got her panties in a twist because of one slight misunderstanding."

"Slight misunderstanding."

"Yeah. He misunderstood the fact that facial

piercings make wonderful targets when you piss off a person who isn't squeamish." Even Dani smiled at that quip, though she had to duck her head to cover it.

"I think I need to come to Grim Road to keep an eye on Lemon," Apple said. "She's obviously having difficulty staying out of trouble."

Lemon's face hardened for a second before she grinned at her twin. "Sure. The more the merrier. Besides, we've not had a girls' night out causing havoc in more than a month. I feel the need."

"Christ," Wylde muttered, scrubbing a hand over his face. "Here comes the *Top Gun* reference."

Lemon and Apple finished together. "The need. For speed." Then the pair of them burst into giggles. This was a side of Lemon I had seen far too little of. She was an adult, but she still needed to have fun.

"Let her come if she wants," I said to Wylde. "If Dani doesn't have any objections, that is."

The look on Dani's face said she didn't like it, but thought it was the best option. I didn't think it had anything to do with Lemon being hurt. It was Apple. "That might be the best idea. Besides, they've never been apart this long. I'm sure they could use some sister time together."

"Me and Lemon will come get her, if that's OK."

Wylde shrugged. "She wants to go. However is easiest for you."

"Pack a bag, Apple." Lemon grinned at her sister. "We'll be there tomorrow night."

"I'll be ready." Apple smiled, but it didn't seem to reach her eyes.

When we hung up, Lemon hopped off my lap and went to the fridge. She snagged a soda before popping the top. "I have the feeling I'm gonna have to cut out someone's balls."

"You got any idea who's?"

"Yep. His name's Deacon. And I will find out what the fuck is goin' on."

And just like that, my little sourpuss turned back into the vice president of Grim Road.

"God, I love you, Lemon."

She turned, a startled expression on her face before her face softened. "I love you too, Rocket."

"I'm not sure I can make you my wife legally, honey. But not because I don't want to. There's still a lot you don't know about me. Things I can't talk about because it's classified and, no matter how much I love you, classified is still classified. I can't tell you."

She shrugged. "I get it. And I don't blame you. Being with you is enough for me."

"Any children we have will have to stay hidden."

"Still not a problem."

"I expected you to at least ask why." I couldn't hide my amusement.

"If you want to tell me -- if you *can* tell me -- you will."

I chuckled, shaking my head. "You continually surprise me, Lemon. I hope you always do. The reason I can't marry you is because the government thinks I'm dead. Hell, they think most of us here are dead. We can't file any paperwork giving that away, and none of us will risk even a false name going on record. All it takes is something to connect a face or a fingerprint to anything, and we're no longer off the radar."

"I'm surprised you feel safe going out anywhere with the city camera system." She took a step toward me. "You know, we don't have to go anywhere. I'm perfectly happy staying here. I mean, after we bring Apple here."

"We're careful and don't go out often. When we do, we tend to avoid interstates or anywhere there is camera surveillance. Obviously we can't avoid everything and the licensing of our bikes has to be done very carefully, but Crush and Byte have some help from a tech company who are pretty savvy about shit like this. I don't understand it and don't really care. As long as it works."

"Come here." Lemon closed the scant distance separating us, moving into my arms. She sighed happily. I felt the same way. "I meant it, baby. I love you. With all my heart."

"I love you too, Rocket. I have one question."

"Yeah? What's that, baby?"

"I get why we can't get married legally, but I'd really like to know your name. What's your real name?"

"Duane." It had been a very long time since I'd uttered that name. "Duane Lexington. Besides Crush, you're the only person in the compound who knows that."

She pulled back slightly and grinned up at me. "I'm glad. Now I've got something none of those fuckin' club whores will never have."

"They sure won't, baby. That's all yours."

"Good. Now. I need more fruit punch, so we can get freaky."

Who was I to argue?

US Agricultural Act of 2018

Author's note -- Lemon's Fruit Punch: As with all hemp products, please partake responsibly. A nod of acknowledgment to *Chronic Guru* (chronicguru.com/apopka-dispensary) for the following information:

US Agricultural Act of 2018: Products contain flower that was grown pursuant to state and federal law (Containing not more than 0.3% delta-9 THC on a dry weight basis) by licensed farmers in accordance with the Agricultural Act of 2018 (and its state law counterparts thus it is not subject to regulation, or control, under the Federal Controlled Substances Act.

Legal Disclaimer: Neither the author nor Changeling Press LLC endorses nor recommends the use of organic hemp products.

Marteeka Karland

International bestselling author Marteeka Karland leads a double life as an action romance writer by evening and a semi-domesticated housewife by day. Known for her down-and-dirty MC romances, Marteeka takes pleasure in spinning tales of tenacious, protective heroes and spirited heroines. She staunchly advocates that every character deserves a blissful ending.

Marteeka finds joy in baking, and gardening with her husband. Make sure to visit her website to stay updated with her most recent projects. Don't forget to register for her newsletter which will pepper you with a potpourri of Teeka's beloved recipes, book suggestions, autograph events, and a plethora of interesting tidbits.

Marteeka at Changeling: changelingpress.com/marteeka-karland-a-39
Wanda Violet O. (Teeka's Dark Erotica side) changelingpress.com/wanda-violet-o-a-226

Bones MC Multiverse

Bones MC
Shadow Demons
Salvation's Bane MC
Black Reign MC
Iron Tzars MC
Grim Road MC
Bones MC Print Duets
Bones MC Audio
Salvation's Bane MC Audio
Iron Tzars MC Audio
Grim Road MC Audio

Changeling Press LLC

Contemporary Action Adventure, Sci-Fi, Steampunk, Dark Fantasy, Urban Fantasy, Paranormal, and BDSM Romance available in e-book, audio, and print format at ChangelingPress.com – MC Romance, Werewolves, Vampires, Dragons, Shapeshifters and Horror -- Tales from the edge of your imagination.

Where can I get Changeling Press Books?

Changeling Press e-books are available at ChangelingPress.com, Amazon, Apple Books, Barnes & Noble, Kobo, Smashwords, and other online retailers, including Everand Subscription and Kobo Subscription Services. Print books are available at Amazon, Barnes and Noble, and by ISBN special order through your local bookstores.

ChangelingPress.com

Printed in Great Britain
by Amazon